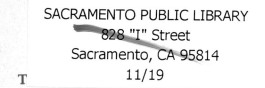
T

"Now you must turn me loose, and you must face me man-to-man, with no tricks." Degas' eyes took on a dark gleam. "For now I must kill you, Senor."

"One-on-one? No tricks?" Shaw asked, letting go of the wad of shirt in his hand. "You're not going to have your pals all try to shoot me down?" As he spoke, he lowered his Colt and eased down the hammer.

Degas watched him almost in disbelief, seeing him lower the Colt back into its holster. A cocky half smile formed as he said, "They go their own way, Senor. I can promise you nothing."

"I understand," said Shaw, watching Degas start to back away and prepare to draw. He sidestepped quickly and spun around, snatching Degas' gun from its holster just as the big Mexican made a grab for it. Degas' hand slapped his empty holster. Shaw spun again just as the three men made a grab for their guns. This time, his arm around Degas' neck, he turned to face the gunmen, using Degas as a shield as he shot the first man down. . . .

ESCAPE FROM FIRE RIVER

Ralph Cotton

A SIGNET BOOK

SIGNET
Published by New American Library, a division of
Penguin Group (USA) Inc., 375 Hudson Street,
New York, New York 10014, USA
Penguin Group (Canada), 90 Eglinton Avenue East, Suite 700, Toronto,
Ontario M4P 2Y3, Canada (a division of Pearson Penguin Canada Inc.)
Penguin Books Ltd., 80 Strand, London WC2R 0RL, England
Penguin Ireland, 25 St. Stephen's Green, Dublin 2,
Ireland (a division of Penguin Books Ltd.)
Penguin Group (Australia), 250 Camberwell Road, Camberwell, Victoria 3124,
Australia (a division of Pearson Australia Group Pty. Ltd.)
Penguin Books India Pvt. Ltd., 11 Community Centre, Panchsheel Park,
New Delhi - 110 017, India
Penguin Group (NZ), 67 Apollo Drive, Rosedale, North Shore 0632,
New Zealand (a division of Pearson New Zealand Ltd.)
Penguin Books (South Africa) (Pty.) Ltd., 24 Sturdee Avenue,
Rosebank, Johannesburg 2196, South Africa

Penguin Books Ltd., Registered Offices:
80 Strand, London WC2R 0RL, England

First published by Signet, an imprint of New American Library,
a division of Penguin Group (USA) Inc.

First Printing, November 2009
10 9 8 7 6 5 4 3 2 1

Copyright © Ralph Cotton, 2009
All rights reserved

Ⓟ REGISTERED TRADEMARK—MARCA REGISTRADA

Printed in the United States of America

For Mary Lynn . . . of course

PART 1

PART I

Chapter 1

Trabajo Duro, the Mexican Badlands

At the end of a clay-tiled bar, Lawrence Shaw lifted a water gourd to his lips and sipped from it. Outside, the shadows of evening had overtaken the harsh glare of sunlight and left the sweltering Mexican hill line standing purple and orange in the setting sun. In a corner of the Pierna Cruda Cantina Burdel, a guitarist strummed low and easy.

Yet even as the music seemed to soothe any tension in the warm air, the player doing the strumming kept a wary eye on the three trail-hardened *americanos* who had arrived only a moment earlier, slapping dust from their clothes. "Like the sign reads, 'Welcome to the Raw Leg Cantina and Brothel,' gentlemen," the owner, Cactus John Barker, had said, translating the name into English for them as the three stood side by side at the bar. "What is your pleasure at the end of this hot, hellish day?"

"Rye whiskey if you got it, mescal if you don't,"

said a man in a no-nonsense voice. A red dust-filled beard covered his face. He wore a weathered duster, and a long riding quirt dangled from his wrist.

Cactus John quickly set three shot glasses in front of them and filled each from a dusty bottle of rye.

"The Raw Leg, huh?" said another of the gunmen, casting a sour look all around the cantina.

"Yes, the Pierna Cruda," the owner said, beaming proudly. "It's your first time here, so I'll tell you—I serve the strongest drink this side of the border. I make it all myself, and I taste it myself, so I know it's the best." He gave a toss of his hand as if saluting his distilling abilities.

"West of the border takes in a heap of land," the red-bearded gunman replied flatly.

The three eyed a couple of half-naked women up and down appraisingly and threw back their shots of rye. The man with the red beard motioned for the owner to refill the glasses. "Pour them to the brim," he said gruffly. "I never liked drinking short."

"Yes, sir. I see you fellows have arrived with a powerful thirst," Cactus John said nervously. He'd taken note that these men had walked in from the hitch rail like men who were there for a reason other than to quench their thirsts for strong drink or to sate their visceral needs for female companionship.

Like the owner and the old guitar player, Shaw had sensed trouble the second the three had pushed aside the ragged striped blanket covering the doorway and stepped inside. He had deftly pulled one corner of his poncho up over his shoulder. Also, like the musician, he had continued on with what he was doing as if they weren't there. Yet, unlike the guitar player and Cactus John, he had little doubt who these men were, why they were there or what was about to happen.

"*Gracias*," Shaw said to the young woman who handed him the water gourd. She stood behind the bar, awaiting its return when he'd finished drinking. The three men had ridden with the late Jake Goshen's gang. They had found the hoofprints of Shaw's and his pal Jane Crowly's horses and begun following them across the border the day before.

Their reason for trailing him was not because they wanted to reap vengeance on him for having killed Jake Goshen and leaving him lying in the dirt. They were following Shaw looking for stolen gold— a freight wagonload of it. There had been wagon tracks leading from Bowden Hewes' spread along Fire River, where they had found Goshen's body. But then the tracks had vanished in the hill country, and only the hoofprints of Shaw's and Jane's horses remained.

The gold had been stolen from the Mexican National Bank in Mexico City more than a year earlier. A week ago, Shaw, along with U.S. Marshal Crayton Dawson and his deputy Jedson Caldwell, aka the Undertaker, and a Mexican government agent named Juan Lupo had taken the gold back from Goshen and his gang. They had retrieved the loot just in time, before Goshen had a chance to melt it all down from German sovereign coins into untraceable ingots. But hanging on to the gold had proven to be no easy job. The borderlands were crawling with gangs of gunmen, outlaws intent on having the gold for themselves.

And here is where they find me . . . , Shaw mused to himself.

"Puedo hacer más por usted, señor?" The young woman asked Shaw with a suggestive smile if there was more she could do for him. She wore a string-tied cut peasant blouse that she kept pulled low and open in front, revealing her wares to the buying public.

"Gracias, no hoy," Shaw said courteously, turning her down but thanking her and leaving her offer open for another day. He laid a coin on the bar for the water and wiped his hand across his lips.

At the end of the bar one of the three gunmen said to the other two in a voice loud enough to make certain he'd be overheard by Shaw, "I hate a place that don't speak American."

The man with the red beard replied, "It is rude and unfriendly in Old Mex, and that's a fact." He dropped a gold coin onto the tile bar top. "Once across the border it appears all civil manners go to hell."

Facing the three from across the tile bar, Cactus John picked up the money quickly and said, "I myself am a born Texan, but I welcome all kinds of talk here." He gave a shrug of acceptance.

"Nobody asked you a damned thing, barkeep!" said the red-bearded gunman. "So keep your tongue reined down, 'less you want to lose it."

Cactus John stared back at him coldly, thinking about the sawed-off shotgun lying under the bar.

The girl standing across from Shaw gasped. She hurried from behind the bar, water gourd still in hand, knowing that at any second bullets would be flying.

Shaw almost sighed. He knew the gunmen would get around to him shortly. First they wanted to make a strong impression, he decided, feeling their eyes all turn toward him. "While we're here, there will be nothing spoke at us or around us but American," said the red-bearded gunman. "Everybody got that?"

Shaw only returned their cold stare.

"You there," one of the men said to Shaw. "Is that your speckled barb at the rail?"

Shaw's reply was no more than a single nod of his head.

"Where you coming from?" he asked.

Shaw didn't answer.

"Mister, I asked you a question," the red-bearded gunman demanded.

"No *hablo*," Shaw said quietly.

The three gunmen looked at one another. "*No hablo?*" one of the men said with a dark chuckle. "He must think we're joshing."

"Aw, to hell with this," said the younger of the three, "let's not pussyfoot around here." He stepped back from the bar and faced Shaw with his hand poised near his gun butt. "You're one of the lawmen, ain't you? One of them who raided Hewes' place over at Fire River. You helped Juan Lupo take back the gold."

Shaw made no move, no corrections in his stance, no drop of his gun hand to shorten the distance between it and the big Colt standing holstered on his hip. It had all been done earlier, in unhurried preparation. "Yep," he said in a calm, flat tone.

The other two stepped back from the bar and flanked the younger gunman. The one with the red beard said in a tight, angry voice, "You fellows thought you'd escape Fire River with a wagonload of gold? You were dead wrong. Now, where is it?"

Seeing that this trouble didn't involve him, Cactus John dropped low and ran in a crouch from behind the bar and out the rear door. The guitar player and the half-naked women seemed to disappear into the walls like apparitions. "I spent it," Shaw said in the same flat tone.

"You spent—!" the third man started to say.

But the younger gunman cut him off. "You're real funny, Mister!" he said to Shaw, his hand grabbing his black-handled Smith & Wesson and raising it.

"Yeah, for a dead man!" said the tall red-bearded gunman, reaching for his Dance Brothers revolver at the same time. The third man took a step back and made his move a split second behind the other two.

Outside, Jane Crowly had seen the three sweaty horses that had shown up at the hitch rail while she'd gone to a small general store for a bag of rock candy. She'd returned with a bulging jawful of horehound candy and heard the language turn heated and loud on her last few steps toward the blanket-covered doorway. *Oh hell . . .*

She jerked to a sudden halt when she heard the roaring gunshots resound so heavily that dust rose from the window frames and plank walkway. Then, recovering quickly, hearing the commotion of falling men and running boots, she raised her shotgun butt and slammed it hard into the striped blanket just as the third gunman came fleeing through the doorway.

Inside, Shaw stood with his Colt in hand. Gray smoke curled from the gun barrel and upward, as if caressing the back of his hand for a job well done. He stared in surprise as the third man flew back into the cantina, striped blanket and all, and landed flat on his back on the dirt floor.

"Is it safe to come in there, Lawrence?" Jane asked, her voice distorted by the lump of candy in her jaw.

Shaw stared at the third gunman lying knocked out cold, his head half wrapped in the dusty blanket. "It's safe, Jane."

Jane poked her head in first and looked back and forth, first at the two bodies lying in the dirt, then at the man she had nailed with the shotgun butt. "Lordy!" she said. "This one won't be coming to before Christmas." She noted a bloody bullet hole in the man's right forearm and inquired of Shaw, "Are you feeling poorly today?"

"I only meant to wound him," Shaw said. "I'd like to know how far word has spread about that gold coming across the desert." He looked all around the empty cantina, making certain no one had overheard him.

Within minutes the cantina had returned to normal. Cactus John Barker was back behind the tiled bar, wiping it with a wet cloth, removing a long streak of splattered blood. The half-naked young women had wandered back in and taken up their places, eyeing the bodies and the bloody bar top, and whispering among themselves as they stared in wonder at Shaw.

"He killed them both?" one of the women asked another in Spanish.

"*Si*, both of them," the other girl replied in the same tongue.

While the third gunman lay limp and unconscious, Jane had cleaned and bandaged his wounded forearm. By the time he began to come around, she and Shaw had propped him up in a wooden chair at a table. Villagers had ventured in and dragged the two bodies out into the dirt to await a hasty burial. Looking out through an open window, Shaw watched a skinny dog creep up and lick dried blood from the face of the red-bearded gunman lying in the street.

Jane, standing next to the wounded outlaw, said, "This one is starting to wake up."

"Good," said Shaw, turning toward them.

The gunman's head bobbed on his chest, and his eyes fluttered and tried to stay open. "I swear I feel almost bad, hitting him so damned hard," Jane said. She winced as she lifted his head with her fingertips and examined the darkening swollen imprint of the shotgun butt across his forehead.

"*Ohhhh*, my head," the gunman moaned. His head lolled to one side for a moment before he collected himself and looked up through bleary eyes. "What—what hit me?"

Jane glanced at Shaw and took on a sharp tone with the gunman. "Hell, I hit you, Mister. You and your pals come in here starting trouble with my amigo. You're lucky I didn't bash your brains out . . . if you had any."

"I'm—I'm still addled," the man moaned, rubbing and batting his red eyes. "I hope this is something that'll go away."

Shaw stepped over to his chair, looked down at him and said, "The only reason you're alive is because I want to know how many of Jake Goshen's gunmen are still running loose out here. Are you going to help us out?"

"There's nothing I can tell you that you don't already know." The man shrugged and held his good hand cupped to his throbbing forehead.

"Give it a try," Shaw said firmly.

"I ain't been riding with Goshen long—just since I got out of Yuma Prison," the man said reluctantly.

"Start with you name," Shaw said. "I don't recall ever seeing you before." As he spoke to the battered gunman he motioned for one of the women to bring over the water gourd. Then he reached out, flipped open the man's vest and pulled a small-caliber hideout gun from a side shirt pocket.

Seeing his hideout gun leave him, the man sighed and shook his head in resignation. "All right. I'm Roy Heaton," he said freely. "I just finished pulling five years, breaking rocks at Yuma, for robbing two stagecoaches over near Cottonwood. They weren't the only ones I ever robbed, but they was the only ones I got caught at and convicted for."

"Roy Heaton, huh?" said Jane, eyeing him up and down skeptically. "Roy *Heathen* is more like it."

"I'm just trying to be honest," said Heaton with a shrug. "I had lots of bad breaks in life. I took to crime as a way of trying to—"

"What about the men left from the gun battle over at Fire River?" Shaw asked, cutting him off, not wanting the man to ramble on about his criminal past.

The gunman had to shake his swollen head a little to get it working. "I can't say for sure," he said. "There's a hell of a lot, though. Twenty or more. Since last year when Jake and his closest circle robbed the depository, everybody and their brother has swarmed in wanting to ride with him."

Shaw started to ask another question, but before he could the man continued, saying, "Your two law-dog pals and that Mexican lawman killed a bunch of them at Fire River, but the ones that got away are all still out here sniffing for that gold. Others have arrived too. Even Garris Cantro, and his old guerilla cavalry."

"Garris the Cat . . . ," Shaw said, contemplating the seriousness of the matter. "I thought he died in a raid over near San Miguel."

"No," said Heaton, "the Cat is still alive. Still commands the Border Dogs. This is his stomping grounds. Even Goshen and his boys gave the Cat wide birth." He looked up at Shaw again as he took the water gourd and sipped from it. "Am I doing myself any good here?"

"Yeah," said Shaw. "Keep talking."

"The Border Dogs was the ones who helped set up the depository robbery to begin with. The way the Dogs figure, since they helped take that gold from the *federales* and the Germans, you and your pals stole it from them." He wiped a hand across his lips. "That's why Red Sage Burke and Sid Nutt was here." He gestured toward the street outside where the two bodies had been laid out, side by side. "They're both Border Dogs cavalrymen. So am I, now that Goshen is dead, I reckon." He shook his head slowly. "I saw how fast you can kill a man with your Colt, but you best hope you don't run into the Cat and his raiders. The killing might go the other way."

Almost before Heaton had finished talking, a young boy came running in from the street and slid to a halt on the dirt floor. "Senor, come quick!" he said, wide-eyed and breathless, to Shaw.

"What is it?" Shaw asked.

"One of the dead men we lay in the street, Senor," the boy said, pointing a trembling finger toward the assembled onlookers. "He get up and ride away!"

Chapter 2

Shaw and Jane hurried from the cantina with Roy
Heaton in tow to the spot where the young gunman, Sid Nutt, lay stretched out in the dirt. But Red
Sage Burke's body was gone from its spot beside
him. Villagers stood staring in awe toward the trail
out of town. With his Colt drawn and ready, Shaw
looked off at the rise of dust left standing in the air
behind where Red Sage's horse had raced away out
of town.

Shaw and Jane hurried from the cantina with Roy
Heaton in tow to the spot where the young gunman, Sid Nutt, lay stretched out in the dirt. But Red
Sage Burke's body was gone from its spot beside
him. Villagers stood staring in awe toward the trail
out of town. With his Colt drawn and ready, Shaw
looked off at the rise of dust left standing in the air
behind where Red Sage's horse had raced away out
of town.

"Damn it all to hell, Lawrence!" said Jane, as awe-
struck as the villagers, staring off beside him. "You
must be feeling off your game today."

Heaton stood in silence, staring down at the
ground.

"I hit him dead center," Shaw said with unwavering confidence. "There's no doubt about that."

"I thought you did, too," Jane said, seeing the serious look on his face. "I saw the hole in his chest. I
saw the blood!"

Shaw thought about it, then said, "You saw the bullet hole and the blood. But was it Burke's blood?"

"The whole cantina is splattered with blood," Jane said. "I saw plenty. So did you."

"Yeah, but what we saw was *his* blood splattered all over Burke," Shaw said, gesturing down toward Nutt, a large bullet hole in the center of his forehead. "We didn't see Red Sage Burke's blood, because he didn't bleed."

"He didn't bleed? Oh my God!" A look of terror came over Jane's face.

"You know what that means?" said Shaw.

"You're damned right I do," said Jane, her voice trembling in fear. She hugged her arms around herself as if for protection. "It means Red Sage is not human! He's some undead voodoo creature from the belly of hell—"

"Whoa, back up," said Shaw, stopping her as she drew closer to hysteria. "That's not what it means at all." He grabbed her shoulders and shook her a little to settle her down.

"I-I'm sorry, Lawrence," she said, "but something spooky like this just goes right through me."

Turning to Heaton, Shaw said, "Tell her why the bullet didn't kill him."

"Damned if I know." Heaton shrugged innocently, taking a step backward.

"Oh, so that's how you're going to be," Shaw said. He raised the small hideout revolver he'd taken off Heaton and cocked it toward the gunman's stomach.

"No, wait! I'll tell her!" Heaton cried out.

Shaw fired three shots in rapid succession. Each bullet hit Heaton squarely in his belly and sent him staggering another step backward.

"My God, Lawrence, you shot Heathen! He's unarmed!" Jane shouted.

"He's not hurt, Jane," Shaw said coolly, lowering the gun. "Are you, Heaton?"

Heaton stood bowed at the waist, his hands clutching his stomach. "No," he said in a tight, strained voice, "I'm all right."

"Straighten up," Shaw demanded of him. "Show her why you're not hurt."

Jane stared, her jaw gaping, her eyes squinting in hard concentration. "Those bullets are *blanks*?" Then she added quickly with a baffled look, "But that don't explain how you shot Red Sage—?"

Shaw cut her off again, this time with nothing more than a critical look. "I said, show her, Heaton, or I'll shoot you again."

"All right, all right." With painful effort Heaton stiffly stood upright and spread his hands. Three bullet holes appeared in a tight pattern in the front of his dirty white shirt. But there was no blood.

"Unbutton it," Shaw said, gesturing with the small gun barrel.

Heaton unbuttoned his dirty shirt, pulled his shirttails from his trousers and spread it open, leather vest and all. Beneath the shirt he wore a thick quilted silk and cotton vest that had the three small bullets embedded in it. "What the hell is this, Heathen?" Jane asked the gunman in amazement.

"He's wearing a bulletproof vest," Shaw answered for Heaton. "So are the other two." He gestured toward Sid Nutt's body on the ground. "This one didn't get much help from his."

"A bulletproof vest! That's damned impossible in these parts," Jane said in disbelief, stepping forward, staring at Heaton's chest in her amazement.

"But you had no trouble believing he was an undead voodoo creature?" Shaw asked, giving her a look.

Jane's face reddened. "Okay, I read the newspapers. I'm not a fool. The French navy took a bunch of bulletproof vests off Emperor Daewongun's soldiers in the Korean campaign."

"Heaton?" said Shaw, giving the nervous gunman a look that demanded an explanation.

"That's where they come from, I expect," Heaton said, eying the gun still in Shaw's hand. "The Border Dogs have been buying military goods and heavy armament from the French for the past year, ever since the big depository robbery. That's where lots of the German gold went."

Shaw contemplated it. "Stolen German coins, minted in Mexican gold, paid to the French, to buy military goods made by Koreans, in order for a group of stubborn Confederates to keep on fighting a war they lost years ago." He shook his head.

"If you think the Border Dogs are just one more bunch of stubborn Confederates, you're in for a hell of a surprise," said Heaton.

While he spoke, Jane stepped closer to him and held out a hand. "If you think you're going to keep wearing that bullet stopper, you've got another think coming to you," she said. "Now skin out of it."

Heaton dropped his vest and shirt to the ground and turned his back to Jane. "I'll need you to untie it for me," he said. "I'm kind of glad to get shed of it, to tell you the truth. The damned thing weighs a ton and it'll sweat a man dry."

Jane untied the three straps holding the vest closed at the center of his back. "You're right about it weighing a ton," she said. "But I expect if it'll stop a forty-five bullet it might be worth all the sweat it takes out of you."

"Yeah, well, good riddance is what I say," said Heaton. "Burke made me wear it, said Cantro has a bunch of his men wearing them just to see how good they work." He fell silent for a moment as if giving the matter some thought. Then he said to Shaw, "What if I hadn't been wearing this thing? You would have shot me dead."

"That's right," said Shaw. "But lucky for you, you're were wearing it."

"Yeah, but what if I wasn't?" Heaton presisted.

"You'd be dead," Shaw said flatly. "That's something to think about the next time I ask you something and you decide to stall on me."

"Yeah," Jane joined in, "and now that you *ain't* wearing it, you might want to answer just that much quicker."

Shaw asked Heaton, "Is there any way it's gotten back to Garris Cantro yet, about us taking the stolen gold back from Hewes and Jake Goshen?"

"Not that I know of," Heaton replied almost before

Shaw got the words out of his mouth. "I met up with Burke and Nutt on the way to Hewes' place. We saw what had happened there, and we came this way. Cantro didn't hear about it from us yet."

"Garris Cantro is not going to stand still for us taking the gold he needs to outfit his rebel army," Shaw said to Jane.

"Sounds like you know him and his Border Dogs pretty well," said Heaton. "They'll be taking that gold back if it's anywhere to be had."

Ignoring Heaton, Jane asked Shaw, "Have you ever crossed trails with these Border Dogs?" As she asked, she bent down over Sid Nutt's body and began stripping his shirt in order to take off the thick vest he wore beneath it.

"No, I've never crossed trails with them," said Shaw. "But it looks like I'm about to. I need to catch Red Sage before he gets word back to Cantro and his men about what happened at Fire River."

Jane rolled the body onto its back, untied the three straps and pulled the vest from his shoulders. Then she rolled the body back over, took off the vest and stood up, holding it out to Shaw with both hands. "You're going to kill him, I expect?" she said quietly.

"That's my plan, Jane," said Shaw, "unless you've got a better idea." He reached out and took the thick vest from her.

"What about this one?" Jane asked. "We can't just turn him loose. He'll go hightailing it straight to Cantro."

"He goes with us," said Shaw. "He might be able to show us where to find Red Sage Burke."

"Huh, I bet," Jane said skeptically. "I can see him doing everything he can to throw us off."

"Now that he sees I'll kill him at the drop of a hat, he'll be more cooperative," Shaw said. "Watch this." He turned to the wounded outlaw, who stood trying to hear them from a few yards away. "Heaton, we're going after Red Sage. Do you want to go with us to show us where he might be headed, or do you want me to shoot you where you stand and be done with you?"

"I know where he's going, sure enough," Heaton said in a nervous voice without hesitation, a hand rubbing three red whelps on his naked torso where the bullets had struck the vest. "I'll take you there straightaway."

"That was easy enough," Jane said with a crooked little grin. "What about Dawson, Caldwell and Easy John? They need to know that the Border Dogs are involved in this."

"They're going to know. We're going to ride back and tell them just as soon as we've caught Red Sage Burke and finished with him," said Shaw.

"They're waiting to hear from us right now," said Jane. "We're supposed to be riding a day ahead, making sure the trail is clear."

"When we don't show up tomorrow, Dawson will know we've run into something," said Shaw. "It's the best we can do for now." He stepped forward, gave Heaton a slight push toward the horses, and said to him, "If Cantro asked you about the vests, what would you tell him?"

Glancing down at the body stretched out in the dirt, the bullet hole in its purple forehead, Heaton rubbed the raised whelps on his belly and said, "I'd have to say it worked better for some than it did for others. Burke is the one who got the best deal on it, and he had refused to wear it until just before we rode into town." He shook his head at the irony of it as he walked on toward the horses out front of the cantina. "It's a strange damned world any way you look at it."

"I'm with you on that," Shaw said, walking along behind him, Jane right beside him, each carrying a bulletproof vest slung up over their shoulder. "And it's getting stranger every day."

Red Sage Burke did not stop until he reached a small muddy water basin at the base of the hill line ten miles from town. When he finally slid down from his saddle, he let the reins fall and allowed the horse to drink its fill while he dropped flat beside it and stuck his face into the water and did the same.

He'd been knocked unconscious by the impact of Shaw's bullet, and by the jar to the back of his head when he'd slammed it against the hard-packed dirt floor. But as soon as his eyes had opened he'd seen Sid Nutt lying beside him, dead in the street with a half-dollar size hole in his forehead. He hadn't needed a second look to realize what had happened—he'd made a run for it.

When he'd sated his thirst, he rolled over, slung water from his red beard, unbuttoned his shirt and reached up behind the small of his back and untied the only two straps he could reach on the cumbersome vest.

Pain pounded deep in his bruised chest as he struggled with the wet, heavy vest. It worsened as he rose to his knees and skinned the vest and his shirt both at once. Groaning, he dropped the vest to the rocky ground and slid back into his wet shirt. Still on his knees he clutched both sides of his ribs. "By God," he said loud enough to cause the tired horse to pique its ears, "I'd sooner get shot clean through." Yet he picked up the vest and managed to throw it behind his saddle.

With painful effort he bowed his head and examined the wide raised red whelp in the center of his chest. In the center of the already darkening whelp he saw the purple-black imprint of Shaw's forty-five-caliber bullet. "Dead center . . . facing three guns," he said almost in admiration of the shooting skills involved.

Loosening the bandanna from around his neck, he dipped it into the water. He squeezed it slightly and pressed it gently against his battered chest. While he held the dripping bandanna in place he looked at the front of the vest lying behind his saddle and saw the bullet half buried in the thirty layers of quilted silk and cotton. "So you're the little killing sumbitch that did all this to me . . . ," he said under his breath.

Still aching, he reached over to the vest and dug out the slug with his thumbnail, noting that the bullet had penetrated less than half of the material before coming to a halt. Holding it in his hand, he looked back along the trail across the wide and endless desert floor. Seeing a thin rise of dust in the distance, he said, "Time to get out of here. . . ."

He looked down at the bullet in his palm. "Since you're the one who could've killed me and didn't, I'm asking you, 'Which way do you want us to go?'" He shook it in his closed hand, then opened it and looked off in the direction the blunted bullet nose pointed.

Burke made a short, painful laugh under his breath and said, "Agua Mala, eh? I have to say that would not have been my first choice." Closing his fist around the bullet, he looked back at the rising trail of dust and considered things for a moment. Then he said, "But come to think of it, that might be as good a place as any, 'til I either lose this man or kill him one."

Burke looked at his closed fist and gave a strange, thin smile. "Obliged, my little killing friend," he said almost affectionately. "You might just be smarter than you look."

Even in his pain he struggled up into his saddle and looked at the vest, which lay wet and smelly on his horse's rump. "Why didn't you say Agua Mala?" he said to the vest. Then he tucked the vest partly under his saddle to secure it in place, shoved the bullet deep into his trouser pocket, turned forward in his saddle and rode away.

Chapter 3

When Shaw, Jane Crowly and Heaton reached the water hole an hour after Burke had left, Shaw walked around the pool and stepped up atop a large rock along the water's edge. He looked all around, his rifle in hand. Noting the hoofprints of Burke's horse leading away, he called down to Jane, "Looks like he's headed north."

"North?" she asked, slapping dust from her fringed buckskin shirt with her hat. In her left hand she held her canteen.

"Yep, north," Shaw said, stepping down from the rock. Turning to Heaton, he asked in a firm tone, "Why's he headed that way?" In the distant southwest a broad black cloud loomed low on the horizon. Shaw noted it but made no mention of it right then.

"I don't know why he went that way, and that's the honest truth, so help me God," Heaton answered quickly, knowing better than to stall Shaw, especially when he held a gun in hand.

"North is to Agua Mala," Jane put in. "Hell, nobody ever goes there. Even the *federales* steer clear of Agua Mala."

"Bad Water . . . ," Shaw said, translating the words to English. He looked closer at Heaton and asked, "There's none of Cantro's men supposed to meet you three in Bad Water?"

"None that I know of," Heaton said, "and that's the truth too."

"Well, it makes no sense that he'd go there without good reason," Jane replied. "Nobody would go to Bad Water unless they had to." She finished slapping dust and put her hat back on. She kneeled down to the water with her canteen and began filling it. Beside her the three horses drew water intently.

"Maybe I ought to mention this to you," Heaton said to Shaw. "Red Sage Burke does not always do things that make sense to the rest of us."

Shaw nodded. "If he's riding into Bad Water, so are we."

"I know I've got no say in where we're headed," said Heaton. "But riding into Agua Mala is a good way to get us all three killed. The only thing in Agua Mala is rattlesnakes and *pistoleros*. If you ain't Mexican, you ain't *welcome* . . . if you ain't *wanted*, you ain't welcome. If you ain't a no-good sonsabitch, you ain't welcome there. Get what I'm saying?"

"Yeah, it sounds like a real nice place," Shaw said, unimpressed.

"You're wasting your breath, Heathen," Jane said to Heaton. She stood up from filling her canteen and hooked its strap over her saddle horn. "I've already learned better than to try and tell him anything." She took Shaw's canteen down from his saddle horn, walked over to the water and bent down to fill it. "He's got a stubborn streak."

Shaw didn't respond to Jane's comment. Instead he thought of the shooting in the cantina and looked out along the trail. "Bulletproof vests . . . ," he said quietly to himself. "What'll they think of next?" He gazed off in the direction of Agua Mala. Then he looked back in the opposite direction, judging how long it would be before the approaching black cloud would reach them.

Twenty-seven miles farther down the trail, Red Burke looked back at the same wide black cloud. "That one's a hell-raiser . . . ," he commented to himself. He slowed his worn-out horse to a halt and stepped down from the saddle. Drawing his repeating rifle from its boot, he levered a round into the chamber and gazed ahead into the wavering heat at the empty street stretched out before him.

"I can kill the first gun-toting sonsabitch who shows his face," he called out loudly. He took quick aim at a faded sign out front of a weathered adobe building and fired a bullet into it. As soon as the sound of the shot fell away across the vast open land, he called out, "Or, I can ride in and offer German gold coins to any *hombre* who wants to earn it doing some hard killing."

After a moment of silence, when no answer came from the row of adobes and shacks lining both sides of the street, he called out, "Have I come to wrong place? I'm on the run. I've always heard that Agua Mala is the place a man comes to when he wants other men killed."

After another, shorter silence, a voice called out from a shadowed doorway, "Ah, you are on the run. Then you have come to the right place, *hombre*. Ride forward. Let us look at the man who tells me he pays in gold, for some killing he wants done."

Beside the Mexican bandit, another bandit whispered to him, "Do you want us to kill him and stick his head on a post, *mi hermano*?"

"No, no, Ernesto," the bandit said to his younger sibling. "If this man has German gold coins, we know where he got them. If he rides with the men who robbed the depository we must allow him in and make him welcome." He gave his brother a sidelong wink. "Who knows, perhaps much of the stolen gold will rub off on us, eh?"

Ernesto turned to the other gunmen spread out in the shadows along the hot, dusty street. "All of you, show your best manners," he called out. "This man will be treated as one of us." Looking back at his brother Sergio, he said with a grin, "Unless my brother and I decide to shoot him and take all of the gold he is carrying."

"Show restraint, Ernesto," said Sergio. "It is time we better ourselves by getting to know these border *gringos*." He spit as if saying such a thing brought a bitter taste to his mouth.

"I cannot believe the words I hear, Sergio," said Ernesto.

"It is true," Sergio replied. "Whether we like it or

not, these *gringos* are the ones who made the biggest robbery in the history of our nation. We must put ourselves in good favor with them if we can."

When Burke stopped his horse in the middle of the dirt street, a hard wind had begun blowing in from the southwest, preceding the coming storm. A dust devil whipped about in the middle of the street a block away. Burke tossed a leather bag full of gold coins to the ground and looked back and forth in the darkened shadows of alleys and blanketed door-ways.

"Don't be bashful, *hombres*," he called out. "You all know there's a hell of a lot more *veinte-dólar*, twenty-dollar, gold coins where these came from." He gave a wicked grin. "All with the compliments of the German government."

Hearing the muffled jingle of gold coins in the bag, Sergio and Ernesto looked at each other. "You ask much of me, my brother," Ernesto whispered, letting the hammer down on his big revolver.

Burke watched the two men step forward into sight. Along the street other gunmen followed suit. "I knew that sound would wake you up from your *siestas*." He chuckled under his breath.

Sergio ignored his words, picked up the bag, loosened the top and looked into it. He fingered the twenty-dollar gold coins and said almost to himself, "*Si*, they are the stolen German coins. . . ." He eyed Burke closely, hefting the bag in his palm and asked, "Who is this lawdog you want us to kill for you, *mi amigo*?"

"I talk better with my hand wrapped around a

bottle for some reason," said Burke, stepping down from his saddle. "I could be talked into bouncing some young senorita on my lap a time or two." He held his reins out toward Ernesto as he spoke. "Take my horse, boy," he added in a tone of authority.

Ernesto gritted his teeth and stared at his brother.

Sergio saw the fury in Ernesto's eyes, but he gave him a nod and said, "Take his horse, *por favor*." Turning to Burke he said, "How do you know we will not take your money, kill you and hang your head on a pole?"

"Ouch," Burke said, with no show of fear. He gave his same grin. "I figure I can take that chance. If you killed me you have this bag of gold. But if you listen to me and play your cards like I tell you, that bag of gold will turn into a whole wagonload."

Ernesto had taken the reins to Burke's horse. But upon hearing his words he stopped as if frozen and stared at Sergio for some clarity. "Oh," said Sergio. "That would be a lot of gold, Senor." Along the street, other gunmen had heard his words. They gathered closer to hear more on the matter. "Tell us where this gold may be seen," Sergio coaxed.

"Not so fast," said Burke. "I want to make sure you boys are worth riding with. Take care of this law-dog and you'll see it, sure enough. It'll be yours— enough German gold to keep all of you in peppers and beans for a hundred years." He let out a laugh and looked around at the solemn faces surrounding him.

Ernesto had to grit his teeth to keep from shooting Burke down where he stood. "Be patient, my

brother," Sergio warned him under his breath. Then
he turned back to Burke with a sweep of his hand
toward a dingy adobe cantina down the street. "Let
us get you that bottle and the young senorita you
thirst for. Then we will talk about gold and how
much of it we will soon have in our hands."

By the time Jane and Shaw had stopped at an
abandoned adobe three miles outside of Agua Mala,
the storm had moved in closer and lay black and menacing almost directly overhead. While Jane stepped
down from her saddle and walked over to a stone-
walled well, Heaton pulled his hat down tight against
a hard gust of sand-filled wind and looked all around.
"We've got a bad one coming," he said sidelong to
Shaw. He looked first at the black cloud, then toward the town of Agua Mala, as if weighing his situation. "By rights, you got no authority to hold me
against my will, do you?"

"By *what* rights?" Shaw asked him with a blank
stare.

Heaton started to say more on the matter, but the
look on Shaw's face made him think better of it. He
gave a submissive shrug. "I'm not making nothing
of it," he said in a meek tone, "just conversing, is
all."

"Don't converse," Shaw said. At the well he saw
Jane spit out a mouthful of water she'd drank from
a gourd dipper that hung by a strip of rawhide on a
pole beside the crumbling stone wall.

"Hell's fire and brimstone!" she said, making a
sour face. "I can see how Bad Water came to get its

name. This water taste like it's been through a sick horse."

Shaw lifted the canteen from his saddle horn and pitched it to her. She wiped a hand across her mouth, uncapped the canteen and took a swig of tepid water. "Can you keep a rifle in his ribs while I ride into Bad Water and take a look around?" he asked.

She wiped her hand across her mouth again and said with sarcasm, "Well, hell no. What made you even think I could do something that requires that much sense?"

Shaw just stared at her blankly.

She stepped over and handed him the canteen. "All right, I expect you wasn't meaning to accuse me of being an out-and-out babbling idiot."

"No, I wasn't," Shaw said with the same flat expression. "Can you do that for me?" he asked with persistence.

"Yes, I will do that, if that's what you want," Jane replied, taking it more serious. "But ain't you taking a mighty big risk riding in there alone?" she asked.

"No, I'm not," Shaw said.

Jane shook her head. "I swear, Lawrence. Sometimes I don't know if you're almighty brave, or if you just don't give a damn if you live or die."

Shaw didn't answer. Instead he said to Heaton, "How much weight does Burke carry with Garris Cantro or the other Border Dogs leaders?"

"Quite a damned bit, to hear him tell it," said Heaton, without stalling.

"How much gold did he have in his saddlebags?"

Shaw asked, gazing off in contemplation toward Agua Mala as he spoke.

"I never got a real good look at it," said Heaton. "But I'd guess him to have five, maybe six hundred dollars stashed there. I understand Cantro was passing out gold coins awfully freely to his better gunmen—keeping his fastest guns happy, so to speak."

"I understand," Shaw said quietly. He gave a nod and said, "Get down off the horse." To Jane he said, "If he makes a move you don't like, shoot him." A gust of cooling wind rushed through the abandoned yard, carrying a harsh blast of sand.

"I hear you." Jane gave the gunman a cold stare, tapping her fingers on the Colt stuck down in her waistband. Then she looked up at Shaw, seeing him pondering something to himself. "Do you care to cut me in on what you're thinking?" she asked.

"Maybe later," he replied. He drew his rifle from the saddle boot and pitched it down to her.

Jane caught the rifle, but looked at it almost in disbelief as Shaw turned his speckled barb away from the adobe. "Wait a damned minute, Lawrence!" she said. "You can't go riding in there without your rifle. Even you ain't that all-fired cocky."

Without reply, Shaw turned his barb and nudged it forward at a walk, the horse bowing its head against the stinging wind. Heaton, down from his saddle, stood beside his mount, the reins hanging from his hand. "What now?" he asked Jane.

"*What now?*" she said, repeating him, giving him an angry glare. "What the hell do you think you're doing, accompanying me to a town dance?"

"I didn't mean nothing," Heaton said quickly, his hands going chest high in submission.

"Go hitch the horses at the rail, Heathen," Jane said angrily. She poked the rifle barrel toward an iron hitch rail. "Then get your sorry ass inside the house before this wind blows us both away." She growled under her breath like a bitch cur as the nervous gunman hurried both of their horses to the hitch rail. "I hope you make a false move," she said. "There's nothing I'd like better than shooting you from a bull to a steer."

As Heaton walked ahead of her toward the open door of the empty adobe, she gave a quick, frightened look over her shoulder toward Shaw as he rode away into a swirl of sand. "Lordy, Lordy," she whispered softly to herself. "What'll I do if you don't come back . . . ?"

Chapter 4

The gusts of wind had grown stronger, more violent, as Shaw stepped his speckled barb onto the swirling street. He guided the animal toward a low-standing cantina where a young woman stood smoking a black cigar, a ragged serape draped around her shoulders. Seeing Shaw arrive, the woman spoke quietly over her shoulder without taking her eyes off him.

"Degas, the lawman is here," she said into the sound of accordion music and men and women's laughter.

The music and laughter stopped. A burly man with a black leather patch over one eye eased up behind her and looked out over her shoulder. "Ah, you have done good, Tetas Dulces," he whispered near her ear. His thick hand squeezed her buttocks for a moment. Then he loosened his grip and patted her firm hip. "You will share my bed with me this night, and I will feed you well."

"But what about *mi* Antonio?" she asked, still

watching Shaw approach, his duster tails standing sideways on the rushing wind.

"Forget about your Antonio. He is nothing but an *alcahuete*," said the big Mexican, Degas Gutierrez. His hot breath caressed the side of her neck. "A woman like you does not need an *alcahuete*. You need a real man, a man like me who can take care of you."

"If Antonio heard you call him a pimp he would kill you, Degas," the young woman whispered in reply, not sounding angry or offended by his words, only challenging him.

"He would try," said Degas, "but I would slap him like the woman that he is. Besides, where is this Antonio of yours? He rides away with the *gringo*, with Sergio and his idiot brother Ernesto and the others. They all want to hang from the *gringo's* teats like suckling piglets. But I stay here, because I am the one capable of putting this *gringo* lawdog in the ground for good."

"You do not impress me with your big talk," the woman said. "We will see what we will see." She jutted her chin and added, "*Mi* Antonio rides to bring me back gold. What do you have for me?"

"For what I do here, I too will have much gold for you when Sergio returns," said Degas, "perhaps even more than your Antonio." His hand came up around her from behind and cupped her firm breast. "Watch what I do to this one for us," he said, gesturing a half nod toward Shaw, who had slowed the barb to a halt and sat calmly looking back and forth. "It is something your *pimp* Antonio would never be able to do. His *cajones* would be too small and delicate for such a task."

"Hello the cantina," Shaw called out, sitting comfortably in his saddle, his poncho down, covering his big Colt. He realized that if Red Burke were still in town he would have already started shooting.

"Hola, señor," said Degas Gutierrez, taking a slow, casual step out of the cantina into the windy street. As he walked toward Shaw, three serious-looking gunmen, two Mexican and one Texan, stepped out and followed him. They stopped a few feet back and spread out as Degas drew closer. With no attempt at pretense, he looked up and said to Shaw, "You are a man who cares little for living, knowing that the *hombre* you are chasing has gold with which to buy himself many amigos here in Agua Mala, eh?"

"Where is he?" Shaw asked flatly without bothering to answer him.

"It does not matter where he is," said Degas with a shrug. He pointed a finger up at Shaw as if taking aim with it. "It is where *you* are that should concern you greatly."

"Not if I'm a man who cares little for living," Shaw replied. As he spoke he slowly lifted his leg over his saddle and slid down the barb's side. He stood close to Degas, too close. But the big Mexican would not allow himself to back away for fear of losing face among his men. That was what Shaw had counted on.

"You must be a foo—" Degas' words stopped short.

Too quickly for anyone to react, Shaw's Colt

had streaked out of its holster, cocked and leveled against the big man's forehead. Degas knew he'd been had. He stood with his hands spread, helpless. Shaw reached out with his free hand and grabbed Degas by the front of his shirt, making sure the man could not get away. "As soon as I pull this trigger all of you go ahead and open fire on me," Shaw called out, staring deep into Degas' eyes. Then to Degas he said quietly, "Isn't that what you'd like for them to do?"

"*Si*—I mean wait! Everybody!" Degas called out in a rattled voice. "Let us all calm down and act like civilized men!"

"If he kills you he is dead, Degas!" a young man called Perro Risueño called out.

"Shut up, Perro! I know he will be dead, you idiot!" Degas shouted. "But so will I. He has a gun to my head, and he is loco out of his mind."

"Two questions, one chance to answer," Shaw said, ignoring the other three men, pressing the tip of the gun barrel a little tighter against Degas' sweaty forehead for affect. "Where's he going and how many men are with him?"

"They go that way!" said Degas, pointing toward a side trail leading out of Agua Mala. "There are five men riding with him. They go to find a wagonload of gold that is headed across the desert." He paused, collected his courage and said, "Now you must turn me loose, and you must face me man-to-man, with no tricks." His eyes took on a dark gleam. "For now I must kill you, Senor."

"One-on-one? No tricks?" Shaw asked, letting go

of the wad of shirt in his hand. "You're not going to have your pals all try to shoot me down?" As he spoke he lowered his Colt and eased down the hammer.

Degas watched him almost in disbelief, seeing him lower the Colt back into its holster. A cocky half smile formed as he said, "They go their own way, Senor. I can promise you nothing."

"I understand," said Shaw, watching Degas start to back away and prepare to draw. He sidestepped quickly and spun around, snatching Degas' gun from its slim-jim holster just as the big Mexican made a grab for it. Degas' hand slapped his empty holster. Shaw spun again just as the three men made a grab for their guns. This time, his arm around Degas' neck, he turned him to face the gunmen, using him as a shield as he shot the first man down.

"Don't shoot!" Degas bellowed. But it didn't help. Shaw put his second shot into the next gunman as two bullets slammed into Degas' big broad chest. Feeling the impact of the shots, Shaw staggered back a step. Steadying himself, he shot the last man standing, turned Degas loose and let him fall. A terrified cur had sped from beneath a broken cooperage barrel and run away, leaving a long yelp resounding behind him.

Degas looked up at Shaw with blood flowing from his lips. *"Por favor* . . . not with my own . . . gun," he said in a halting voice.

Shaw pitched the Mexican's gun aside and redrew his Colt. "I can stop it here," he said, the Colt hanging loosely in his hand.

Cutting a short glance toward the cantina, Degas shook his head and said to Shaw, "No . . . finish it. I deserve to die."

Before the dying Mexican's words left his lips, Shaw's Colt bucked at his side. As Degas fell limp in the dirt, Shaw looked up and saw the woman walking toward him from the blanketed doorway of the cantina. "Do not shoot, Senor!" she called out to him, seeing him turn toward her, the smoking Colt in his hand. "I only come to see what you have done, and to make you welcome in Agua Mala." She skidded to a halt a few feet away, one shoulder of her blouse lying seductively low on her shoulder.

"Do not trust that one, Senor," said a gravelly voice from the corner of a low plank porch out front of a crumbling adobe. "She is a slippery little *puta* who will cut your throat in your sleep."

Shaw's eyes snapped toward a bent old man standing beneath a wide battered sombrero. He stood barefoot, wearing a loose black suit and leaning on a long walking stick.

"Pay the old fool no mind," said the young woman with a smile. "You can call me Tetas Dulces, like everyone else does. I will be yours while you are here with us."

Sweet Teats . . . Shaw translated the woman's name in his mind. As he removed the empty brass shell from his Colt and replaced it with a new one from his belt, he ignored the woman and asked the old man, "How long have men like these held their boot on the neck of Agua Mala?"

"For much too long, my quick-triggered friend,"

the old man said. He stepped down and shuffled forward. "Some ride away earlier with the *americano* . . . then you kill the rest of them." He spit down on Degas' bloody body, then looked back up at Shaw and gave a tired grin. "I think this is all of them."

"Obliged for the information," said Shaw, taking a searching glance along the alleyways and side paths leading off the dirt street. The wind from the coming storm grew more intense. The old man swayed sideways and caught himself on his walking stick.

"It is a good day for us," he said. "By the saints, please tell us that you are not like them. There are still some of us who want to live in Agua Mala and turn it back into the peaceful place it once was." He shook the walking stick toward the young woman. "Now that they are gone, the *putas* who follow them will leave as well."

"How dare you call me whore, old man!" the woman shouted, taking a step toward the Mexican. Shaw caught her by her forearm and stopped her. Still she leaned and continued to the old man, "When Antonio and the others get back I will have them slit your throat and bleed you like pig!"

"Antonio is not coming back," the old man said with confidence. "You and your *puta* friends must leave here if you value your lives."

"What do you mean he is not coming back?" the young woman asked, still enraged, seeing a few more weathered old faces begin to appear like ghosts along the dusty street.

"None of them will be back," said the old man, his voice stronger, "because this one wants them dead, and I believe when this one wants a man dead, so it will be."

"You can go to hell, old man!" she shouted, pulling free of Shaw's grip and taking a step backward toward the cantina. "You can all go to hell! That is what I have to say to you!"

From out of nowhere a rock sailed in and struck her on the leg. She looked stunned.

"I think it's time for you to go, Tetas Dulces," Shaw said. "These folks seem a little edgy right now."

"And take the rest of the thieving *putas* with you!" a voice shouted from along the dirt street.

Looking out across the sandy, rolling land between Agua Mala and the line of low hills where he'd left Jane to watch over Heaton, Shaw saw the black storm cloud hovering lower and closer. "I need some food and supplies," he said to the old man. "Can I get it here?"

"For you, anything you need, *nuestro amigo*," the old man said with a sweep of his hand toward the long dirt street running through Agua Mala. "This humble town is at your service."

A full hour after Shaw had ridden off into a swirling netherworld of dust and whipping wind, Roy Heaton stood staring out the window in deep thought. Beyond the adobe, the wind whistled and roared. Jane had stood leaning back against a wall, facing him from across the littered room. Once satisfied that the gunman wasn't going to make a move against her, she stood away from the wall and dusted the seat of her trousers. "The wind's turning cold . . . ," she commented to herself.

Shaw's rifle cradled to her breast, she kept an eye on Heaton as she gathered twigs, dry brush and scraps of wood into a pile beneath the half-missing ceiling and built a small fire.

"I still want to know what right he thinks he's got holding me prisoner like this," Heaton said over his shoulder.

"Well, let me see . . . ," Jane said. "Maybe the same right all you sonsabitches think you have, killing and robbing, then running across the border, figuring nobody can do anything about it. Now you're whining because somebody finally comes along and puts a stop to it?"

"Two wrongs don't make a right," Heaton said in response. "Just because men like me break the laws, it doesn't mean it's all right for him to. He's a lawman, damn it."

"'Two wrongs don't make a right . . . ,'" Jane quoted in a mocking tone. "Heathen, that's some powerful philosophizing." Then she searched all around on her fringed buckskin clothes and added in a mocking tone of voice, "Damn it, I never have a pencil and paper handy when I need one."

Heaton turned from the window facing her and said bluntly, "What's he got on you, anyway?"

"He's got nothing on me," Jane replied. "I'm only doing the same as I'd do for any man I'm riding with."

Reading something in her tone of voice, Heaton cocked his head curiously. "Are you telling me the two of you are *man and woman* . . . ?" He let his words trail. He took a short step forward.

"That's none of your *damned* business, now, is it?" Jane said, her face reddening. She stood up beside the small flickering fire, rifle in both hands, her face carrying a silent warning for him to keep his distance.

He stopped in his tracks and lifted his hands chest high. "No offense, but I always heard you had no interest in men."

"That's a hell of a thing for you to say to me," Jane spat back, his words having an effect on her. "What do you know about me anyway?"

"Hell," said Heaton, "I've heard all the stories about Jane Crowly. You once posed as a man to work as a teamster." He gave a thin, knowing grin. "You got drunk and got caught naked, taking a bath with the rest of the bunch." He eyed her up and down with a distasteful look. "I also heard the story about you and a dance hall girl in Abilene—"

"You listen to too many stories, Heathen," Jane said, cutting him off. "I once *worked* as a dance hall gal to feed my little brothers and sisters after my folks died. But I worked lots of jobs to feed them little ones, and I'd do it again if I had to. Now keep your mouth shut before I feed you a lead dinner."

"I'm just repeating what I heard," said Heaton.

Jane held the rifle pointed at him with both hands. He saw her knuckles whiten on the gun stock. "If I'm what you're saying I am, I wouldn't be living as man and woman with Lawrence Shaw . . . the man I just *so happen to love*," she added, lying before she could stop herself. "Now, would I?"

A stunned look came upon Heaton's face. He seemed to forget anything they had been talking about and asked in a wary, lowered voice, "Lawrence Shaw? *The* Lawrence Shaw . . . Fast Larry? The Fastest Gun Alive?"

"All of that, and then some, smart-ass," Jane said with her chin jutted. "Don't you feel stupid just now figuring it out? Haven't you heard me calling him Lawrence all this time?"

"Yeah, but . . ." Heaton fell silent for a moment, then said, "Damn, no wonder he shot the hell out of everybody!" He looked away as if trying to get a grip on things. Then he asked, "So, you and him . . . ?" He slid a finger back and forth between two fingers of his other hand.

"That's right, genius," said Jane. "See how smart you are when you really work at it?" She took a deep breath and extended her lie. "Now, would he and I be lovers if I was what you and some other pecker-heads think I am?"

Heaton didn't reply right away. He stood in stunned silence for a moment. Finally he said, as if something else had just dawned on him, "Fast Larry Shaw is going to kill me dead, ain't he?" A panicky look overtook his hardened beard-stubbled face. He took another step forward.

"No," said Jane. "Because I'm going to kill you myself if you don't settle down and keep your mouth shut."

Heaton stood staring at her for a moment as if resolving a question in his mind. Finally he did settle down a little and said, "You won't shoot me, Jane Crowly. I've figured you out. You're all spit and bluster. You won't kill a man." He advanced a step, then another.

"You're making a bad mistake, Heathen!" she warned, taking a step backward, but cocking the rifle hammer as she did so. "I've already killed once. The second time won't bother me none." She recalled shooting the Widow Edelman down in her own front yard when the woman was about to shoot Shaw from behind. *All over that damned gold . . .* , she recalled instantly, not liking the feeling that came over her as she'd watched Lori Edelman fall dead in the dirt.

"I'm leaving. Give me that rifle," Heaton demanded boldly, seeing something in her eyes that made him think he could get away with it. His advance on her quickened. She saw him making a move for the rifle,

"No, stop, *please!* Damn it all to hell," said Jane, holding the rifle tight, cocked, aimed and ready, but not certain she could use it even though her finger lay tense on the trigger.

Her words showed her weakness. "*Please?*" Heaton said with a dark chuckle as he reached out and grabbed the rifle barrel in order to wrench it from her. "I said give me that rifle, you stinking she-man!" he growled.

"Get back, I'm warning you," Jane said, her tough voice turning to a terrified sob.

"*Warn* me!" Heaton grasped the barrel with his good hand. With his other hand he backhanded her across her face and jerked the rifle at the same time.

Jane fell backward; her finger pulled the trigger before she landed on the littered dirt floor. She heard the blast and felt the rifle buck in her hands as she held tight to it. She saw Heaton turn the barrel loose. He jerked backward a step as the bullet went through him, then jackknifed as a red spray rose and trailed behind him to where the bullet struck the earthen adobe wall.

"You shot me!" he gasped in a strained, stunned voice. In disbelief he clasped both hands to the bullet hole in his belly, then raised one hand and stared at his own blood.

Jane shook like a person with an affliction. "Damn it, Heathen! Why'd you do that?" She managed to lever a fresh round into the rifle chamber and struggle up onto her knees.

Heaton backed away toward the door in a crouch, realizing she'd had no intention of pulling the trigger. "You . . . crazy bitch," he said.

"Don't try it, Heathen! I'll shoot you again! I swear I will!"

But Heaton didn't believe her. He turned and ran out through the rear door, still bowed at the waist. Jane fired the rifle wildly and saw the bullet strike high above the doorway. "Damn it!" she cursed. "What's wrong with you, Janie?"

She shakily levered another round into the rifle chamber. But instead of going to the rear door for another shot at the wounded, fleeing gunman, she backed away to the open front window. Hugging the rifle against her like a child's comforter, she peeped out and watched him grapple with his horse until he finally crawled up into the saddle.

Tears streamed down her face as she hugged back against the wall and heard him ride away. "What the living hell is wrong with you?" she said again, bellowing long and painfully against the hard roaring wind. Then she sank to the dirt floor, sobbing, clutching the rifle to her bosom, repeating the same question over and over under her breath.

Chapter 5

When Shaw returned, the black storm cloud lay low and growling overhead. Rain and hail began to beat down mercilessly as he stepped down from his saddle, noting that Heaton's horse was missing from out front of the adobe. "Easy, boy," he said soothingly to Jane's horse, unwrapping its reins while the animal ducked its head and stomped a hoof against the stinging hail.

He led both horses to a partly collapsed lean-to alongside the adobe and left them beneath the shelter of a sagging roof. With a cloth sack full of trail supplies slung over his shoulder, he checked his Colt beneath his poncho and walked to the front door, listening intently.

Inside the adobe he found Jane lying in a ball on the floor, his rifle clutched to her chest. She appeared to be neither asleep nor awake, her red-rimmed, half-open eyes staring lost and aimlessly across the dirt floor. Shaw swung the cloth sack of supplies onto a battered table. "Janie, are you all right . . . ?"

he asked barely above a whisper, not wanting to startle her. But in spite of his effort Jane let out a shriek and jerked the rifle around toward the sound of his voice.

"Whoa," said Shaw, catching the rifle barrel with his hand. He held it down and pointed it away from him as a shot exploded from the barrel. "You best give me that," he said, yanking the rifle quickly from her hands. "What's gone on here?"

"Oh Lordy, Lordy, Lawrence," said Jane, "thank God it's you!" She scooted up onto her knees and rubbed her face with both hands. Shaw saw the whelp left across her cheek where Heaton had backhanded her.

"Where's Heaton?" Shaw asked, checking the rifle as he spoke. He glanced all around as if expecting to see Heaton waiting to surprise him.

"He's—he's gone, Lawrence," Jane said with a worried look. "I failed you. I let that heathen bastard get away."

Shaw noted the large spots of blood leading to the rear door. "But you're not wounded, are you?"

"No, that's not my blood; it's his," said Jane. She settled down and took on a bolder attitude. "He bolted on me. I managed to put a bullet in the sonsabitch before he got away," she said, her voice sounding stronger as she talked about it. "I would've shot him again, but he'd busted me a good one in the jaw and I felt myself slipping fast. By the time I got aimed and ready, he was in the saddle and gone into the dust." She spit with disgust. "The low *poltroon* bucket of scum."

Shaw helped her to her feet and seated her on a rickety wooden stool. "You shot him, then he hit you?" he asked, not getting a clear picture of what had happened. He examined her bruised cheek and the dried blood on her lower lip.

She pulled her face away from his gloved hand. "Don't fret over me none. I'm okay," she said, avoiding the question. "How'd things go for you in Bad Water?"

"Not too bad," said Shaw. "Red Burke was already gone. He's got some local cutthroats riding with him. He left a few behind, but now they're gone too."

"Meaning you shot them," Jane said flatly.

"Yep," Shaw said.

She shook her head in awe. "You never cease to amaze me, Lawrence."

Shaw freed his bandanna from around his neck. He touched the edge of it to his mouth, wet it, and dabbed at the dried blood on her chin and cheek. "The town is most grateful to be shed of them." He gestured toward the sack of supplies. "I've brought back some food—some peppers and beans, and coffee. We're welcome in Agua Mala as soon as this storm blows over."

"Are we going there?" she asked, "now that Heathen has got away?"

"No," said Shaw. "We're not going there. We're going to stick here for a while and let everything and everybody settled down some."

"It's my piss-poor luck that brought this on,"

Jane said, as if offering an apology. "The weather never carries on like this except when I'm here."

"If you're not here, how do you know?" Shaw offered in her defense.

"Anyway . . . ," she said, having no comeback. "I expect I should have warned you about riding with me."

Shaw ignored her words and looked down at the waning fire she'd built earlier. "I'll stoke the fire up and boil us some coffee if you're all right now," he said.

"Ah, hell, Lawrence, I told you I'm all right," Jane said, sounding a bit put out by him attending too closely to her. "I'll rustle up some wood for the fire." She stopped as if his words had just registered to her, and said, "What do you mean 'let everybody settle down some?'" She gave him a questioning look.

"It came to me riding back here," said Shaw. "This storm is going to wash out the tracks of Red Burke and his bandit pals. Everybody gets a fresh start. I'm betting Red Burke is not hurrying back to Garris Cantro and the Border Dogs."

"You figure with his new *bandito amigos* he'll go searching after the gold himself?" Jane asked.

"For all we know that's what him, Sid Nutt and Heaton were all up to in the first place—going after the gold for themselves," said Shaw.

"Well, if they were, you shot that idea plumb to hell for them," Jane said.

"I busted them up and slowed them down. I didn't stop them," said Shaw.

"I don't know." Jane shook her head dubiously. "Going after all that gold without Cantro and the Border Dogs is mighty ambitious of them."

"Gold makes men ambitious," said Shaw. "Dawson, Caldwell and John Lupo will be waiting out this storm too. When it's over they'll also get a new start. They know we're ahead of them, keeping watch on the trail. We'll give Red Burke time to stick his head up. Then we'll chop it off. Same goes for Roy Heaton if he makes it to Garris Cantro and tells him what's going on." He paused in reflection, then added, "That is, if Cantro doesn't already know."

"Lordy," said Jane. "It sounds like you're itching for a fight with somebody, and you don't much care who."

"I agreed to work the law with Marshal Dawson and Deputy Caldwell," Shaw replied. "We're here to clean up along the border. I don't care how it gets done."

"Then you ain't awfully upset with me, over Heathen getting away?" she asked meekly.

"No," Shaw said. "As much gold as there is involved, it'll draw him back to us sooner or later." A crash of thunder roared overhead. "Meanwhile, we sit out this storm, rest ourselves and the horses."

Overhead the storm had turned more severe. Hail pounded the walls and half roof like bullets. The wind had lessened, but only a little as the sky turned dark as night. Lightning split the dark, boiling clouds, followed by cannon-fire thunder that shook the crumbling adobe. The horses whinnied in protest from within their lean-to shelter.

"It's going to be tomorrow morning before this sky-buster is over," Jane calculated, looking up at the black heavens through the missing part of the ceiling. She stooped down to the smoldering fire and blew on it, then stopped as if in deep contemplation. She touched a hand to the bosom of her fringed buckskin shirt and let her fingers toy idly but nervously with the top button.

In the late evening, when the storm had slackened to a hard, windless rain, Shaw sat on his blanket in a dry spot on the dirt floor and sipped coffee in the glow of firelight. He cleaned and checked his big Colt, while to the northeast thunder still growled low beneath an occasional faded steak of lightning.

In a rear corner of the adobe Jane had stretched a ragged, discarded blanket she'd found in the rubble across two rickety chair backs. She undressed behind the blanket and bathed herself with fresh rainwater she'd collected in a large clay urn. She used a small bar of lye soap Shaw had given her from his saddlebags. "Lawrence," she said quietly, out of the blue, "before Heathen got away, he and I were talking some."

"Yeah?" Shaw didn't look up. He sat checking the action of his Colt by turning the cylinder slowly between his fingertips. "Is that what helped him get away—he caught you off guard?"

"Hell no," she snapped back at him. "He didn't get the drop on me."

"I understand," Shaw said, not trying to pursue the matter.

"I—I told him something that maybe I shouldn't have," she said hesitantly.

"What's that?" Shaw asked, his attention still drawn to the revolver in his hand.

"I told him you and me are man and woman," she said, almost holding her breath after saying it.

A silent pause followed.

"Was that all right?" Jane asked after a moment, her voice sounding anxious, unsteady.

"Was what all right?" Shaw asked quietly, "us being man and woman . . . or just you telling him that we are?"

Jane breathed a short sigh of relief and smiled demurely to herself. "Either one . . . *both*," she said, quickly catching herself. "Damn it . . . It would be all right, that is, as far as I'm concerned. You know, the two of us, together?" She paused and listened intently, not daring to look around the edge of the blanket and face him. "I know there's been some bad things said about me . . . things that ain't true. I'm as normal as the next person. I want you to know that."

"You don't have to prove anything to me, Janie," Shaw said. "I put no stock in stories passed along bars and gambling tables." He finished with the Colt and slid it into his holster.

"Well, thank you very damn much," Jane said with sarcasm. She grumbled and cursed under her breath, then said, "I'm not trying to *prove* a damned thing. I just figured you're here, and I'm here. I just went a little soft for you for a minute—" She cut herself short and said, "Aw, hell, forget it."

She stood up, naked above the top edge of the hanging blanket. She began pulling on her buckskin trousers. "Don't go thinking you'd be the first hardheaded gunslinging fool I ever let crawl up my leg. You wouldn't—and you won't be the last, either. I've always had a partiality for misfits and idiots...." Her words fell back into a muffled grumbling.

Shaw sat in silence. He watched as she struggled with the close-fitting buckskin, seeing her firm, bare breasts without the binder she usually wore to keep them flattened. *Jesus* ... He set his tin cup down and rose to his feet. He'd never realized what a shapely woman she was beneath her men's trail clothes and breast binder.

With her trousers up but not buttoned, in a huff she gathered her hair back and began tying a strip of rawhide around it. "I'll tell you another damned thing, too, Mr. Fastest Gun Alive," she said. "When I was a schoolgirl, I had men come to court me the likes of which—"

This time it was Shaw's finger on her lips that cut her off. "Are you going to talk all the while?" he said quietly, standing close to her.

"No, I'm not," she said, taken aback at his sudden appearance. She raised a hand as if to cover her bare breasts. "But I just wanted to let you know—"

Shaw cut her off again, this time with his lips

pressed to hers. He kissed her long and deep, at first feeling some strange awkward resistance from her. But it quickly passed, or melted away, as she moaned and let go of something inside herself. She had clenched her fists when he'd begun the kiss, but she opened her hands and let them fall upon his shoulders.

When the kiss ended, she gasped for breath and held him at arm's length. Her hair fell undone around her shoulders, the rawhide strip clinging to it. "I—I wasn't prepared . . ."

"Are you now?" Shaw asked. He looked deep into her eyes in the soft flicker of firelight.

"Yes, I am. I mean, I think so," she said, sounding not quite certain. She shrugged clumsily and started to say more, but before she could, he swept her up off her feet and carried her to his blanket. "Oh my . . . ," she said as he laid her down gently but firmly.

She writhed out of her unbuttoned trousers as Shaw pulled them down and off and pitched them aside. "You do move fast when you've put your mind to it," she gasped, spreading her legs and pulling him down between them.

He wanted her to shut up, but he had a feeling she wasn't going to.

"I hope you . . . don't think that this is something I let everybody in the world—" Her words stopped again, this time in a deeper, louder gasp. "Oh my!" she repeated, this time crying out the words. She felt the heat of him, the hard powerful presence of him, and she gasped wide-eyed, staring off through the missing roof at the darkness overhead. "Oh yes, Lawrence! Oh, damn it, yes . . ."

He'd been right. She wasn't about to shut up. This was how it was going to be all the way.

Moments later, when they had finished and lay side by side looking up at the dark, clearing sky, she reached a hand over and drew circles on his chest. "Was it . . . good?" she asked.

"Yes," Shaw said, feeling strange, being asked something like that, "it was good." He stared straight up, trying to remember whether she had talked all through their lovemaking. He believed she had.

"Just good?" she asked.

Here we go. . . . "No, it was better than good, Janie. It was *really* good."

"Because that was the first time in a long time for me," she said, relaxing against him. She laid her head on his chest and said, looking up at the clearing sky, "Look, the stars are coming out." She paused and smiled to herself. "We made love in the desert, under the stars, didn't we?"

"Yes, we did." Shaw wondered if this had been a mistake. But he stroked her naked back, felt her breasts warm against his chest and put aside any doubts. "I know you're tired," he said. "Go on and get some sleep. I understand."

After a pause, Jane said quietly, "I'm not tired at all."

Shaw lay gazing at the stars through remnants of drifting clouds.

"I always worry afterward, what a man thinks of

me. I don't want to be looked at like I'm some kind of line whore," she said.

"I don't look at you like that at all, Janie," Shaw offered, hoping it would do, yet knowing somehow that it wouldn't.

"Ever since I was a young girl I've worried about that." She paused in reflection. "I took over raising five brothers and sisters when I was just a strip myself, so I didn't get much time to figure how men and women ought to act with one another. You could say I missed out on some things." She shrugged. "Anyhow, I always got along better riding and hunting with the men than I ever did sewing and chatting and taking tea with the lady folk. Is that wrong . . . ?"

"No," Shaw said quietly. He could tell it had been a long time since she'd talked to anybody this way. He let her get it all out. He continued listening as his eyes fell closed. He drifted with the dark passing clouds. He felt Rosa warm against him, then Rosa's sister, Carmelita, with whom he had lived for a while following Rosa's death.

"I took what men's work I could find to feed my orphaned brothers and sisters, because women's work didn't pay worth a squat. . . ."

It was the same with the women in his life, Shaw reminded himself, nodding, seeing countless other faces of women come and go behind his lowered eyelids. And now among those faces, Jane Crowly, he thought, hearing her voice grow farther and farther away as sleep overtook him. Jane continued talking for a while. She raised her head from his chest enough to look up at his face and see that he had fallen asleep.

"Well, I can't say it's the first time I've talked one under the table," she whispered to herself. Snuggling back onto his chest, she turned her eyes to the dark, clearing sky and sighed. "It's still a beautiful night. . . ."

Chapter 6

Just before dawn Shaw opened his eyes to the smell of boiling coffee. Jane was already up. She looked over at him from where she sat stooped beside the fire. Seeing him return her gaze, she looked away, lowering her head, her floppy hat brim shielding her eyes from him. "I figured you'd be waking up hungry this morning," she said. Reaching out a hand, she stirred beans and peppers in a small tin skillet over the low fire. "I know *I* did."

Shaw looked at her, not knowing what to say and not really wanting to say anything. He thought about the night before and felt strange now seeing her back in her buckskins, wearing her big heavy miner's boots, her breasts flattened by her binder, her hair back and pushed up under her hat.

Jane stood and walked over and stooped beside him with a cup of steaming coffee. "Here, drink this. It'll make you feel better about last night," she said as if reading whatever concerns might be crossing his mind. She gave a slight grin, holding the cup out to him. "Don't worry, I ain't holding nothing over you. What happened last night don't make us married."

"Obliged," Shaw said, referring to the coffee, not sure how else to respond to her. He took the cup, blew on the brew and sipped it.

"Although," she continued, "I can see how this kind of partnership could be good for both of us if we wanted it to. I bet there's many a pilgrim wishes he had a pard he could trail with all day and rub bellies with all night."

"I never gave it much thought," Shaw said. He didn't like the image her words conjured up in his mind now that she was back in her buckskins and miner's boots. He paused for a moment, then said, "Look, Jane, last night was something that maybe we—"

"I know what you're going to say, Lawrence," Jane cut in, "but lest you think I'm going to go getting all moony-eyed and talking stupid, let me tell you straight out: I'm free as a bird and I intend staying that way. What happened last night was really good—you said so yourself. But it might happen again or it might not."

Shaw sat staring, lost for words.

"So let's neither one go counting on anything from the other, okay?" She pushed a stand of hair from his eyes and smiled. "Ain't that sort of what you were fixing to say?"

"Yeah," Shaw lied, "something like that." He wasn't clear on what she was saying or why she was saying it, but he breathed a silent sigh of relief hearing her lay to rest any notions of romance between them. With that, he decided it best to sip his coffee and let her clear the air on the matter.

"You see, Lawrence, I've never allowed myself to be hurt by a man, like some women have. I've never had time for it. I pull my trousers on when I'm satisfied, and I go on about my business. Do you understand me?" She offered another smile. It was stiff and unconvincing, but Shaw decided it would have to do.

"Yeah, I understand," said Shaw. How much of this was the plain truth, and how much was Jane's tough-sounding pretense, he didn't know. But this was neither the time nor the place for him to sort through it. She offered him a way out and he took it.

"Good," Jane said, standing, backing away. "Now, I expect we can eat breakfast and go on riding together without any foolish expectations of each other."

Enough said . . . Shaw nodded. Standing, he pulled on his trousers and his bib-front shirt. He tucked the shirttail in, buttoned his fly and hooked his gallowses over his shoulders. He picked up his gun belt, slung it on and buckled it. Jane watched him draw his Colt, check it, then slide it back into the holster.

After a breakfast of peppers and beans, they attended to the horses and were on the trail before the first rays of sunlight rose above the eastern horizon. They rode upward into a low line of jagged hills. When they stopped at daylight, they stepped down from their saddles and scooped up hailstones into their hats and held the offering up to the horses' muzzles.

Crunching on a piece of hail herself, Jane gestured toward a stretch of flatlands below to the northwest of the hill line. "After that storm your pals and the wagon will do well to keep to the foot of the hills, at least until the sun dries things up some."

"Yeah, that's what I figure," said Shaw, gazing in the same direction, realizing that the lawmen and the wagonload of gold lay somewhere out there, hidden in the vastness of the rugged desert hill country. "We'll keep scouting east of them until we find some fresh tracks or turn something up. As long as we keep ourselves between the wagon and the thieves, we'll have the upper hand."

"I've rode enough for the army to know that 'scout' is ofttimes just another word for 'decoy.'"She offered a crooked smile. "Hell, sometimes all it means is 'live bait.'"

"Then let's make sure we do all we can to keep the 'live bait' *alive*," Shaw said. He slung a few remaining hailstones from his hat, placed the hat back atop his head and swung up into his saddle.

"I'm with you on that, pard," Jane said, slinging water and crunched ice from her hat. She stepped up into her saddle next to him and the two nudged their horses forward onto a path leading down to the desert flatlands.

"There's three villages over there?" Shaw asked, gesturing toward the rolling hills east of the flatlands.

"Yes," said Jane. "The first is Suerte Buena, meaning Good Luck." She gave her crooked grin. "I was through there once, but no good luck rubbed off on me. What about you?"

"I was too drunk to remember what my luck was at the time. Good or bad, I managed to ride it out." Nodding off into the distance, he said, "There's two more towns past Suerte Buena." He searched his memory. "There's Mal Vuelve. . . ." He stalled, having a hard time remembering the third.

"Ciudad de Almas Perdidas," Jane said, helping his memory along, "the City of Lost Souls."

"That's right," Shaw said, "it's Ciudad de Almas Perdidas." He spoke the three names in order. "Suerte Buena, Mal Vuelve and Ciudad de Almas Perdidas."

Jane translated the names to English, saying, "Good Luck, Wrong Turn and City of Lost Souls." She smiled, nudging her horse forward. "Sounds like some kind of dark prophecy, don't it? Life wishes you good luck, then sends you down the wrong trail, then ends up sweeping you in with all the other lost souls."

Shaw didn't respond.

"But I never blame life for my making any wrong turns," Jane added, feeling a need to lighten such a hopeless line of thought. "Seems like wrong turns is where I always developed a keener sense of direction."

"Let's hope this trip does the same," Shaw said as they rode on.

When Red Burke and the five Mexican *banditos* rode into Suerte Buena, they watched doors and windows slam shut along the narrow dirt street lying before them. A man wearing a stove-pipe hat and carrying chickens by their feet scurried into an alley. Guitar and accordion music coming from within a cantina stopped suddenly. Sitting atop his horse between the Alevario brothers, Sergio and Ernesto, Red Burke slapped dust from his shoulder and said, "We just got here and I already feel unwelcome." He gave Sergio a grimace. "I hope you boys' cloudy reputation hasn't dampened any chance of a warm reception."

Sergio spit in disgust. "These stinking piglets," he said, staring from one closed door to the next. "They will pay for shaming me this way in front of an amigo." He looked at Ernesto. "Take this pigsty apart, my brother. Perhaps the next time we come here they will remember this lesson."

Ernesto started to spur his horse forward. But Burke stopped him with a raised hand. "Hold it. . . . What have we here?" He gestured toward a spindly legged old man who stepped out into the street thirty yards away with a large, ancient shotgun in his hands. He wore a drooping gray suit with a red sash around his waist and a tin badge pinned crookedly on his lapel. Atop his head was a wide flat-crowned hat, like the kind worn by lawmen on the American side of the border.

Sergio chuckled and said, "Oh no, they have elected another lawman for us to shoot."

"*Si*, and I will shoot him right now," said Ernesto, "so he does not have to walk all this distance in the afternoon heat." He drew his long Remington from his waist and cocked it.

"No, wait," said Red Burke. "Let's talk to him, hear what he might have heard about the stolen gold. He could be of some use to us."

"What? This one?" Ernesto laughed. "He will do us no good. They are hardheaded, these old ones. They take upholding the law much too serious."

"In that case we can always kill him," said Burke, sounding firm on the matter, "but for now we'll talk, and see what he has to say."

"*Hola, hombre viejo,*" Sergio called out, holding up a hand in greeting.

"Do not call me 'old man,'" the aged lawman replied in a scorching tone. He stopped a few feet away and planted his feet firmly. "I am a *diputado alguacil* here in Suerte Buena. Show respect for the law."

"Oh," said Sergio, a bit taken aback by the fire in the old man's voice. "I offer my apology to you," he said humbly, eyeing the shotgun in the man's hands. "But tell me then, *Diputado*, if you are the *deputy* sheriff, where is the sheriff himself?"

"Our beloved sheriff is dead and in the ground," said the old deputy in a grave tone. He made the sign of the cross on his chest in respect. "He is dead because desperados like you killed him."

"Desperados? No, not us, Deputy," said Sergio. "You are mistaken. I am a businessman from Agua Mala. These men are my associates." He pointed quickly all around at Red Burke and the others.

"No businessman comes from Agua Mala," the old deputy said firmly. "Only *banditos* and *putas* come from Agua Mala. Anyway, I know of you and your brother." He wagged a finger back and forth between Sergio and Ernesto. Red Burke only watched in silence. "I have seen wanted posters of the two of you. There is a price on both of your heads, here and across the border in Tejas."

"It is true there have been some misunderstandings regarding me and my brother," Sergio said, jutting his chin proudly. "But we are both bold men and it is by our hand that we have kept our freedom. Do not be foolish enough to think about collecting the rewards for us."

"I am old and I know I am no match for the two of you. I seek no reward. But it is my job to keep you out of my town and by the saints I will do so." His grip on the shotgun tightened.

Turning sidelong to Red Burke, Ernesto said under his breath, "Please, we must kill this old fool, Red. I think he is going to cause us trouble if we let him live."

"Take it easy," Burke replied. He stepped his horse closer and said down to the old man, "I'm not from Agua Mala, but I am a businessman, and I have a serious question for you, Deputy. Have you heard any rumors about a freight wagon full of stolen gold trying to cross the desert anywhere near here?"

"You are talking about the gold stolen from the depository in Mexico City last year, eh?" the old lawman said.

"*Si*, that's right," said Burke. "I'm willing to pay you for any information you have."

"Of course I have heard about the gold stolen

from my government," said the deputy. "But do you think I would tell a piece of border trash like you what I might know about it?" He shook his head. "No, not for any amount of money."

"That's that," said Burke. He raised his Colt and fired one quick, decisive shot. The old man had no chance to swing the shotgun up to defend himself. He hit the ground dead. A braided stream of blood rose, then fell from the bullet hole in his heart. Burke said calmly to Ernesto, "That didn't take too long."

Ernesto and Sergio and the other three gunmen grinned among themselves. "You are one wild *loco hombre*, Red," said Ernesto. "I think you are going to be our good *americano amigo* even after this gold hunt is over."

Red returned the grin. "I'll settle for being your rich amigo," he said, nudging his horse forward at a walk.

Over his shoulder he said back to Sergio, "Have Antonio, Rollo and Little Jose open this town up and tell these folks we're their friends. I want a belly full of mescal and an arm full of warm senorita before sundown gets here."

"You got it, Red," said Ernesto. He turned to the other two, Rollo Barnes and Little Jose Montoya, and waved them along behind him. Sergio rode up beside Burke, and the two stepped their horses around the dead deputy and rode to the cantina.

They tied their horses' reins to an iron hitch rail and walked inside the silent cantina, hearing shoes and boots scuffle across the dirt floor as they pulled open a rickety wooden door. "All right, all of yas,"

Burke called out, "I better see some happy faces welcoming me. I'll start shooting some sonsabitches right here and now!"

Sergio stepped over to the plank and tile bar and reached around and lifted a guitar player by the scruff of his neck. "You heard him, music man. *Musica, musica por mi amigo!*"

"Si, *musica*, right away," the guitar player replied in a nervous voice. He pulled the accordion player out from behind the bar and the two hurried to the corner and fell right into a snappy tune.

"That's more like it," said Red Burke with a wide grin. He leaned both hands down on the bar and said to the empty air in front of him, "If there's not a bottle of mescal standing at attention here in two seconds, I'll start shooting anything that's got a heartbeat."

A bald bartender sprang up, bottle and wooden cup in hand and shakily poured the cup full of mescal. "I am at your service, senors," he said. "Please excuse our ignorance here in Suerte Buena. It is not every day that we have such important guests in our humble village." His eyes flashed back and forth between Sergio and Burke.

"Is that a fact?" said Burke. He pulled a fistful of black cigars from a cigar holder on the bar top. He stuck all of the cigars but two down into his dusty shirt pocket. He stuck one of the two between his teeth and handed the other to Sergio.

"*Si*, it is true, Senor, we only want to make you happy while you are here." The cantina owner eyed the empty cigar holder, then quickly produced a long match and struck and held it up, lighting each man's cigar in turn.

"I'm going to suggest that you get some women and food laid out here, pronto," said Burke. He grabbed the man's wrist and forced him to hold on to the match as the fire traveled closer and hotter toward his fingertips. "You do not want me leaving here with anything but fond memories. I'll burn this town to a cinder."

From the end of the bar two identical young women stood up and ventured over to Burke and Sergio. "Welcome to Suerte Buena, senors," one of them said in stiff English, hoping to direct Burke's attention away from the cantina owner. "I am Falina, and this is my sister, Malina. Here, let us show you something." In unison the two pulled the tie strings loose on their blouses, spread them open and let their ample breasts spill forward.

"Good gawd almighty! Twins!" said Burke, his eyes lighting up with a lustful gleam. "No wonder this little pigsty is called Good Luck." He lifted his Colt from his holster and fired it into the soot-smudged ceiling. "*Yiiihiii!*" he shouted, gathering the two bare-breasted young women against him. "I just got here and I feel lucky already!"

"I knew we would feel welcome here," Sergio said, reaching a gloved hand over and roughly patting the cantina owner's tense beard-stubbled cheek. "You have done well for yourself. Now you can take the rest of the night off." His hand went around the cantina owner's throat and yanked him over the bar top and threw him toward the door.

"Please, Senor, my cantina," the man begged even as he crawled through the dirt toward the darkening street.

"Do not worry about this place. We will look after it for you as if it were our own," said Sergio. He grabbed a bottle of mescal by the neck, jerked the cork from it with his teeth and spat it away. He turned his big pistol toward the two terrified musicians who had stopped playing as they watched the owner being dragged over the bar. "What is wrong with you two?" Sergio shouted, waving the gun menacingly at them. *Musica! Musica por mi amigo!* He fired at the dirt beneath their bare feet.

Hugging the twin whores to his chest, Burke grinned and said, "I want you gals to start calling me Daddy right now."

Chapter 7

In a shack behind the town livery barn an old German mining engineer named Adolf Herzoff stood in the glow of candlelight listening to the men of Suerte Buena. The old men talked barely above a whisper even though the gunmen were over a block away inside the cantina. In their midst stood a goat chewing a mouthful of brittle hay. Nudging the goat aside, the old stoop-shouldered German walked to an open window and looked through the evening gloom toward the dimly lit cantina.

"Poor Deputy Leone," he said quietly, hearing the music resound gaily along the empty street. "And Leone did nothing to provoke these men?"

"No, nothing," said one of the village elders who, along with the others, held a machete at his side. "And even if he did, they had no reason to kill him. He was doing his job, standing up to them, trying to keep this kind of border trash out of Suerte Buena."

"Our quiet little village is no place for such men as these. They are killers and pillagers, and we know what they always do," said another man, this one holding a short-barreled homemade gun, made for hunting wild pig. "Before they stepped down from their horses, poor Leone was dead." He crossed himself, adding, "May God take his spirit."

"And we must do something," said the other man. "We are not men if we do not avenge poor Leone." He looked all around at the other town elders for support. They nodded their agreement and grumbled in unison.

The old German looked hesitantly at their faces. After a moment of grave silence he said, "We wait until they have sated themselves with mescal and the brown coco powder. Then we will swoop down upon them and confront them severely. We will make them pay for what they have done."

"*Si*. We will do to them what the people in Flores Pequeñas did to the same kind of outlaws who crossed the border and violated their women and stole their horses. We will sink their severed heads on a stick at the entrance to our town as a warning to others of their kind."

"*Si*," said another of the men, raising his machete over his head and waving it back and forth, "and I will personally do the cutting. Leone was once married to one of my wife's cousins, so I stand as family to him."

"We will cut off their heads, but only after we hang them," said another old man, also waving his machete.

"I have a rope. I will go get it," said the first villager.

"Yes, go get it, Carlos," said the old German. "We will wait here until the time is right. Then we will strike without mercy." He held up his shotgun with a somber look on his weathered face. "What we do, we do for the sake of Suerte Buena!"

"For Suerte Buena!" the men said with determination.

Inside the cantina, Red Burke lifted his face from between Malina's legs and stepped back from the bar. The young woman hopped down from the bar and pushed her dress down over her thighs. She reached a hand up to close her open blouse, but Red grabbed her wrist, stopping her.

"Leave them puppies out where they can breathe. I'll keep them from running away," he said. His eyes were bloodred and wild. Brown powder streaked his beard from beneath both nostrils. He reached his free hand back and groped behind him for the other twin. "Falina," he said, "powder me down some. I feel a darkness coming on."

When Falina didn't answer he turned and saw her lying on a table in a far corner, Antonio standing hunched between her legs. Through a thick haze of cigar smoke he saw what the two were doing and a blind rage swept through him. "You sonsabitch!" he shouted. "Get your own whore! These two are mine!" Drunkenly, he raised his Colt and began firing wildly. His first shot hit the wall above Antonio's head and caused the couple to scramble away, their clothes half off and their private parts exposed.

This time the musicians knew better than to stop

playing. They kept up their lively music as shot after shot exploded, leaving an uneven line of bullet holes in the wall, following the half-naked fornicators all the way to the rear door.

The men hooted and roared with laughter as Antonio and Falina vanished into the darkness. Red waved his smoking gun and said loudly, "Somebody go get my whore and bring her back here. Tell her I want us to kiss and make up."

Sergio had left for a few minutes. He and his brother had retuned just as Red sent Antonio and Falina running out the back door. They had returned with a short, somber-looking American with large watery eyes and a drooping mustache that ended down past his chin. Above the music, Sergio called out to Red, "Amigo, this is River Johnson. He wants to talk to you."

"River Johnson, I've heard of you. . . ." Red spoke drunkenly. "You burn stuff down." He staggered in place and looked the man up and down. Seeing River Johnson standing with a long black wool coat buttoned all the way up the front, he said, "Are you warm enough? Do you need to build yourself a fire?"

Ignoring Burke's remark, Johnson said in a stern tone of voice, "I'm looking for work."

Red Burke shrugged and tossed a bleary-eyed look all around the cantina. "I haven't seen any."

River Johnson turned on his heel and started to walk out the door. "Hold up, Johnson," Burke said with a dark chuckle. "I'm just having some fun with you."

"Fun . . . ?" Johnson stared flatly at him through his watery eyes.

"Hell's fire, man, don't be so damned serious," Burke offered, his mind boiling with cocaine, mescal and rye whiskey. "We're all just having a little *fiesta* here, in honor of me shooting the living hell out of an old deputy."

"I know," said Johnson, "I saw it from my room. You shot him down like a dog."

"Yeah, I did," said Burke, "does that not bode well with you?"

"I can't give a damn," said Johnson. "I told you I'm looking for work."

"Do you know who I ride for?" Burke asked.

"Who?" said Johnson.

"Garris Cantro's Border Dogs, is who," Burke replied. He stared hard at Johnson, waiting for a response. "What does that do for you?"

"It suits me," said Johnson. "I always wanted to ride for a big guerilla band like the Dogs. I missed out on the war myself, owing to bad health."

"Bad health? When did bad health ever stop a man from fighting in a war?"

River Johnson didn't reply. Instead he repeated bluntly, "I'm looking for work. Got any?"

"No, I've got no work that I can think of for you today," said Burke, in a taunting voice. "But let me think on it. Hell, I'm just here following orders myself," he lied, "doing what Cantro wants me to do here."

"He's got you here raising hell and killing the town deputy?" Johnson eyed him skeptically.

"Yep, I'm only following orders," Red said, "strange as that might sound." He swung an arm toward the barful of mescal bottles, both empty and full, and said, "I never get in a hurry hiring a man. You'll have to wait awhile, let me see what I come up with." Still in the taunting voice he added, "Meanwhile, you're welcome to join us in a drink or two while we're here."

"Obliged," said the serious-looking gunman, "I don't mind if I do." He stepped closer to the bar and picked up a wooden cup and a bottle of mescal.

Burke nodded. "Make yourself to home. But you'll have to excuse me. I've got a couple of sassy twin whores here." He reached and snatched Malina by her arm. "I might just skin and eat one of them right here."

"*Bon appétit.* Enjoy yourself," Johnson said dryly, raising the wooden cup as if in a toast.

In the dark hours of early morning the old German and the group of ten town elders converged on the cantina with weapons and torches in hand. One man carried a coiled rope on his thin shoulder, one end with a noose, which he swung back and forth with each step. When the group stopped, they were twenty yards from the cantina. They stood in silence for a moment, listening to the two worn-out musicians play slowly and quietly inside.

With a gesture of his hand, the old German sent a townsman forward in a crouch. The man first handed his hat and his machete to a friend standing beside him, then eased forward as silent as a ghost.

He took a position at the edge of the door frame, where he inched the wooden door open slightly and peeped inside.

At the far end of the bar the only man left standing was River Johnson. The bottle standing before him was still half full. The wooden cup sat close to his fingertips alongside a big Remington revolver he'd drawn from his coat pocket and laid on the bar top earlier. He still wore his big wool coat fully buttoned. Not a hair stood out of place atop his bare head. He'd seen the front door creep open an inch, but he deliberately ignored the matter and gazed away toward the tired musicians.

The guitar player saw Johnson raise his hand and give them a dismissing sweep toward the rear door. "Holy Mother be praised," the guitarist murmured. He tugged at the half-asleep accordion player's shirtsleeve and the two eased across the dirt floor without a word and slipped out into the chilled morning dark, stepping over the sleeping bodies of gunmen on their way.

From the front door, the townsman watched the musicians leave. Then his eyes went to a dim candlelit corner where some goatskins and blankets had been spread on the dirt, forming a sleeping pallet. On the pallet he saw Red Burke lying half naked in the shadowy light. Burke lay entwined between the naked twins. He wore nothing but his dirty trousers, the fly blaring open revealing a red tangled patch of hair deep on his lower belly. His gun belt lay close beside him on the dirt floor.

The townsman stared intently. On the bare dirt floor another naked young woman lay with a sleeping gunman's arm thrown over her, and her dirty foot in the face of another snoring gunman.

Red raised his head for a moment, long enough to grumble at the loss of the music. Then his face fell to the tip of a large breast and laid there as still as stone. Before the townsman backed away and scurried back toward the others, he watched River Johnson pick up his pistol and the bottle from the bar and walk toward the rear door.

"Well, are they all knocked out?" Herzoff asked in a nervous whisper.

"*Si*, they are asleep," the townsman said, out of breath. "They are drunk and naked and unarmed, all but one and he is leaving even now." He shot a glance toward the dimly lit cantina. "He is the one who has been staying here this past week—the silent one."

"Oh, him," said Herzoff. "His name is Moses River Johnson. Perhaps he will go away and not take their side."

"Perhaps," the townsman agreed, then said, cautioning the old German, "But he is not drunk. He is as wide-awake as we are."

"Even so," said Herzoff. "We came here to do a job and so we will. If he gets in our way, it will be his mistake."

From within the dark shadow of an alleyway, River Johnson stood within listening range, chewing on a long unused wooden match. He smiled thinly to himself upon hearing them discuss him. He didn't care. He had no dog in this fight, he reminded himself—at least none that he held any attachment to. He backed a step as the group walked forward and the flickering glow of torchlight moved past the corner of the alley. . . .

Inside the cantina, Red Burke opened only one eye, halfway, when he felt Falina's hand shaking him roughly by his shoulder. *"Por favor,* Daddy! Wake up! Wake up! There are men here!"

Burke mumbled groggily, unable to pull himself together. "Tell them . . . come back . . . ," he moaned.

"Daddy, they have a rope!" Falina said, sounding shaky and alarmed.

"Whoa!" said Burke, snapping up into a sitting position, both eyes wide open. His hand went instinctively for the gun beside the pallet, but he felt only an empty holster lying there.

As one, the rest of the knocked-out gunmen awakened and tried to rise. To their shock they found themselves held down in place by the rounded tip of machetes pressed firmly to their chests. Sergio, realizing his guns had been lifted from his side, stared up at the men standing over him and said, "Swing your blade, old man. You better hope to the saints that you can kill me with one blow—"

"Shut up, Sergio Alevario. You and your brother's reign of terror in this desert is over," Herzoff called just as the old man with the machete pushed the blade more firmly.

"Fellas, I'm afraid there's been a terrible mistake here," said Red Burke, his hands spread wide in a show of peace. "The Alevario brothers and I came here to see what it's going to take to help this community get back up on its—"

"Hang them quickly," Herzoff said, cutting Burke off. He dealt Falina and Malina a searing stare. "You twins are going to watch this, and I hope that seeing it changes what you both have become."

"Damn it all," Burke said, rising from the pallet with two of the old men pulling him to his feet. His loose trousers dropped to his knees. "What's everybody so damned angry about? You're all acting like somebody pissed in your whiskey!"

"You murdered our deputy!" said the old German. "And for that you will hang!"

"Easy does it," said Burke, glancing all around, taking close note of their situation, who was there and who wasn't. "I shot that lawman in self-defense, fair and square. He drew first."

"He carried a shotgun," Herzoff countered. "You do not even remember the circumstances!"

"Yes, you're right, a shotgun, and he intended to kill me with it, that's the gospel truth," Burke said quickly as one of the townsmen jerked his hands behind his back and tied them tightly with a stripe of rawhide.

"You can tell all of your lies to the devil when you get to hell," the townsman behind him cut in, pushing him forward toward the door. From all corners of the cantina the other townsmen shoved the bound gunmen forward until the drunken half-naked outlaws stood in a lineup on their way out the door.

"We will hang them at first light," said Herzoff, shoving the outlaws forward to the street, "so all can see and know what we do to those who harm one of our own."

Chapter 8

Out front of the livery barn the old German and the rest of the townsmen lined up all the outlaws except Red Sage Burke along a corral fence rail. They ran one long rope behind the outlaws' backs between their tied wrists and tied them all as one to the corral. Next to the outlaws they tied the twins and two other young women who had spent a night of drunken debauchery at the cantina. The young women stood naked save for whatever shawls or blankets or table-cloths they'd managed to grab and pull around them-selves on their way out of the cantina.

"You still have time to ask God for forgiveness for the wrongs you have down, Senor," a religious townsman said to Burke.

"I wouldn't know where to start," Burke replied with a tight, devilish grin. He stood alone, barefoot and shirtless beneath a lifting timber sticking out from the roof of the barn with a hemp rope hanging down from a large pulley. A noose hung around his neck.

By dawn, the township had gathered at the barn to watch the hanging and along with it the beheading that would follow. As the first glimmer of sunlight rose along the eastern line of the earth, Herzoff stepped away from Burke and gave a nod to three of the elderly townsmen holding the working end of the hemp rope.

Feeling the rope pull him up slowly, Red shouted to the other outlaws watching, "So long, you bad sonsbitches . . . my brothers in arms, the meanest, dirtiest best bunch of sonsabitch—" His words ended in a squawk as the rope lifted him two inches off the ground and continued higher.

"Wait—" he managed to croak as he began kicking back and forth, his bare toes searching and scratching toward the ground beneath him.

"My God, the church is on fire!" a woman screamed. All eyes turned from the hanging to stare at the tall licking flames reaching up from the adobe church's modest steeple.

"So is my cantina!" shouted the cantina owner. As one the townspeople turned and bolted toward the two raging fires boiling upward fifty yards away.

"Tie him off," Herzoff shouted at the three men holding the rope to the pulley, Burke dangling and kicking on the other end only six inches off the ground.

Quickly the three townsmen reached down and tied the rope to a thick ring on the end of a long iron tie-off stave driven deep into the ground.

"*Pleaaa—!*" Burke managed to grunt, his eyes bulging, his face turning a deep red-blue.

But the men didn't even hear him. They turned and ran toward the fires.

Along the corral the unattended outlaws began immediately struggling with the long rope holding them to the fence rail, their tied wrists rendering their hands useless. "Hold on, Red!" shouted Sergio. "We're coming! We're coming to you!"

"Yeah, but when?" River Johnson replied calmly. He stepped out from around the corner of the barn with a cigar in one hand and a rifle in his other. "I don't believe ole Red here can hold out much longer." He stopped in front of Red Burke, looked him up and down and asked, "Can you?"

"Waghhgahh—" Burke rasped, his bulging eyes pleading with Johnson. Bloody saliva swung from his twisted, gaping mouth.

"Cut him loose, damn you!" shouted Sergio. The others strained against the rope. The four young women watched in rapt horror.

Johnson blew out a stream of smoke and stepped closer to Burke. He looked up at him with a flat expression and said quietly, "I'm still looking for work. Got anything for me today?"

"Waghhgahh—," Red repeated. "Cuuut-meee-loo—" He grunted.

Johnson took his time. He turned to the other outlaws and asked Sergio, "Did you understand any of that?"

"Cut him loose, damn your eyes! Cut him loose! You will ride with us!" shouted Sergio.

"Well, all right then," Johnson said coolly. He reached down, grabbed the loop of a knot holding the rope and jerked it quickly. Burke hit the ground with a solid thud and rolled onto his back, wheezing, gasping and gagging violently.

Johnson stuck his cigar in his mouth, stepped forward and stood over Burke as he pulled a big knife from under his long buttoned coat. With his boot toe he rolled Burke onto his side, reached down and, with one slash, severed the rawhide binding his wrists together. "I hope things don't always go this way, riding with you boys," he said.

Burke rolled up onto his behind, yanked the noose from around his neck and sat choking and rubbing his throat with both hands. "Come cut us all loose," Sergio shouted to Johnson. "Hurry, before someone returns!"

River Johnson seemed not to hear him. He stuck the rifle barrel down and tapped it on Burke's shoulder. Burke looked at it, then realized it was offered to help him to his feet. He grabbed the barrel with both hands and pulled himself up, still gasping and wheezing.

"You . . . ever, slow walk me like that again . . . I'll kill you," he rasped at River Johnson. He swallowed a hard, bloody-tasting knot in his throat, looked at Johnson with red, watery eyes and said, "Obliged."

"Don't mention it," said Johnson. He walked to where Sergio stood straining against the long rope. "I stashed all of your guns back behind the barn." He slashed the long rope holding them all to the corral fence, then shoved Sergio around backward and slashed the rawhide binding his wrists. "Figured once you got freed up, you might want to do a little shooting on the way out of town."

"Oh, *si!* Indeed we do! You can bet your mother's ears we do!" Sergio growled, staring toward the running townspeople who were busily fighting the fires. He rubbed circulation back into his raw wrists and walked hurriedly to the barn, where the townsfolk had taken their horses. "Follow me, all of you! Now the killing is going to start!"

The small church in Suerta Buena sat off to itself in a wide sandy fenced lot, making the flames easier to contain. But the cantina sat in a crowded block-long stretch of buildings. Three of the buildings had thatch roofs instead of tin or clay tile. Those buildings had ignited like dry fire kindling. Within minutes, even as a bucket brigade brought the fire inside the cantina under control, the rest of the block lay beneath a long blanket of licking flames.

Running back and forth from the church to the cantina, trying to carry water and keep everybody fighting the fire, Herzoff shouted aloud, "Fortunate for the old *padre* that he is dead. Seeing this church burn would have broken his heart."

"What about my poor Suerta Buena Cantina?" the cantina owner cried, running along beside Herzoff with a bucket of water. "It has always been an important part of these people's lives!"

"It's gone now," the old German shouted, arriving at the burning building.

"I must rebuild!" shouted the sobbing cantina

owner even as the fire had begun to wane inside the adobe structure.

"And I will help you," said Herzoff. "We will all help you!"

"Gracious," said the cantina owner. But no sooner had he gotten the words out of his mouth than he turned with the empty bucket and staggered backward as a rifle shot exploded and slammed into his shoulder.

"Holy Hannah!" the old German engineer shouted, seeing the storm of angry, yelling riders swoop down on the defenseless townsfolk from the direction of the livery barn. "Now we will all die."

Out front of the burning church, three men and a woman turned to run when they saw the outlaws coming. Red Burke led the charge, riding shirtless and barefoot, yet firing the rifle with deadly accuracy. "Kill them all!" Sergio shouted. He fired three shots in a row and watched two of the three men and the woman fall to the ground.

While Burke and the others rode back and forth wildly, firing and killing at random, River Johnson walked along at his leisure, leading his horse behind him, whistling to himself. When a man appeared in an open doorway and pointed an ancient shotgun at him, Johnson turned and fired three shots rapidly, sending the man scrambling back inside.

"Hose! Look at River!" shouted Rollo Barnes to Little Jose Montoya. "He's cooler than a fat rattler!"

"*Si*, a fat rattler," said Hose with a puzzled look, having no idea how cool a fat rattler might be. But he didn't contemplate it for long. Instead he shrugged, let out a yell and drew aim on a man running at them waving a machete in the air.

Rollo Barnes fired with him, and the two watched the man fall and roll and slide the last few feet, the machete flying from his hand and bouncing across the dirt. *"Yi-hii!* That's just what I've been looking for," said Rollo. He bolted his horse past the machete, dropped down low on the running animal's side, snatched up the long, sharpened steel by its handle and sat upright swinging the wide blade overhead.

"Look out!" Hose warned. He fired at a man who ran toward Rollo with a raised shovel and sent him sprawling in the dirt.

"Yes, sir! This place is Good Luck!" Rollo grinned wildly, still swinging the blade. "Now, where's the son of a bitch who was going to hang us and cleave off our heads? I want him to step up and get himself some of this!"

River Johnson watched the gunmen race past him, firing, killing, trampling over the bodies of the wounded and the dead alike. "What did you old people expect," he murmured with disgust, "trying to fight off a bunch like this?" He took out an unused wooden match and stuck it between his teeth.

By the time he arrived at the burning church, the fight was nearly over. The gunmen were busily herding the townsfolk into a circle in the middle of the street. Herzoff put himself between the townspeople and the gunmen and spread his hands as if that would protect them. "Do not kill them," he said boldly for a man with no power to stop or change anything. "None of this was their idea. It was all mine. I talked them into this! Let it be me who dies, not they!"

"There's my ole pal," said Rollo Barnes, gigging his horse in closer to the old German. He reached down with the machete and flipped Herzoff's black cloth cap from his head, revealing a pile of stringy snow-white hair. "Hold real still, I'm betting I can swath off your head with one swipe." He reached down and grabbed a tight handful of Herzoff's hair. "Hang me, you flathead old son of a bitch." He drew back his arm in a wide arch. The old German stood rigidly and closed his eyes.

"Let him go, Rollo," Burke said in a hoarse voice. He rode in fast and slid his horse to a halt.

"Naw, sir, Red," said Rollo. "I aim to dabble my fingers in this old turd's brain pan—"

Before he got his words out, he was on the ground, the German falling with him before Rollo could turn loose of his hair. "I said *turn him loose*, damn it to hell!" said Burke, barely able to speak with his injured throat.

"Yes, sir, Red, there, he's loose," said Rollo, seeing the killing rage in Red Burke's eyes. "I meant no harm. I was just going to cleave his head off. I figured it was all right with you."

The gunmen fell silent and watched, their guns aimed at the remaining townsfolk. "Kill somebody else. Not him," said Burke, staring coldly at the old German. He rubbed his reddened throat for the old man to see. "Nobody wants him dead worse than I do." He had held his rifle pointed at Herzoff. But he tipped it up and fired a shot in the air as if to release some of his rage.

"Kill me if you will," said the old German, not flinching, not backing an inch. "But I die proud of what I did to you here today. The *federales* will be coming. They will see to it you pay. You will not get away with what you do here."

"Yeah, the *federales*." Red Burke seemed to calm down some. "About them ..." He looked all around, singled out an old man standing a few feet away from the others, raised his rifle and shot him down. Women screamed; men cursed under their breath and stood staring with frightened looks on their drawn and weathered faces. "You tell them what happened here. Tell them I'm one of Garris Cantro's Border Dogs ... one of his *main* men."

"I will tell them, make no mistake about that," the old German said with bitter determination.

"Just to make sure ..." Burke gave a harsh grin, turned the rifle on the old man and sent a bullet slicing through his foot. "There, that ought to seal the deal." Burke laughed.

The old man had let out a loud grunt as he hit the ground. But once in the dirt he clenched his teeth and refused to reveal his pain. Instead, he struggled to his feet, shooing away two townsmen who reached out to help him. Managing to stand on his own, blood running freely from the bullet hole in his foot, he jutted his chin in defiance, as if nothing had happened.

"You're a hardheaded old sonsabitch." Burke laughed aloud. "Be sure and tell the *federales* that

Garris Cantro knows there's too many of us for them to handle. Tell them the Border Dogs said if they know what's good for them, they'll turn tail and run back home to their women. . . . Tell them Cantro says to leave the fighting for all us real *hombres*."

Standing back a few feet, River Johnson watched and listened curiously. With a slight shake of his head in disbelief, he stepped up into his saddle, smoothed back his dark well-trimmed hair atop his bare head and nudged his horse forward. "That's one surefire way to get the *federales* on your ass and keep them there," he said under his breath.

From the cantina, Falina came running, still wearing only a flimsy shawl pulled around her. She carried Burke's boots under an arm. In her other hand she carried the rest of his clothes wadded into a dusty ball. "Wait, Daddy! Don't go!" she yelled, afraid he might leave without his clothes.

Red Burke swung his horse around and looked at her, seeing her breasts bob and jiggle wildly as she bounded along the dirt street. "Twins . . . ," he said, smiling in reflection. "Damn, it's hard to leave here."

He reached out a bare foot and Falina rolled his dirty sock on, then shoved a boot onto his foot. As she circled to his other foot, he asked Sergio, "Which way to the next town?"

Sitting atop his horse, reloading his smoking revolver, Sergio pointed southeast. "That way, to Mal Vuelve." He closed the freshly loaded revolver and looked at Burke. "But it is wise to ride around Mal Vuelve. A high-ranking *capitán* has family living near there."

"Does he, now?" Burke grinned. "Then I'd consider it a pleasure to go meet those good people."

Finishing with Burke's other boot, Falina looked up and pleaded with him, "Take us with you, Daddy, *por favor*, take us with you. My sister and I will be beaten and treated badly for being so friendly with you."

"Is that fact?" Burke eyed the old German, who stared back at him coldly and unafraid. "All right, darling," he said to Falina. "Swing up here. We'll find you some clothes along the way." He reached down and helped her scurry up behind him. She readjusted the shawl to cover her nakedness.

"What about me?" Malina yelled, running along the dirt street, holding scraps of clothing to her naked breasts.

"You too, darling," said Burke. To Sergio he said, "Give her a ride until we get some extra horses."

Sergio nodded. He reached down and caught Malina by her arm and swung her up behind him.

"Let's ride!" Burke shouted. He sent his horse lunging forward, stirring dust behind him. The others followed, racing out of town single file, then spreading abreast onto the desert floor.

Watching them ride away, the old German said, "May they all burn in hell."

In the glittering morning light the townsfolk watched Falina pull the shawl from around herself. She held it up and let it stream overhead behind her. She rode naked, staring back, laughing toward Suerte Buena until she disappeared into a rising swirl of dust.

PART 2

PART 2

Chapter 9

The Badlands Hills, Old Mexico

Jedson Caldwell, aka the Undertaker, sat his horse atop a cliff, gazing out across the rolling desert below. With a brass-trimmed field lens to his eye, he watched a long line of dust move along behind a column of uniformed soldiers as they crossed the desert floor. Behind him the large freight wagon groaned to a halt, being driven by Juan Lupo, respectfully known along the Mexican side of the border as Juan Facil, or simply Easy John by his *americano* colleagues.

No one knew exactly what Juan Lupo's official title might be. Because he offered little on the subject of himself, most lawmen on both sides of the border considered him a spy, something Lupo himself neither confirmed nor denied. If pressed on the matter, he always gave the same short, crisp response, accompanied by a humble and courteous nod: "I serve at the behest of the emperor of Mexico under *Generalissimo* Manual Ortega."

Enough said . . . , thought U.S. Marshal Crayton Dawson,who rode alongside the big, heavily loaded wagon. Juan Lupo had proved himself, fighting his way across the border on the trail of robbers and killers, helping Dawson and Caldwell find the gold that had been stolen from the Mexican National Bank in Mexico City over a year earlier. Dawson had no fondness for either the Emperor of Mexico or *Generalissimo* Manual Ortega. But he had gained all the respect in the world for Juan Lupo, spy or no spy—*with guarded circumstance, of course*, he reminded himself.

Dawson stopped his horse and stepped down from his saddle. Rifle in gloved hand, he led his horse forward the remaining few yards and stopped beside Caldwell's mount.

"Where is Shaw?" Caldwell asked, hearing Dawson walk up beside him.

"That's anybody's guess," Dawson replied.

"You don't suppose he's gotten down drunk again, do you?" Caldwell squinted straight ahead into the harsh wavering sunlight, his hands crossed on the saddle horn. Beneath his shirt he still wore a bandage covering the bullet wound he'd taken at Fire River, where they'd wrenched the gold back from some of the men who'd stolen it and begun their escape. Beneath his patched trousers he wore another bandage, this one covering a bullet wound in his thigh.

"Ordinarily, I wouldn't rule it out," Dawson said,

he himself wearing a bandanna serving as a bandage around his left upper arm. "But Shaw knows what's at stake here. He's never let me down in a tight spot."

"I know," said Caldwell. "Forget I said that. It must be the heat making me edgy." His eyes searched back and forth across the empty desert floor. From here, with the position of the sun, he ran no risk of being sky-lighted. Yet he stopped scanning the desert and backed his horse a few steps—a man could never be too careful. He swung a leg over his saddle and stepped down. "There's no man I'd rather have scouting my front trail than Lawrence Shaw."

Dawson and Caldwell had been scouting the day before when they'd spotted a small band of Apache moving northwest. To make sure the hostiles hadn't spotted them, they had stashed Juan Lupo and the wagon in the rocks, rifle in hand, while they shadowed the men a full six hours until they decided the band wasn't going to circle back on them.

"Jane Crowly has done her share of trail scouting too," said Dawson. "I figure the two of them laid up somewhere out of the storm. I figure they're onto something now though. The difference between Shaw and a good tracking hound is that he doesn't bark when he's got something treed." His eyes continued to scan the desert as he spoke. "They figured we laid up too. They know we're all up and moving now. Everything is going about as well as it can. So far he's kept a clear trail ahead for us. That's what their absence is telling us."

"That could change anytime," said Caldwell. "It might have changed already. Maybe that's the message Shaw's sending us, hanging away this long."

"I don't think so," said Dawson, "but we'll find out soon enough I expect." He looked up as Juan Lupo approached from the wagon. Lupo wore a long faded black riding duster and black wide-brimmed hat. For a big man, he moved with the ease and poised agility of a mountain cat.

"Where are Shaw and Jane Crowly?" he asked quietly, almost to himself as he stopped and looked out across the desert, barely seeing the column of *federales* with his naked eye.

"We just asked ourselves that same question," said Caldwell, handing him the long telescope. Lupo raised it to his eye and looked back and forth along the dust-covered *federales*.

"The red plum of the *capitán's* hat tells me they are from the southern command—a long way from home," Lupo offered. He lowered the lens. "What else were you talking about?"

Dawson realized that Lupo might have assumed they'd excluded him from their conversation. He didn't need that kind of thinking to set in. It was shaky enough, three men traveling with a freight wagon loaded heavily with gold coins. "We decided Shaw and Jane will show up while we're crossing to the hills unless there's something wrong. In that case they'll pull up and stay away from us, protect our flanks. We might not know what good they've done us until after it's done."

"*Si*, I understand," said Lupo.

Dawson noted the grave expression on the Mexican's face. "It's not too late to lay low right here. One of us can ride to these *federales* and tell them we need their help. They're probably combing the towns and villages for this gold anyway."

"No *federales*, not yet anyway," Easy John said quickly. "There is too much gold involved. We are too far from Mexico City to trust the *federales*. Until I can get word to *Generalissimo* Ortega that the gold is in my possession, we can trust no one."

"It's your call," said Dawson, although he found such thinking questionable. He wasn't going to mention the fact that Lupo was trusting two American lawmen more than he trusted his own countrymen. But he knew that the thought had just gone across Lupo's mind.

"If I could not trust you two, I would have known it by now," he said, almost as if the matter had been spoken aloud. He managed a grin. "We would have already been killing one another. With these southern *federales*, I include yet another unknown element into this situation."

"Our trust is mutual," Dawson acknowledged. Changing the subject, he gestured in the direction of the column of *federales* who had ridden out of view over the crest of a sand hill. "Are we going to be able to keep out of their sight? I expect they're just as hot after the gold as every outlaw gang on both sides of the border."

"So long as we slip unnoticed across the desert and back onto the hill trails we can avoid them," said Lupo. "I have traveled in this hill country for weeks on end without seeing anyone." He collapsed the telescope and handed it back to Caldwell.

"Yes," said Caldwell, "but was half the gold of Mexico's depository out here, everybody and their brother knowing about it?"

"No," said Lupo, "and the gold is what makes the difference. When a man has a little gold, everybody around him is his friend. But when a man has *this much* gold, the whole world is his enemy."

Dawson and Caldwell both nodded. "What lays beyond the hill line?" Dawson asked, trying to get an idea of what to expect once they crossed the desert floor.

"Small villages, towns that grew with the French and German mining business. They have been trying to hang on since the silver and copper mining companies pulled stakes and left."

"If I know Shaw, him and Jane will have those towns checked out good before we start across," said Dawson.

"Perhaps that is what has kept him from riding back to us yet," said Lupo. Without waiting for a reply, he turned and walked back toward the wagon. "We will do well to cross at night while the eyes of the world are closed."

Dawson and Caldwell looked at each other. "What have Shaw and Jane Crowly run into out there?" Caldwell asked.

"I don't know," Dawson said, "but whatever it is, they're right in the middle of it." He gazed off across the desert toward the hill line.

"Since we're talking about Jane Crowly anyway, what's going on between those two?"

"Again, that's anybody's guess," said Dawson.

"I shouldn't have asked," said Caldwell, "but you've heard the same rumors I have about her."

"Yep," said Dawson, "and *rumors* is just how I counted them, nothing more."

"I'm not passing along gossip," said Caldwell. "It's just you and me talking here."

"I understand," said Dawson. "But it's still just rumors until I see something to tell me otherwise. Far as I'm concerned, she's just a rough-edged gal who's playing the hand that's been dealt her, same as the rest of us on this earth."

"I know," said Caldwell, "but her and Shaw? It can't get less likely than that, can it?"

"She's known for being soft on gunmen," Dawson said. "Shaw is the Fastest Gun Alive."

"He also has his *pick* of the womenfolk," replied Caldwell. He avoided mentioning that Jane Crowly wasn't the kind of woman to turn heads, at least not for her poise and beauty.

"It's true, he does have his pick," said Dawson, "and maybe Jane Crowly is *it*."

Caldwell kneaded the bandage on his wounded thigh and looked out across the desert. "I can't argue that," he said quietly.

Lawrence Shaw and Jane Crowly had seen the smoke rising from the two fires in Suerte Buena just before first light, yet it would be close to midday

before they rode onto the dirt street and saw the
burned-out hull of the adobe church and the roof-
less, half-collapsed walls of the black-charred cantina.

From his saddle, Shaw studied the sweat-smudged
faces of the elderly townsfolk who eyed the two
strangers with suspicion. "Stick close," he warned
Jane. "It looks like Red Burke hasn't done much to
boost their attitude toward us *gringos*."

"Don't you have a badge or something?" Jane
asked under her breath.

"It's in my hand," Shaw said, having already anticipated such a situation.

"Well, would it disturb you *awfully* to pin it on
your shirt?" she asked. "I know this is Old Mex, but
damn, let's take what we can get." She cleared her
throat and added, "Meanwhile, I suppose I best
sweet-talk them some."

"Yes, you do that," said Shaw. He reached up under his ragged poncho and pinned on his deputy
marshal's badge as they saw a few of the elderly
townsfolk gather out front of the burned Suerte
Buena Cantina. Using a long walking stick, the old
German hobbled out in front of the others and
stopped as if to bar them from coming any closer to
the cantina.

He said to Shaw, "If you *hombres* come to drink
and *raise hades*, our cantina is not open right now . . .
as you can see." He swept his free hand toward the
cantina. "We have had our fill of strangers for a
while."

Shaw and Jane stopped their already slow-walking horses and looked down at the old German. Before Shaw could speak, another elderly man, this one an American, stepped forward and barked, "In plainer words, ride the hell on. We don't want you here."

Ignoring the warnings, Shaw flipped his poncho up over his shoulder and said to the German, "I'm looking for an *americano* who has a red beard. He's riding with Sergio and Ernesto Alevario and some of their men."

The badge on Shaw's chest changed everything. The old German let out a sigh and said, "They are the ones who did all of this."

The American wasn't through yet in spite of Shaw's badge. "You should have been a day sooner, lawman."

"That would've meant they were chasing us, instead of us chasing them, you old fool." Jane cut in.

The old American's eyes flared and he took a step toward her horse, his crooked finger raised accusingly. "Let me tell you something, Mister," he said to Jane. "That deputy marshal badge your partner is wearing don't cut any fat down here. This is the Mexican badlands. The Alevario brothers and their men will chew yas both up and spit yas both out—"

As he'd spoken Jane had reached up, pulled off her hat and shook out her hair. "Call me *hombre* again, see if I don't box your damned jaws for you."

Shaw gave her an incredulous look. "*Sweet-talk . . . ?*" he said under his breath.

Seeing her hair fall to her shoulders, noting her features without the low, floppy hat brim partially hiding her face, the old American said, taken aback, "Jane? Jane Crowly . . . ?" He staggered back a step in his stunned surprise. "Begging your pardon, ma'am," he said, his attitude suddenly changing.

To Shaw, Jane said under her breath, "Sweet talk is as sweet talk does, I reckon." She gave a demure little grin and added, "It's good to hear that I'm also known here 'bouts."

"Please forgive us," said the old German, stepping closer. "Wherever your badge is from, it is welcome here in Suerte Buena until our *federales* arrive to help us. If you are hunting these men, you are our friends. What can we do to assist you?"

"Gracious," said Shaw. He and Jane both swung down from their saddles. "We won't be here any longer than it takes to water and rest our mounts. Did they mention anything we might need to know?"

"No," said the old German. He swept a hand toward the damage the men had left in their wake. "Like most men of their kind, they drank, ate dope and played with some *putas* who came here on word that a column of soldiers will be arriving from the south."

"Oh?" Shaw said, interested in knowing the whereabouts of any *federale* troops. "When might that be?"

The old German shrugged. "We only know what we heard from the whores when they arrived here last week," he said.

The bald cantina owner stepped forward from the gathered townsfolk. "But now two of the *putas*—

beautiful raven-haired twins all the way from Tampico—have gone off with Red Burke. He has them calling him Daddy." He spit in disgust and disappointment. "I hope you kill all of them, including River Johnson."

"River Johnson?" said Shaw.

"*Si*," answered the cantina owner. "He is a man who rode away with them. We believe he started these fires in order to keep us from hanging Red Burke." He looked at Shaw. "Do you know this man?"

"By name only," Shaw said. "If there's a fire involved, you can bet he started it. He's an arsonist. He's also a paid killer for the mines and railroads . . . used to be anyway."

"And now he rides with border trash," said the cantina owner, "so I hope you kill him too."

"That's a possibility," said Shaw.

"But you will have to hurry in order to do so," said the old German, cutting back in. "Red Burke was acting on orders of Garris Cantro. Once Burke and the Alevarios meet with the rest of the Border Dogs, they will become much harder to kill."

Shaw considered things for a moment. "Red Burke told you he's acting on Garris Cantro's orders?"

"Yes," said the German, "although I do not see why Garris Cantro would bother with such a place as our dying little town."

Shaw gave Jane a look. "Neither do I," he said. Turning to Jane as the two led their horses to the iron hitch rail, he said, "Just like I speculated. Burke wants to set the *federales* after Cantro's Border Dogs while he and the Alevario brothers find the gold wagon and make a move on it for themselves."

"Sounds like Burke's got it all figured out," said Jane. "There's a hill trail the other side of Mal Vuelve. If they figure they lost us to the gunmen in Agua Mala, my guess is they'll take that trail down onto the desert and search for the wagon tracks."

"Then so will we," said Shaw with finality. He asked the old German, "Are there any good spare horses we can buy here?"

While Herzoff considered the request, the cantina owner cut in and said, "I have some fast horses that I used to race in Esperanza. You are welcome to pick two of them for yourselves. Anything to help you catch this 'Daddy' Red Burke," he added. Again, he spit in disgust.

"When the *federales* arrive," Shaw said, "tell them we are after the same men they are. Tell them we chase Red Burke with the approval of Juan Lupo himself."

"You work with Juan Facil? Lupo?" the cantina owner asked, impressed at the mention of the name.

"Yes, we work with Easy John," said Shaw. "Be sure and tell the soldiers, so they won't be shooting at us." He gave Jane a look and said, "We'll try to leave the *federales* a little better message than Red Burke left them."

Chapter 10

———

Roy Heaton had no idea how far he'd traveled with the bullet hole through his belly. He knew only that he'd managed to get away from Lawrence Shaw and Jane Crowly before one of the two killed him. He'd made it off the desert floor and into the base of the hill country where he'd taken shelter in a wide arroyo. On the rocky banks of a shallow stream, he lay dipping water with his cupped hand and letting it trickle down onto the blood-crusted wound in his belly.

The flesh surrounding the wound had turned rosy red and was hot and tight to the touch. Yet it looked and felt better than it had the day before. For the time being, *better* would have to do, he told himself. The main thing is he'd gotten away. He managed a weak smile, thinking about how he'd slipped away from Jane Crowly, rifle and all. To hell with her . . . and Fast Larry Shaw too.

"Fastest Gun Alive, my ass . . . ," he murmured to himself. Reaching around behind him, he examined the hard swollen lump where the bullet had failed to bore its way out of his back. "I guess I showed you both, you can't hold ole Heaton down." Beside him his horse drew water deep and steadily from the cool running stream.

Ten yards away in a stand of dry bracken palo chino and Mexican ironwood, a Border Dog gunman named Elijah Chase whispered to the man named Arnold Stroud standing beside him, "He's lost his mind—he's babbling to himself."

"He's shot, Eli," Stroud replied. "What do you expect from a man, a bullet in him in this kind of heat?"

"All right," Chase said, "but let's watch him close. Heaton's never been real sane even when he's at his best game."

Stroud raised a hand and gave a signal to three other men standing spread out and hidden among the low-standing ironwoods and bracken on the other side of the stream.

"To think this ornery belly-shot sonsabitch used to be married to my sister," Chase whispered to himself.

"I never knew that." Stroud studied him as the men across the stream returned his signal and stood ready to make their move.

"Well, you know it now," said Chase. "Anyway, look at him, gut shot and most likely dying. My ma—God rest her soul—would have given anything to seen this."

"Yeah, well . . . ," said Stroud, "let's get to it. Cantro is waiting to hear what happened to those three." He stepped away silently in a low crouch.

At the stream, Heaton caught the slightest rustling of dried brush behind him. He stopped dipping the water onto his wound and lay listening intently, his bloodstained shirt off, lying in the gravel and rocks beside him.

Seeing Heaton freeze and listen, Stroud said, "He's caught us!" He ran onto the open stream bank, his rifle up but not pointed, Chase right behind him. "Heaton, wait, it's us!" he called out.

Feverish and scared, Heaton bolted up, snatched up another small hideout pistol he'd kept stashed in his saddlebags and fired a wild shot at Stroud as he leaped into his saddle, his side and back throbbing with pain.

"Don't kill him, Pond!" Stroud shouted out across the stream.

Heaton was on his way, his horse splashing through the braided shallow water. But on the other side of the stream a young, solemn gunman named Elvis Pond appeared as if from out of nowhere and swung his rifle around by its barrel. The blow lifted Heaton from his saddle and sent him sprawling backward into the running water.

"Well, he's dead . . . ," Stroud remarked.

"Good riddance," Chase whispered with a smug little grin.

Yet, walking quickly forward, Stroud saw the shirtless Heaton rise up onto both palms and shake his head, slinging water from his wet hair, trying to maintain consciousness.

"Elvis! Don't kill him!" Stroud shouted again as the young southern gunman stalked forward to-

ward Heaton, the rifle raised for a deadly blow to
the back of his head. "Jesus, is he deaf?" Stroud
shouted to the other two gunmen running from the
ironwoods toward Heaton in the stream.

"Hold it, Elvis," said an older ex-Confederate sergeant named Bale Harmon. He ran up in time to put
himself between Elvis Pond and Heaton and raised
a hand to hold Pond back. "We need him alive!"

Pond didn't reply, but he backed off grudgingly
and stood staring down coldly at Heaton as the
wounded man fell over onto his side and clasped his
belly wound. Fresh blood seeped through his fingers. "I'll kill . . . you," Heaton managed to squeeze
out through his pain.

Elvis stepped forward again, expressionless, this
time drawing back his boot to kick Heaton. But
again Harmon interceded. "Elvis! That's enough!"

Running up, Stroud looked down at Heaton, then
at Elvis Pond. "Didn't you hear me, Pond? We need
Heaton to tell us what they learned out there."

Pond stared blankly.

Helping Heaton up into a pained crouch, Stroud
and Harmon half assisted and half carried him to
the bank of the stream. They lowered him onto his
knees, looking down at his bleeding wound as he
bowed forward, clutching his stomach.

Chase walked up slowly and looked down at Heaton. "Yep, you're dead, Roy, end of string." He couldn't
completely hide a slight smile of satisfaction. "I'll tell
Althia how it happened if you want me to."

"I'm . . . not . . . done," Heaton said. He rose slightly,
gave Chase a dark, hateful stare, then turned the

same look toward Pond. "If you can keep this jackass . . . from killing me."

Before anyone could stop him, Pond planted his boot toe firmly into Heaton's blood-soaked belly.

Heaton screamed loud and long. Stroud and Harmon grabbed Pond and pulled him back. Heaton screamed again. But this time anger overcame his pain and he grabbed a palm-sized rock and started to rise to his feet. "I'll bash your—"

Pond shot his boot toe between the two men holding him and kicked Heaton again. Heaton fell back screaming, a wide stream of fresh blood spilling down his stomach.

"Jesus! Elvis. Damn it to hell, what's wrong with you?" Stroud shouted, shoving Pond backward, snatching the rifle from his hands. Pond didn't respond but he stood staring in defiance.

"He's new, Roy," said another gunman, Corey Trent, stooping down and helping Heaton back onto his knees. He took Heaton by his arm and helped him uncoil enough for him to take a look at the wound.

"Why does . . . he keep kicking me?" Heaton gasped, opening his fingers for Trent to see better.

"I told you he's new," said Trent, wincing a little at the red swollen flesh surrounding the wound. "He's some kin to Lewis Davenport, a nephew, cousin or something." He leaned and looked at the hard reddened lump on Heaton's back. "You've got a bullet that needs cutting out." He looked back at Heaton's face. "You're full of lead fever too."

"Just keep that jackass away from me," said

Heaton. He looked up at Pond's leering, mindless stare. "If I need cutting, let's get it done," he said to Trent. "You're never going to believe who shot me. . . ."

"Yeah, who's that?" Trent said, pulling him up into a crouch. He looked at the others for support as he turned Heaton and walked him farther away from the stream.

"Jane Crowly," said Heaton, almost proudly.

"*The* Jane Crowly?" Harmon asked, walking alongside him opposite of Trent, keeping an eye on Elvis Pond. "The half-man, half-woman Jane Crowly?"

"*The* Jane Crowly," said Heaton in a strained and rasping voice, "leastwise the only Jane Crowly I ever heard of."

"He's awfully fevered," said Trent, looking dubiously at Stroud and the others.

"I'm not out of my mind," Heaton insisted, his strength seeming to rise a little as he defended his mental capacity. "It was her . . . she's traveling with Lawrence Shaw."

Trent considered it as they walked along; so did Stroud and the others. "You don't mean Fast Larry Shaw, do you?" Stroud asked.

"One . . . and the same," said Heaton, sounding better still.

"Hell, Fast Larry's dead," offered Harmon, walking along beside Elvis Pond to keep him out of trouble. "He was held captive and eaten by a bear up in the high country as I recall."

"You best recall all over again," said Heaton. "Shaw's alive . . . he's a lawman . . . rounding up curs along these badlands. Take my word . . . for it."

"Sure thing, Roy, whatever you say," said Trent. Looking at the others, Trent shook his head, keeping Heaton from seeing him. "You'll feel better once we get this bullet out of your back and get your fever down."

"I don't have the fever . . . damn it to hell," Heaton insisted, struggling along toward a clearing inside the stand of ironwood and palo chino.

"Let me cut it out," Pond said in a flat but menacing voice.

"What the hell is wrong with you, Elvis?" Harmon asked, giving the young Southern gunman a look of disbelief. He'd never seen the newcomer act this way toward anybody.

Pond stared back as if in defiance. "Nothing's wrong with me. I don't like this son of a bitch," he said, turning a hate-filled gaze down toward Heaton.

When Trent had finished working on his wound, Heaton sat slumped, a cup of coffee in one hand and a bottle of whiskey in the other. Trent had sliced an inch-long incision in his back, a quarter of an inch deep, and let the bullet plop out onto his palm. Then he'd washed the incision with hot water heated sterile over a small fire Harmon had built.

"And that's the whole of it," Heaton said in conclusion, having told Stroud and the others about what happened in Agua Mala. He'd told them about Shaw saying he'd spent the gold, about Shaw killing

Sid Nutt, and about his being captured by Shaw and
Jane Crowly. Finally he'd told them about his escape, and getting shot. "I got to my horse and made
flight. Here's where I ended up."

"You're lucky to be alive," said Stroud, watching
Trent wind stripes of cotton cloth around Heaton's
waist, covering both front and back wounds. "I've
never seen a rifle shot from that close not go all
the way through a man."

"You've seen it now," Heaton said, sipping the
whiskey, feeling himself getting stronger, feeling the
heat of his fever starting to wane.

"He's lying," Pond said flatly, standing back from
the others.

"Damn it, Elvis," said Harmon. "I don't know
what to do about you."

"Lying, am I?" Heaton struggled to stand, but
Stroud and Trent both held him down in place.

"Take Elvis and go tend to the horses," Stroud ordered Harmon, starting to get testy over the young
gunman's surly attitude toward Heaton, a man he
didn't even know.

"Let's go, Elvis," said Harmon, wanting to keep
down any trouble among the men. He pulled the
young man away by his arm, toward the horses a
few yards away. Pond kept looking back over his
shoulder with a hard, angry stare.

"Are you sure you don't know him?" Stroud asked
Heaton, trying to get an idea as to why Elvis Pond
hated him so badly.

"I've never seen him before in my life," said
Heaton. He gestured toward Chase. "Ask Elijah

here. He knows near everybody I do. We're from the same hilltop in Arkansas. I was married to—"

"Eli told me," said Stroud, cutting Heaton off sharply. "Forget Pond. Tell me this. Did you, Red Burke and Sid Nutt intend to come back to the rest of us Dogs with news about the gold?"

Heaton heard the accusation in Arnold Stroud's voice. Stroud was one of Garris Cantro's right-hand men, a captain in the Border Dogs fighting ranks the same as he'd been in Cantro's regular command during the war. "I raise my hand to heaven, Captain Stroud," Heaton said, "that was our intention. If Red Burke was here he'd attest to it."

"Where were you headed when we caught you?" Trent asked, finishing up with the wound.

Heaton gave him an irritated look. "I'm obliged for you cutting my bullet out and trussing me up, Corey. But I wasn't *caught* by you. You *found* me . . . and I was on my way back to the Dogs when you come upon me." He turned to Stroud and said, "As you can tell by my direction." He gestured the whiskey bottle toward the hills.

Stroud studied the trail both ways, looking back and forth across the desert floor. "You could have been headed either way," he said quietly. Before Heaton could argue the point he asked, "What about Jane Crowly and Fast Larry Shaw?"

"What about them?" Heaton asked, determined to weigh each word carefully until he found where he stood with Stroud.

"Were they really with the wagonload of gold, or was Shaw saying all that to throw us off?"

"I don't follow your thinking," said Heaton, his expression turning curious.

"It's a big desert," said Stroud. "Maybe Shaw was saying it to draw us after him, while Juan Lupo and the American lawmen cut across the desert with the wagon and up off these badlands." He turned and walked away a few feet and stood staring out across the rolling desert below.

Heaton sipped the coffee and watched Trent walk over and stand beside Stroud. "Maybe Shaw wasn't lying, Captain," Trent said, "maybe he did spend it."

Stroud's silence let the young Mississippian know that his humor wasn't welcome. "That gold is the difference between us keeping the war alive or going down in defeat, Corey."

"Yes, sir, I know that. I apologize," said Trent.

But his apology went unacknowledged. "Take the best horse we have and prepare to ride," Stroud said.

"Ride, sir?" said Trent. "Where am I headed, Captain Stroud?"

"Back to get word of the gold wagon to Cantro. We've got to stop that wagon before it crosses out of these badlands." He took a deep breath and continued to stare out across the wavering heat. "Tell Cantro it's time we let the Dogs out."

Chapter 11

In Mal Vuelve the twin whores dropped down from behind Burke and Sergio's saddles, giggling playfully. No sooner than their bare feet touched the ground, they padded away from the hitching irons and into an adobe brothel owned by a one-eyed Frenchman named Cluteau LaPrey. He was better known as Clute by the few remaining miners and settlers in the fringe of the higher Mexican badlands.

The commotion of clattering chickens, barking dogs and squealing pigs in the street of Mal Vuelve brought Clute to the open doorway. He stepped out into the harsh sunlight to meet the giggling twin whores, his arms resting around their still naked waists. The women had not bothered to stop long enough to dress on the dusty ride along the hill trail.

"Well, well, well, but aren't the two of you some *durty-gi-rils* . . . ," Clute said in a lewd, suggestive voice, looking them up and down.

Staring down at Clute's black-gray hair sticking

out from beneath a yellow, curly wig, Red Burke asked River Johnson in a lowered voice, "What the hell is this?" Clute wore purple stage makeup on his lips and sported thinly blackened eyebrows.

Sitting on his horse beside Burke, Johnson gave a slight smile. "It's ole Clute LaPrey himself. Don't worry, once you get past his perfume and peculiarities, he sort of grows on you."

"If he does, I'll scrape him off with a skinning knife," Burke replied.

"Gentlemen, Gentlemen!" said LaPrey, his arms still around the whores. Burke noticed warily that the man's thumbnails were painted black with silver dots in their middles. "Welcome to Wrong Turn! I always say, 'Every turn is a right turn in Wrong Turn!'"

"I already want to kill him," Burke whispered sidelong. River Johnson chuckled.

On Burke's other side, Sergio said to his brother Ernesto, "He is an idiot, I think."

"I see you have brought along your own entertainment, eh?" said LaPrey, a hand sliding up each of the whores' dusty sides. He grinned. Each hand jiggled a firm dust-coated breast.

"*Si*," Ernesto said in hushed reply to Sergio without taking his eyes off LaPrey.

"If this *francés raro* tries to take our twin whores, I will torture him so slowly he will be an old man when he dies," whispered Antonio.

"But that suits me fine, gentlemen." LaPrey continued rattling on regarding the two new whores' arrival in town. "The more the merrier, I always say.

In fact, if you'd like to do some trading, I'm always open to any—"

"Turn loose of my wives," Burke said testily, cutting him off. "What have you got to eat in this shithole that ain't crawling off the plate?"

LaPrey's hands came down off the twin whores as if the women had turned red-hot. He left imprints in the dust on their breasts and long streaks down their sides. He could not tell if Burke was joking or not, but from the looks of the trail-hardened gunman he didn't want to find out. "Oh, we have much good food for you here, *monsieur*," said LaPrey. "Good food, good drink, dope, more *wives*, for you, if you want more *wives*!" He stopped short of reaching his arms back around the twin whores.

"We're not his *wives*," said Falina in a pouting tone.

"Oh . . . ?" LaPrey gave her an uncertain look.

"No, he is our Daddy," said Malina, smiling, cocking a well-rounded hip toward Burke.

"Ah, I get it," said LaPrey, giving a Burke a sly, knowing grin. "You are the Papa! *Uhhh*, yes, of course. How lewd. I like that." He raised a long-nailed finger for emphasis.

"I'm not pretending I'm their Pa, you filthy-minded turd," said Burke. "I'm Daddy to them. There's a hell of a difference."

"*Oui*, of course," said LaPrey, "how stupid of me." He slapped himself on his purple-painted lips. "I chastise myself!"

"I bet that ain't all you do to yourself," said River Johnson, having stepped down from his saddle and walked over to LaPrey. "How are you, Clute?" He grabbed the brothel owner in a firm headlock and scrubbed his fist back and forth on top of the curly wig.

"I—I am good, River Johnson," LaPrey said, a bit startled and shaken by Johnson's rough greeting. He straightened his curly wig and touched his fingers to his smeared purple lipstick. "I hope you are too?"

Johnson hung his arm loosely around the Frenchman's neck, leaned against him and grinned up at Burke. "Ole Clute never knows if I'm going to kill him or just cut him real deep and watch him bleed, right, Clute?" He shook the tense brothel owner roughly.

"I'm afraid it is true," Clute said to Burke as Burke and the others stepped down from their horses. "With this one, I never know."

"You'll know with me," Burke said bluntly, walking up and putting his arms around the nearly naked twins. "*Mr.* Frenchy, I'm Red Sage Burke, leader of the Border Dogs."

Burke's lie caused Johnson to give him a bemused look.

But Burke went on, saying boldly, "We are killers and thieves, the lot of us." He gestured a nod back toward the rest of the men. "In Good Luck, we killed a town *guardia* dead, and burned the church and cantina to the ground before we left, and I have to say"— he paused and gave LaPrey a hard, cold stare—"I liked all those folks better than I like you, so far."

LaPrey swallowed a dry knot in his throat.

"Aw, now, look you've scared him," said River

Johnson with a laugh. He took LaPrey's rouged cheeks between two fingers and squeezed them until the Frenchman's lips formed a tight, twisted O. "Don't worry, Clute—he's only funning." He paused, then added, "Maybe . . ."

"There'll be soldiers coming after us before long, for what we did in Good Luck," said Burke. "If you're still *alive*, what will you be telling them about us?" He continued his hard stare, his hand raising his revolver an inch from its holster in expectation.

LaPrey touched a smeared rouged cheek when Johnson turned his face loose. He said haltingly, "What-whatever you want me to tell them, *monsieur*. Or may I call you Daddy too?"

"Damn right, good answer," said Burke, letting his revolver fall back into place in his holster. "Yes, you can call me Daddy, but don't let it go getting inside your head." Burke tweaked his cheek roughly. "Now get your yellow-curly-ass busy—get us fed, bred and drunker than blind wild hogs."

"*Yii-hiii! Fiesta!*" bellowed Rollo Barnes. He raised his Colt and fired shot after shot into the air. At the iron hitching rings the others followed suit, catcalling and firing wildly in every direction, sending the few pedestrians running and leaping for cover.

Turning to Sergio and Ernesto, Burke gestured toward Rollo Barnes and Jose Montoya and said quietly, "Let those two get all the piss and fore out of themselves, then send them out two miles to cover our back trail."

"*Si.*" Sergio nodded, but said, "Two miles? Why so far back?"

Burke responded with only a glare.

"So we can hear the shots and have time to pull our britches up," River Johnson cut in.

From the open window of a dusty adobe, an elderly town leader named Esta Uzanda looked out at the naked twins, hearing the gunshots, the cursing and yelling. Then he looked back at his aged wife in bewilderment.

"Now they come here naked," she said, turning away. "They do not even bother putting their clothes on. This is what our village has become." She crossed herself and walked away, shaking her head. She drew her shawl tighter around her shoulders. "Soon Mal Vuelve will change its name to Ciudad de Extraños Desnudos."

Her husband took her words like a sharp slap on his face. "It will not be the City of Naked Strangers so long as I have any say in it."

"Do you still have any say in it?" she snapped. "If not, perhaps we must all throw off our clothes and become animals, like the rest of this wicked world around us."

"I am going to do something about this," said her husband. "I will call together the men of Mal Vuelve to see what we must do. But I cannot fight these men alone. What good can I do us if I am dead?"

With two spare horses they'd purchased from the cantina owner, Shaw and Jane Crowly shortened the time it took to ride upward and along the hill trail from Suerte Buena to Mal Vuelve. Four miles from the small Mexican mining town they heard the distant rumble of gunfire while they stopped to switch their saddles to the fresh mounts.

Shaw noted the concerned look on Jane's face as he drew his saddle cinch. "That's drunken wildfire."

"Oh, I see, just a bunch of drunks shooting bullets all around," said Jane with a note of sarcasm. "Nothing for the townsfolk to worry about, I suppose."

"You know what I mean," Shaw said. He started to say more, but a sound from around a turn in the trail caught his attention. He swung around toward a large rock blocking the view of the trail, Colt out and cocked.

"Don't shoot!" an old man cried out, his bony arms stretched in the air, holding a long walking stick. His sombrero fell from his head and landed amid a gathering of goats crowed around him. "I have no money! No whiskey! No dope! Nothing that you want, only these stinking worthless goats that are not fit to—"

"Take it easy," Jane called out, stopping him. "We're not *banditos*."

Shaw's Colt uncocked and lowered into its holster as he looked around past the old man and farther along the empty trail.

"Thank the Virgin Mother," said the old man, crossing himself quickly. He reached down and retrieved his sombrero from where it had landed squarely atop a spotted goat's head. The goat shook its ears and bleated under its breath. "I have had enough gunfire and violence to fill this old belly forever."

"You're coming from Mal Vuelve?" Shaw asked in his easy border Spanish.

But the old man gave his reply in smooth accented English. "*Si*, and none too quickly, I must tell you." He cocked his head and squinted slightly, not sure of who he was talking to. "Are these people your amigos? If they are, I have nothing bad to say of them."

"Speak freely, Senor," said Shaw. To shorten matters, he flipped the edge of his poncho up over his shoulder and revealed the badge still pinned to his chest. "We've been trailing these men up from the desert."

"Ah, an *americano* lawman," said the old goat herder with a wizened look. "It is about time we have *americano* law here. The Germans, the French, the *americanos*, all have come here in my lifetime to make this country like their own. Only now that they have all given up do we get the law, eh?"

Shaw let him spill it out, then said, "I don't know about all that, Senor, I'm just trailing the men who are shooting up your town."

"My *town*! There, you see?" said the old man, wagging a bony finger. "Before the Europeans and *americanos* came, these hills were filled with villages. In order to be more like our *Inglés* neighbors, we built villages to look like places in *Tejas* . . . and we started calling them towns. Now the mines are closing. . . . Soon we will call our towns *villages* once again."

"Things change, that's a fact," said Shaw, wanting the old man to finish and move along.

"*Si*, 'things change, that is a fact,'" the old man said with a shrug of resignation. He raised his sombrero and placed it back atop his head. "The closer my people move to the border, the more quickly things change, and that too is a fact."

Hearing enough, Jane blurted out, "Is this your way of telling us you don't want us here, old man? Because, as I recall, it was your leader who invited the Germans, the French, us *americanos*. Don't blame us for the prosperity not making it down to yas."

"*Prosperity*?" said the old man in a humble tone, shaking his lowered head. "What does an old man like me care for prosperity? What good does it bring to my goats?" He walked forward on the trail, leading his small herd around him. "Go with God," he said sidelong to Shaw and Jane as he passed. "Suerte Buena in Mal Vuelve."

"*Gracias*, Senor," Shaw said respectfully.

"Same to you, goat herder," Jane called out a little testily, Shaw thought. Walking away, one of the goats bleated back long and loudly over its shoulder as if replying to her. "Yeah yeah, you little sonsabitch," Jane grumbled. "I'd like to see you turning over an open flame with onions stuffed in your belly."

Shaw looked at her. "What got you so upset?"

"Didn't you hear him?" said Jane. "Suerte Buena in Mal Veulve." She gave Shaw a look. "Meaning, good luck in Wrong Turn."

"Yeah, I heard him. So what?" said Shaw. "He didn't mean anything."

"Oh, I beg to differ with you, Lawrence," Jane

said ardently. "I think he knew full damned well what he was saying."

"Let's go," Shaw said, not wanting to discuss it with her. "Maybe we'll get lucky and catch Red Burke and his pals and end this in the streets of Mal Vuelve."

"Maybe," said Jane, swinging up onto the newly saddled horse, the reins to the other in hand.

"We're veering off the trail up ahead," said Shaw, also swinging up into his saddle. "We're riding the high ridges up there the rest of the way to Mal Vuelve, in case Burke left some trail guards lying in wait for us."

"Both of us, huh . . . ?" Jane looked him up and down closely.

"Yeah, both of us," said Shaw. "Why? What's the look for?"

"It's the look I always give a man who thinks he wants to protect me from harm . . . like I'm some delicate flower unable to take care of myself."

Shaw gave a sigh. "I never thought that, Janie. I just figured we'd both ride up there and save ourselves any trouble."

"Even though it would best if one of us stayed down here on the trail to draw out any ambushers?" she asked critically.

"No," Shaw replied. "I figured if we could slip around, avoid any gun play, we'd keep Burke from hearing it and know that we're coming."

Jane gave a forgiving little grin, realizing she might have been wrong. "All right, I see your point," she said.

They rode on until they reached a high, narrow game path winding up into the rocky hillside. They climbed the path until they stopped a few yards short of the crest, lest they skylight themselves to anyone lurking in the rocks below. Then they rode on quietly toward Mal Vuelve, keeping a close watch down the steep sloping hillside.

Chapter 12

―――――

Perched on a partially hidden cliff, invisible from the lower trails, Rollo Barnes said aloud to Jose Montoya, "Does it cross your mind that the ones *Daddy* Burke is worried about dogging us have already turned tail and gone home?"

"Keep your voice down," cautioned Jose. "And if I were you, I would not call Burke Daddy. I think he might cut your tongue out if he heard you."

"Why?" said Rollo, indignantly. "LaPrey and the twins call him Daddy; he seems to like it."

Jose shook his head, gazing down at the trail with his rifle in hand. "If you do not see the difference, I would be wasting my breath explaining it to you."

Rollo spit and sat silent and restless for a moment. Finally, he said, "Aw, hell, I can't stand sitting up here like some damned trail vulture, everybody else getting their skins pulled back and living it up back there." He gestured a thumb toward Mal Vuelve.

"I feel the same, but I keep it to myself," said

Montoya. "That is what *hombres fuertes* must do, in order to be respected by all around them."

"Are you saying I'm *not* a strong man, a *hombre fuertes*?"

"Take it as you will," Montoya answered with a shrug, keeping his gaze on the trail below. "I am sent to do a job. I will do the job without complaining."

"Shi-iiit," Rollo grumbled under his breath. He absently picked up a small stone and tossed it off onto the rock hillside, not expecting it to go bouncing noisily downward until it stopped with a *clunk* against a half-sunken boulder. "Whoa!" Rollo said in surprise.

"Are you loco?" said Montoya, shooting him a critical stare.

"Sorry, Hose," said Rollo. "*Damn*, I can't stand sitting here all this time. . . ."

Above the two ambushers, Shaw jerked his horse to halt when he heard the crack of the falling rock, then the sound of Rollo's voice below and ahead of them. He held up a hand to Jane, and they slid down from their saddles as one. They stood in silence beside their horses, Jane's spare horse standing right behind her.

Without a word, Shaw pointed in the direction of the sounds and slid his rifle from the saddle boot. Jane nodded, and removed her own rifle from her saddle boot. As one they eased over to their left, to the wall of rocky hillside flanking them and tied their horses' reins to some dry stubs of creosote bush.

Following Shaw in a crouch, the two moved along the rocky path until they saw the two half-hidden gunmen on the cliff below.

Shaw gave a sign with his gloved hand for her to prepare herself to fire. She nodded and eased her thumb over the rifle hammer and pulled it back slowly and quietly. "Ready when you are," she whispered, stepping over to the edge of the rocky path.

Shaw raised his cocked rifle and took close aim at Rollo Barnes just as the gunman stood and turned and looked up at him. "Holy Je—," Rollo managed to say before Shaw's shot nailed him in his chest and sent him flying off the cliff.

Jane took quick aim on Montoya as the Mexican gunman turned. Before he could raise and fire his cocked rifle, Jane's shot hit him high in the shoulder. Although the shot itself didn't kill him, it spun him backward off the cliff and sent him screaming into thin air. His rifle flew from his hand, hit the ground and fired wildly.

Shaw stood in the ringing silence, his rifle still up, scanning back and forth for any other gunmen. "Good shot, Janie," he said over his shoulder.

"Yeah . . . you too," Jane replied in a strange voice.

Something about her tone caught Shaw's attention, and he turned to face her. Jane's pale face wore a stunned expression. A wide circle of blood was forming on her fringed buckskin shirt, just beneath her left breast. "Janie—!" he managed to say.

"Don't start on me, Lawrence," Jane said, stopping him short. "I know I've been shot. I'm not a fool." She slumped sidelong against the steep wall of rock. "Don't go making . . . nothing of it."

"Here, Janie, sit down!" said Shaw, moving in quickly, grabbing her before she slid to the ground. Once he'd seated her, Shaw pulled her shirt open. He unclasped the binder around her breasts and pulled it off. He looked at the bullet hole as it bled slowly and steadily. Grateful that the wild shot had missed her heart, Shaw stretched her down onto the ground and stuffed his hat and hers beneath her head. "Lay still. I'll be right back."

"It's not a bad wound, is it?" Jane asked. "I mean how damned bad can it be? I'm still able to talk and cuss. . . ." Her voice trailed as she struggled to retain consciousness. "Of all the rotten damned luck. This damned fool drops his gun . . . shoots me all to hell. . . ."

Shaw returned and stooped down to her, a canteen in one hand, his saddlebags in the other. "Here, I brought you some water." He raised her a little, scooted her around and leaned her back against the wall of rock. But she had drifted into unconsciousness. "All right, maybe it's best if you're asleep," he said, laying the canteen aside.

Taking off his trail gloves, Shaw reached a hand behind her back and felt the warm bloody spot where the bullet had exited. Incredibly, the exit wound was a full eight inches below the entrance wound in her chest. "You must be one hard-boned gal," he said quietly, realizing that the bullet must have hit an upper rib and been diverted down away from her heart. He flipped open his saddlebags and took out a roll of cotton dressing and pulled her against him enough to wrap it around her and slow the bleeding.

"Don't be ... feeling my teats, Lawrence," she said in a groggy, half-conscious voice.

"I won't—I promise," Shaw replied, working fast. He knew he had to get her to town and get her properly attended to before she lost too much blood.

"No ... it's okay," she murmured faintly. She raised a weak hand, placed it on his bloody fingers and pressed them to her pale bosom. She gave him a tired smile, her eyes closed, her face white and drawn. "You beat all ... I've ever seen."

"Stop fooling around," Shaw said. He finished wrapping her in the cotton dressing and lifted her, saddlebags, canteen and all, and hurriedly walked over to the horses.

In Mal Vuelve, Red Burke had just stood up from a pallet in one of the brothel rooms and started taking a long swig from a bottle of mescal when he'd heard the rifle shots in the distance. On the pallet, the twins lay naked, sweaty and giggling, picking at each other playfully. "Shut the hell up!" Burke demanded. He listened intently for more gun shots. But upon hearing none, he slung his gun belt over his shoulder, shoved aside a wooden-beaded curtain and walked back out into the cantina.

"I heard it," said River Johnson, standing at the bar, a bottle of mescal before him. "Do you want to hightail it or stick and kill them right here?" Next to him a young whore stood with her hand inside his shirt.

"It could be more than just the lawman from Agua Mala," said Burke, not liking either the question or Johnson's way of asking it. "It could damn well be the *federales* catching up to things."

"Three shots?" Johnson asked in disbelief. "Naw, I don't think so. If it was *federales* they'd keep firing 'til they ran out of bullets—then they'd send for a wagonload and start over." He turned his gaze to the whore and gave her a wink. "I like what you're doing there, sweetheart," he said, nodding at her hand on his chest.

Across the room, Sergio and Ernesto came out of separate rooms, each shoving their shirttails into their trousers. Antonio walked in from another room. A young dark-skinned Indian girl looked out of the doorway behind him. Clute LaPrey hurried from a small room at the rear of the cantina, his makeup fixed and his curly wig back in place.

"I hope you will not allow them to shoot up the cantina, Daddy," he said to Red Burke.

"You're on your own, Frenchy. We're leaving," said Burke, tweaking the man's cheek roughly between his thumb and finger, smearing his thick rouge all over again. "All right, men, let's ride," he said to the others, snatching up the rifle he'd leaned against the bar.

"What if I lag behind long enough to kill this lawdog for you?" Johnson asked, still standing quietly at the bar while the others began to hurry toward the door.

Burke grabbed his shirt from where he'd laid it on the bar earlier. As he pulled it over his head he said to Johnson, "I don't know that you're up to it with this man, River. I'd be dead right now myself had I not been wearing a Korean bullet-stopping vest."

"I'm up to it," said Johnson, "without wearing a whatever-it-was you said you wore." He gave a slight grin and sipped mescal from the bottle.

Burke shrugged. "Yeah, sure—why not?" he said. Then he stuffed his shirt into his trousers, saying, "But I thought you wanted to ride with us, track down this gold?"

"I'll have the killing done and catch up before you reach the desert floor," said Johnson. "Have no doubt about that."

"If you say so," said Burke. "We'll be looking for you." He buttoned the bib of his shirt, picked up the gun belt he'd taken off his shoulder and laid on the bar. He swung the belt around his waist and buckled it. "I know you ain't doing this killing out of the kindness of your heart. What's it going to cost me?"

River Johnson shrugged and grinned. "A bigger share is all . . . say Rollo and Hose's cut if they don't make it back alive?"

"What makes you so sure they won't be coming back alive?" Burke asked.

"Nothing," said Johnson, "just me playing a gambler's hunch. If they come back and have done the killing already, we stay even. If those don't come back, I kill your lawdogs and get both their shares."

"Hell, you're on," said Burke, bending and tying his holster to his thigh. "Only don't sell this man short if he shows up here. He's fast on the draw, maybe faster than any man I've ever seen."

"Fast won't help him with me. I'll kill him my own way, before he knows what's hit him," said Johnson. "Don't even worry about how."

"In that case I won't," said Burke. He picked up his hat from the bar and shoved in down atop his head. He turned to the twins, who had walked out of the room and to the bar buck naked. They had washed each other free of the trail dust while Burke lay watching with a bottle of mescal in hand.

"It looks like this is where I'm leaving you, little darlings," Burke said.

"But, Daddy," said Malina, "we have only been here a short while. We know no one here. We have no clothes, only a shawl and a blanket."

"Yeah, but you girls make friends easy enough," said Burke. He pitched a handful of heavy jingling gold coins onto the bar top. "There's enough gold *monedas* to get you dressed proper like and take you all the way to San Francisco if you wanted to go." He turned to Johnson. "See you down on the desert floor."

"Adios," said Johnson. He raised the bottle of mescal as if in salute and watched Burke walk through the open doorway to the horses, where Sergio, Ernesto and Antonio had already mounted and were ready to ride.

When Burke stepped up into his saddle he reached back, picked up the bulletproof vest from behind his saddle and slung it over his lap until he could stop long enough to put it on. Hot and sweaty was better than cold and dead, he told himself, spurring his horse along the street.

LaPrey stood at the bar, the naked twins flanking him, the gold coins having been snatched up and clutched to their bosoms. "I have a wonderful idea!" he said with a wide, glistening purple smile.

"Yeah, let's hear it," said Johnson. He turned up a swig of mescal, keeping his drinking in check until he took care of business. Either the law or Rollo and Hose would be coming into Mal Vuelve shortly. Whichever it was, he was all set to do some serious killing.

LaPrey said, "We have these two lovely girls who seem to always be naked, and we have Gina here and myself." He gestured toward the whore standing beside Johnson with a black and silver thumbnail. "I say we all take a room together, eat some dope and do whatever we want to do."

"Jesus, Clute . . ." River Johnson stared at him with a look of disgust. "Sometimes you make me sick." He reached out and tweaked his cheek roughly. "Other times, I think you're the smartest man I've ever seen."

"Then we are all set?" LaPrey said with excitement. He started to hurry the naked twins off toward a room.

But Johnson stopped him. "No, we're not all set. You'll all have to carry on without me right now. I've got work to do."

Johnson turned and walked out the front door. He unhitched his horse from one of the iron rings and walked with it, leading the animal off the street. As soon as Johnson was out of sight, Esta Uzanda and a group of incensed townsmen and -women assembled up the dusty street. They walked toward the cantina with broom handles and switches and leather straps in hand.

Chapter 13

An hour later, Shaw stopped his horse and the three-horse string behind him at the edge of Mal Vuelve. An angry crowd was gathered in the street, their fevered movements raising a billowing cloud of dust. Watching the squabble in disbelief, he was surprised to spot two nude young women amid the mob. He nudged his horse forward, hearing their cries above the slap of leather and the angry hiss of switches slicing through the air.

Shaw kept an eye on the commotion as he sidled his mount over to a man standing out front of a small dusty adobe watching the fray himself. A sign on the adobe behind him read ALMAND CORD PHYSICIAN.

"Pay them no mind, sir," he said to Shaw, rolling up his shirtsleeves. "They're correcting a social matter that has cropped up in Mal Vuelve." He gestured to Jane, who Shaw cradled across lap. "What have we here?"

"A gunshot in the chest," said Shaw. He leaned

down, passing Jane's languid form to the doctor's waiting arms. "It happened a couple of miles back. I slowed the bleeding some, but she's still lost a lot of blood."

"I'll determine that," he replied crisply. He cradled Jane in his arms. She looked small, weak and pale, Shaw thought, glancing down at her. The front of her fringed buckskin shirt lay open. Her breasts were partially exposed above the bloody bandage on her chest.

Shaw slid down from his saddle and hitched the horses quickly to an iron hitch ring. The two turned and hurried into the adobe. Shaw watched him lay Jane on a canvas gurney and start loosening the bandage from around her chest. "I'm a lawman tracking some men from Agua Mala," said Shaw, cutting another glance toward the thrashing going on up the street. "The leader is an American named Burke. He sports a red beard."

"You don't look like a lawman," the doctor said over his shoulder as he checked Jane's pulse and wiped her hair from her eyes. Shaw knew he was referring to the ragged poncho, hat and trail clothes. "But I suppose I don't look much like a doctor either," the man added, tossing him a quick smile.

"I don't care what you look like, so long as you can help this woman," said Shaw.

"The men you're tracking were here, but I believe they've left now. I saw them ride out right after we all heard some rifle shots from along the high trail."

"That was our gunfire," said Shaw. "I figured Burke left a couple of men to tip him off when we

got close." He looked Jane up and down and asked,
"Is she going to be all right, Doctor?" Shaw asked.
"Are you going to need my help?"

"The bullet glanced off a rib and went down at an
angle," he replied. "If it had hit any vitals she'd be
dead by now. You did good slowing the bleeding—
she'll be all right. I won't need any help. Get out of
here; see if you can keep those twin *putas* from being
skinned alive."

"The *putas*?" Shaw asked.

"The whipping going on up the street ... that's
two young *putas* who rode in with the man you're
after," he said. "They might be able to tell you where
he's headed, if you get there before the town has
them beaten into a stupor."

"Obliged, Doctor," said Shaw, turning and heading out the door.

Out front of the cantina, the twins thrashed back
and forth in the dirt as the townsfolk struck them
with switches and leather straps. Shaw watched the
fray as he approached, seeing an old woman repeatedly stab at the twins with a broom handle. "Help
me!" screamed Malina, writhing as a razor strap came
down with a crisp slap on her naked rump.

"*Por favor!*" Falina pleaded. "He forced us to come
with him! He threw away our clothes!"

"Yet look at this!" shouted Esta Uzanda. "You
have money with which to purchase new clothes!"
He shook the leather coin bag the twins had found
in the cantina and placed their money in for safe-
keeping.

As he reached the boiling mass, Shaw first glanced

down at the cluster of fresh hoofprints leading away from the hitch rings out front of the cantina. He noticed a single set of prints that diverged from the others and turned into an alley. Then he pushed his way into the circle of angry townsfolk and forced himself into the middle, where the twins lay sobbing and trying to cover themselves with their forearms.

"*Detenga! Ahora mismo!*" Shaw shouted, telling the townsfolk to stop. "They've had enough." He grabbed Uzanda's raised arm before the town leader had time to bring the leather strap down onto Falina's back. "*Por favor*, for me," Shaw added, easing his tone of voice a bit.

"And who are you?" Uzanda demanded, backing away but still ready to continue the whipping.

"I'm a lawman," Shaw said, lifting the corner of his poncho and showing the badge on his chest.

"Ah, an *americano* lawman," said Uzanda in a dismissing manner. He started to take a step forward toward the frightened twins.

Shaw stepped forward too, a bit menacingly. "Let's get along," he said through clenched teeth. "I want to talk to these two about the men who brought them here."

Uzanda considered it. Finally he nodded and said quietly, "All right, Lawman. We have proved our point to these two." He tossed the bag of gold coins into the dirt near the huddled twins. "Both of you, find some clothes and get yourselves dressed, or we will come back and whip you even harder."

"Women's clothes, coming right up," said LaPrey,

nudging his way through the crowd until he stood beside Shaw, two plain white cotton dresses draped over his forearm. "Here, girls, slip these on, pronto, pronto! Before anyone else gets an urge to start whipping somebody." He cast a condemning look at Uzanda and the other townsfolk. To Shaw he said in a guarded, lowered voice, "Watch your step, Lawman. Red Burke left a man here to kill you."

"Obliged, Clute," said Shaw without looking all around. "Where is he?"

"You know me, *monsieur*?" LaPrey said, looking surprised.

"I know you from Eagle Pass, Texas," said Shaw. As he spoke he tipped his hat up slightly to give the man a better look. "I'm Lawrence Shaw," he whispered.

"Fast Larry!" said LaPrey, barely able to keep his voice down. "But I thought you were dead, *mon ami*—eaten by a bear, I believe?"

"As you can see, I wasn't," said Shaw. "Now, who is the man I'm looking out for here?" He lifted the two dresses from LaPrey's arm and tossed them in turn to the naked twins. "Get dressed, girls, while everybody catches their breath," he told them.

"It is River Johnson, the fire starter. He is a longtime friend of mine," said LaPrey. "But I no longer feel safe around him. He pinched my face too hard and at times does other things that gives me pause and frightens me."

"I've heard of River Johnson," Shaw said, "a back-shooter and an arsonist, as I recall."

"I do not judge a man's character, having so little

myself," LaPrey offered. "But he has agreed to kill you, so you must be careful of him. He is a very tricky man. One of the most slippery I have ever seen."

"I will be careful," said Shaw. He suspected that the prints he'd seen leading into the alleyway belonged to Johnson's horse, but he was careful not to tip off his stalker by scanning the alleys, windows, and rooftops. He'd just have to be ready for him when the time came.

The townsfolk began to disburse as the twins stood up and wiggled into the dresses, gathered close to LaPrey and Shaw for protection. Falina clutched the bag of gold coins to her bosom. "The gold came from Red Burke, I take it?" Shaw asked, nodding at the bulging leather bag.

"*Si*, he is most generous to those he loves," said Falina, jiggling the gold coins. She batted her dark eyes and smiled. "I hope you are generous as well, Senor. We will call you Daddy if you want us to—"

"Easy," said Shaw, stopping her. "I'm here on business."

"Red has them call him Daddy," LaPrey explained with the toss of a slim hand. "Of course, any of my girls will do the same thing if I tell them to . . . for a little *extra*, of course."

"I'm busy tracking down the man you've both been calling Daddy," Shaw said to the twins, ignoring LaPrey's offer. "Did he tell you he's headed to the desert?"

The twins looked at each other, then at LaPrey. "Is it all right to tell him?" Malina asked.

Instead of answering her, LaPrey replied to Shaw, saying, "Yes, they have both heard him say that he is headed to the desert to search for the gold. I heard him say so myself. He's talking about the stolen gold from Mexico City, *oui*?"

"Yes," said Shaw. He looked toward the cantina and said, "I have a woman with me. I'm leaving her here with Dr. Cord to be cared for. One of Burke's men shot her. I want you and these girls to help the doctor look after her while I get on Burke's trail. Will you do that for me?"

"Of course," said LaPrey. "Tell me then, will she be looking for work when she gets better—"

"No," said Shaw, "she's not that kind of girl. It's Jane Crowly."

"Oh my," said LaPrey, "Then you are right, she is not that kind of girl. In fact, I have heard she is . . ." He wagged a hand back and forth with a knowing grin. "Is it true?"

"No." Shaw gave him a flat stare. "She's with me. You understand? If there was any truth to that *I* would know, wouldn't I?"

"Yes, you would, and I apologize," said LaPrey. "I am such a terrible degenerate that I think everyone is as deplorable as I am. But you must forgive me. Anyway, you must rest assured, when Dr. Cord gets back, the three of us will pitch in and take good care of Jane Crowly for you."

"Obliged," said Shaw. Only then did he take a guarded glance along the roofline and alleyways. But as his eyes made a sweep along the far end of the dusty street, he froze. A sharp chill ran up his spine as realization set in. He snapped around toward LaPrey and grabbed him by his ruffled shirtfront. "What did you say?"

Startled, LaPrey tried to pull back; but Shaw held firm. "Please, Fast Larry! I only said we would help take care of—"

Shaw turned him loose quickly, and LaPrey stood staring, stunned into silence. He and the twins watched Shaw turn and stalk back toward the doctor's office. "Ah, but look," said LaPrey, pointing in the same direction, toward the doctor's adobe. "Here comes the doctor now, wearing his surgical apron. He must have returned in time to attend to her."

"Yep, just in time," Shaw murmured, walking straight and unhurried, keeping himself from breaking into a run until he saw the situation more clearly.

Ahead of Shaw he saw the long, dark surgical apron sway back and forth on a warm breeze, drawing closer along the street. "I have good news—she's doing fine," a cheerful voice called out. "She's awake now, and she asking for you!"

"That's good news, Doctor. You're the best," Shaw called out at thirty yards. Then, in a blur, he drew his Colt from its holster and fired one round—a head shot that found its mark and sent the dark apron flying backward in a flurry.

LaPrey came at a run along the street. "You have killed the doctor!"

"Not so," said Shaw as he approached the body. He stared down at the bullet hole in River Johnson's forehead. Lying in the dirt before his feet was a sawed-off shotgun that had fallen from beneath the surgical apron. "I only killed a snake."

Shaw smelled smoke, and looked up to see a curl of smoke rising from the doctor's adobe. He shoved his Colt into his holster as he raced to the door of the building. It was locked. From inside, he heard Jane's muffled voice. "Hang on, Janie, I'm coming!" he shouted, hurling himself shoulder first into the wooden door.

On his third try the door broke away from its frame and swung open. Smoke billowed out around him. He ran through the smoke, seeing flames already licking up the rear wall in the next room where Jane lay strapped down on the gurney. Rubbing her cheek frantically against her bare shoulder, she managed to pull down the gag from her mouth just as Shaw reached her.

"Get me the hell off of here!" she shouted, even in her weakened state.

"I've got you, Janie," said Shaw. He grabbed a knife up from his boot well. Instead of taking the time to untie the strips of cloth, he sliced through them and jerked her up into his arms. Turning, coughing and choking in the thickening smoke, he hurried from the adobe, into the street and collapsed to his knees. Behind them, the flames raced across the floor and roiled upward out the front door.

As townspeople raced past them with buckets of water to fight the fire, Shaw let Jane down gently onto the ground and said in a hoarse voice, "Are you all right, Janie?"

"Hell no! Do I . . . look all right?" Jane coughed and choked and held her arms across her bare breasts, fresh blood trickling down from the darker blood that had dried on her bullet wound.

LaPrey and the twins ran up and stooped down around the two. "I had no part in this, Fast Larry!" LaPrey said, looking worried. "I had no idea!"

"I believe you, Clute," said Shaw, his eyes watering from the smoke. "It was you who tipped me, saying 'When the doctor gets back.'"

"Than I have some done something good for once in my depraved and shameful life," said LaPrey.

"Yes, you have," said Shaw. "Now help me get her to your cantina. We've got to dress this wound and—"

"Hell, my wounds . . . will be healed by the time you get me taken care of," Jane said, sounding weaker again now that she was out of danger.

"Of course, to my cantina," said LaPrey. "We will get her taken care of."

"Here, put this on her," said Falina, beginning to wiggle out of her dress.

"No, stop," said LaPrey, grabbing her forearm. "You must stop going naked in public." He turned back to Shaw and helped him stand, Jane cradled in his arms.

"How long have they been gone?" Shaw asked.

"Two hours, three at the most," said LaPrey.

"Where are you . . . taking me?" Jane asked, her face resting against Shaw's chest as he hurried along with her in his arms.

"To LaPrey's Cantina and Brothel," LaPrey answered. "Is that all right with you, Jane Crowly?"

"A brothel . . ." Jane tried to chuckle, but it came out as a cough. "Riding with Lawrence . . . a person might end up anywhere."

Chapter 14

———

By the time Shaw, LaPrey and the twins had gotten Jane Crowly settled into a bed in one of the brothel rooms of the cantina, the people of Mal Vuelve had the burning adobe under control. Sipping from a water gourd, Jane said to Shaw, who stood at the side of her bed, "That sneaking son of a bitch meant to burn me alive." Her voice sounded stronger than it had earlier. Malina had changed the bandage on her chest.

On the other side of the bed, LaPrey said through smeared purple lipstick and melting makeup, "I cannot tell you how many times I have stayed awake at night, in fear of River Johnson wrapping me in my blanket and burning me up in my sleep."

"Well, he's out of business now," Shaw said. "I have to admit he slicked me good, standing out front, looking as much like a doctor as any I ever saw."

"What put you wise to him?" Janie asked.

"Lucky for both of us, Clute here happened to

mention that the doctor is away right now," said Shaw. "Otherwise, you'd be burned to a crisp and I would've walked into a load of buckshot." He gave LaPrey a nod of gratitude.

"Obliged," Jane said to the Frenchman.

"I am only too happy to be of assistance to you, Fast Larry, and you, Jane Crowly," said LaPrey with a hint of a French accent.

"Okay, *Dr.* Shaw," Jane said, feeling better enough to take on her skeptical attitude, "what's the verdict? How bad am I hit? If I drank whiskey, would it pour out quicker than I can pour it in?" She started to sit up on the side of the bed, but Shaw stopped her with a firm hand on her shoulder.

"Lay back and settle in," said Shaw. "You're doing good, but you lost enough blood to keep you off your feet for the next few days."

"The next few days?" Jane protested. "That's no clear answer. How many days is 'the next few days?'"

"Three days," Shaw said.

"Bull, you made that up," Jane said as Falina stepped in from beside her sister and adjusted a thin pillow beneath her head.

"Maybe so," said Shaw, "but three days it is. I want your wound healed enough to not start bleeding all over again. We can't have you out there weak and sick and getting yourself hurt."

"Well, hell, all right, if you say so . . . ," Jane grumbled, but gave in and relaxed, staring up at the cracked adobe ceiling.

Shaw had looked at Jane's wound closely before

Malina covered it with fresh cotton cloth bandaging. The bullet had broken the skin but traveled around a rib without going into her chest. It had struck her at an upward angle, but had cracked the bone and took a downward turn around her side cage and exited from her lower back. Shaw traced its path by following the purple bruise line it drew around and down her rib cage.

"I'm leaving you here with the twins while I go on ahead and try to head Burke and the Mexicans off before they get out on the desert floor. Maybe the doctor will be back and take a look at you before you leave."

"I'm not accustomed to people heaping so much concern and attention on me," Jane said. She sighed. "I suppose I best get used to getting shot now and then, riding with you."

Keeping the conversation serious, Shaw overlooked her quip and cautioned her, saying, "When you get back on the trail, you keep a close watch for *federales* as well as outlaws. Burke and his pals have stirred the Mexican troops up enough to make it dangerous for anybody riding the trails right now."

"I'll watch my trail both ways," Jane said. "You be careful yourself." She reached a hand out to him.

"You can count on it," said Shaw. He took her hand gently for a moment, squeezed it slightly and turned it loose. Turning to the twins and LaPrey, he said, "And I'm counting on the three of you to take good care of her."

"You don't have to tell them that, Lawrence," said Jane. "Damn it all to hell, you're embarrassing me."

Shaw added, "If she tries to get out of bed too soon, knock her in the head with something."

"There," Jane said, grinning crookedly, "that's more like it."

The three stood beside the bed and watched Shaw turn and leave the room. When he had disappeared across the cantina floor and walked out onto the street, Jane said to LaPrey with a sigh, "I suppose this would be a good time to get caught up on some serious drinking, wouldn't it?"

"No!" said LaPrey with a startled look. "Not in my place! I do not want Fast Larry Shaw finding I have let him down!"

"Just checking, Clute," Jane said with a quiet chuckle. She settled back onto her pillow and looked up at the twins. "My, but you two are some beautiful angels," she said with a sigh. Then she closed her tired eyes and drifted off to sleep.

She did not hear Shaw riding by only moments later atop his speckled barb. He looked at River Johnson's body as two old men carried it off the street. He gave a glance toward the cantina and nudged the barb into a faster pace. Leading a fresh horse behind him, he rode away onto the same hill trail Burke and his men had taken, leaving a drifting cloud of dust in the air behind him.

Fifteen miles along the steep hill line, Burke brought the Alevario brothers and Antonio Lero to a halt and gazed ahead, saying, "What have we here?" They stared at a narrow rope bridge that stretched across a deep gorge thirty yards ahead of them. In the middle of the trail stood a rifleman. He stared back at them, his feet planted firmly.

"It is one of the Paylo Gang," Sergio said. "They are always taking over bridges and ferries and charging people to use them." With a shrug he added, "But we will kill them and go across." He turned and started to gig his horse forward, Ernesto and Antonio flanking him. But Burke stopped them.

"Hold back, Sergio," he said. Then he looked back in the direction of Mal Vuelve for a moment as if in contemplation. "Are these Paylo boys any good?"

"Good in what manner?" Sergio asked. "They will kill to get what they want, as most men will."

"Then they'll kill for money," Burke said, answering his own question.

"*Si*, all men will kill for money," Sergio said, his brother and Antonio nodding their agreement with him.

Burke gave a thin smile. "Follow me; keep me covered," he said, nudging his horse forward. "They're bound to have heard about the stolen gold." A few yards closer he called out, "Howdy!"

Instead of returning Burke's greeting, the rifleman answered, "That's near enough, pilgrims. Read the sign and start scratching through your pockets. No money, no crossing."

Smiling, Burke eyed a large wooden plank sign with words crudely carved in misspelled English. "One dollar *toel* fee," he read aloud, managing to discern the word "toll" from it. He grinned at the gunman. "That's a steep fee. You own this bridge, I take it?"

"Take it or leave it," said another rifleman who stepped up from a path beside the bridge. "Yeah, you could say we do own it, *now* leastways."

"*Los testículos* of these *hombres*," Sergio whispered sidelong to the others with a dark chuckle. "They charge Mexicans to use Mexican bridges and tell them so in *Ingles*." To Burke he whispered, "Are you sure you do not want us to kill them?"

"I'm sure," said Burke. He reached into his trouser pockets, pulled out a stolen gold coin and said, "This is the only size coins I have. How else can we cross?"

Sensing something underway, two more riflemen stepped into sight. The four spread out across the mouth of the bridge in a show of strength. The last man to step up, a tall Mexican with a scraggly black beard, replied matter-of-factly to Burke, "You can ride to the next switchback. It is twenty miles."

Burke appeared to consider his situation. "Well, it looks like you've got us," he said finally. He gave the coin a pitch and watched it land at the Mexican's feet. The tall man glared at Burke, stooped and picked up the coin and examined it closely. Squinting at Burke curiously, he passed the coin over to a broad-shouldered Texan, Fitz Paylo.

"I thought that might grab your attention," Burke called out. "How much would it take to buy this bridge from yas?"

"This bridge ain't for sale, pilgrim," said the first rifleman.

"Hush up, Ted," said Fitz Paylo with a short, stiff smile. "Of course it is. Let's hear what the man has to say." Holding up the shining coin, he called out to Red Burke, "To a man carrying these babies, we might be willing to let this bridge go at a bargain."

"There's plenty of those shiny babies waiting to be had where we're headed," said Burke. "My question is, does the Paylo Gang have the kind of sand it takes to help me collect it?"

"You're Red Sage Burke, ain't you?" said Fitz Paylo, cocking his head slightly for recognition. He squinted in the harsh glare of the sun.

"Yep, that's who I am," said Burke. "Are you the leader here?"

"Yep, I'm Fitz Paylo," the gang leader replied. He gave a wide sweep of his gloved hand. "This is just one of my enterprises. I've got bridges, ferries and whatnot everywhere I go." He grinned. "I'm what you might call a toll baron." He gestured toward the other three. "These are my associates, Teddie Hugh, Morgan Gadler and Mexican Carlos."

"Are you in or out, Toll Baron?" Burke asked with a flat stare.

"Do I look loco to you, Burke?" said Paylo. "Hell yes we're in. I been smelling the air in every direction ever since I heard about that robbery last year, trying to get a sniff of that gold. Who do you want killed?"

"Every poor mother's son that gets in our way," Burke said. "Is that easy enough?"

"It is to us," said Paylo. "Let us gather up our gear and horses; we'll shut this operation down and skin out of here."

"Not so fast," said Burke, him and the others sliding down from their saddles. "Let's all take a look at this bridge first."

"What the hell for?" said Paylo. "When you've seen one bridge, you've seen a dozen."

"Never know," said Burke, "I might want to go into tolling bridges myself someday."

Gathering warily, the entire group of gunmen walked out onto the bridge and stood in a long line gazing down into the deep, treacherous chasm beneath them. At the distant bottom a narrow stream of water rushed along and disappeared out of sight around a turn. "Damn," said Burke, spitting and watching it plunge to the water below. "How far do you suppose that is?" he asked Teddie Hugh, leaning out and staring down beside him.

"How the hell would I know?" said Hugh, leaning with him, gazing down.

As quick as a snake Burke grabbed his belt and kicking ankle and hurled him over the rope edge. Hugh bellowed loud and long, flailing his arms and legs wildly. Paylo and his men instinctively started to make a move, but they found themselves staring into the three Mexican's revolvers. "Take it easy, *hombres*," Sergio warned them in an easy, calming voice, beneath Hugh's final blood-curdling scream.

"*Whoo-iiii!* Look at him go," said Burke, staring down, the rope bridge swaying a bit with all of their weight. "Uh-oh! He's landed," he chuckled, hearing Hugh's voice stop as he splattered on the rocky edge of the stream. He turned to Paylo; his smile was gone. He said in a serious tone, "When I tell a man *howdy*, I expect a reply."

The men stood in silence for a tense second until Paylo finally let out a breath and said, "I know what you mean. I'm much the same way myself."

"All right, then," Burke said, closing the matter. He looked down at the thick rope and plank weaving that lay beneath their feet. "Where's the best place to cut these ropes some if we wanted to make sure they'd break on somebody coming along behind us?"

"Right back there where it starts," said Paylo. He turned and hurried along, walking upward from the sagging belly of the bridge until he stood at the entrance pointing down at four thick ropes supporting the swaying plank floor. "Cut these main ropes more than halfway in two. As soon as some weight gets on, down she'll go, quicker than ole Ted Hugh."

"Let's get across, partner," Burke said with a grin of admiration. "Then leave a man to cut these ropes where you tell him to. He can ride around the long way and catch up with us."

"You got it, partner," said Paylo.

"Good," said Burke. "Now let's get moving . . . go get that gold I'm talking about."

Chapter 15

It was late evening by the time Shaw reached the swinging bridge. He stepped down from his saddle and led the two horses across without incident, more concerned with keeping his eyes on the shadowy darkness rather than the bridge itself. When he'd walked across the bridge and climbed back onto his saddle and rode away, he heard a creaking sound along the ropes and planks. But he only looked back in mild curiosity. With no reason to think the sound was anything other than normal, he nudged the speckled barb beneath him and rode on.

Throughout the night he stopped only long enough to change horses or allow the animals to water themselves. The rest of the time he pushed on, keeping the animals at a quick pace in the thin light of a half-moon amid a blanket of glittering stars.

At the first ray of dawn on the horizon he crept forward and stopped at the edge of a steep crag. His spare horse drawn up close beside him, he sat partially hidden by a stand of scrub cedar and pine.

Watching closely, he counted seven men as a ghost-like procession filed slowly around a bare ledge on a trail beneath him.

Seven men . . . ? Somewhere, Burke had managed to take on three more riders. Shaw didn't bother to speculate as the where, or when, or how the outlaw had come upon three more guns. He knew *why*. It was because of the gold, or the promise of gold, he surmised. Gold had a way of drawing men to it like a magnet drew nails.

Patting the necks of both horses in turn, he whispered, "Good boys . . ." Then he backed the horses silently, turned and rode on at a lessened pace until grainy morning light seeped down from the higher edges of cliffs and rock ledges above him.

Judging the men to be no more than an hour's ride ahead of him now, Shaw took it easier. He could see they were headed for the desert floor. He wanted to trail them for now, keep them in his sights and be ready to strike when he had the advantage. That would be on the open desert floor, he told himself. Seven men would not expect to be attacked by one rifleman in miles of open rolling sand.

Their mistake, he thought, nudging the barb forward.

At midmorning he'd followed their tracks down a long trail that turned to sand and eventually spilled onto the great desert basin. There the tracks had gathered as Burke and the men had stopped for a moment. Then the hoofprints stretched out again and wound off through endless sand hills dotted with mesquite brush and barrel cactus.

Shaw stopped long enough to draw his rifle, check it and lay it across his lap. He had no idea where Dawson, Caldwell and Juan Lupo were out there. But judging from where he'd known them to be before the storm, he calculated they could not have gotten much farther than this wide stretch of desert lying before him. Not with a wagon full of gold, he told himself.

He stared across the desert and saw a small, thin outline of hills at the end of his vision. In his saddlebags he carried a telescope. But there was no need to dig it out just yet. He knew that these were the hills he and Jane had trailed down and crossed before the storm caught them. This was good enough for now. He had Burke's trail, and Burke was looking for the same thing he was. Burke and his men were no more than an hour in front of him still.

This was scouting, he reminded himself, tapping his boots lightly to the horse's sides. Keep an idea of where the party you're scouting for might be, and take on any threat that gets near it. He gave himself a grim smile and rode on. . . .

At a narrow wash cut deep between two steep mounds of sand, Mexican Carlos pressed an empty canteen in a soft, shaded strip of darkened sand, and stepped all of his weight down near the open cap. After a few heavy steps a small puddle began to form in his boot prints.

"A Mexican can find water in hell, blindfolded," said Fitz Paylo, watching from where he sat in the thin shade of a large half-sunken rock.

"I expect anybody could after that gully washer

the other day," said Burke, sitting beside him, sipping tepid water from a canteen. "But it ain't like we need it." He sipped again and spit a stream. Raising his voice for Mexican Carlos to hear, he added, "We've got plenty of *agua fresca* to get us across!"

"My people know that an *hombre* must search for fresh water when he does not need it, in order to be able to find it when he *does* need it," Mexican Carlos replied, still pressing his boot sole down on the canteen.

"How fresh is it, if you're squeezing it up out of the ground?" Paylo mused.

"*His people . . . ?*" Sergio said quietly, he, Ernesto and Antonio watching stone-faced.

"He is no *Mejicano*, this one," Ernesto whispered to the other two. "No *Mejicano* squeezes water from the dirt when the needles of plump cactuses are sticking him in his rump at every turn."

The three nodded in silent unison.

"I think you are right—he is no *Mejicano*," Sergio replied, after a moment of keeping his eyes on the theatrical stampings of Mexican Carlos. "No *Mejicano* names himself 'Mexican.'"

"Unless he is an idiot," Antonio put in, speaking in Spanish in a lowered tone.

"He is trying too hard to show us what he is," Antonio said. His hand went to the revolver stuck behind his belly sash. "I think I will shoot him and watch him die. If he crosses himself . . ."

"No, wait, *mi amigo!*" said Sergio, seeing that Antonio was serious. "Let this *idiota* do his dance in the sand. When we find the gold, perhaps we will need him."

"Need this *necio*? I don't think so," said Antonio, even as he pulled his hand away from his revolver and put aside the notion of shooting Mexican Carlos.

Sergio gave him a smile. "We will need some red meat to feed to Juan Facil when we find him."

"*Si*, Juan Lupo . . . ," said Antonio, settling back to watching Mexican Carlos go about his unnecessary water raising. "We must feed someone to Easy John," he said.

At the sound of a gruff voice calling out, "Hello the camp," the men came to their feet and stared in anticipation toward a turn in the wash. Guns slipped free of holsters, belts and belly sashes.

"Hello the wash," Burke and Paylo replied almost at the same time.

"It's me, Gad Man. Don't shoot at me," the voice called back to them as Morgan Gadler stepped warily into sight and walked forward, leading his sweaty horse. Seeing the guns drawn and aimed at him, he said, "I knew I better call out first."

"What's going on out there? Did you find any trace of the wagon?" Burke asked.

"It's hotter than nine kinds of hell in a brass bucket out there, I'll tell you that," said Gadler. He took off his broad-brimmed black hat and fanned himself.

"Is that all you brought back for us, a report on the weather?" Paylo asked sharply. "If it is I wish you'd stayed."

Gadler stopped and stared at them, his face and full beard covered with a thick cake of dust, veneered over in layers by dried sweat. "I found the wagon," he said flatly.

"You did! Jesus, man!" said Burke. Paylo and Burke both rushed forward. The other men—except Mexican Carlos—lunged forward in anticipation.

"Hold it!" Galder said, looking frightened, raising a protecting hand to ward them back. "What I shoulda said is, 'I found the wagon *tracks*!' " He looked back and forth among the sweaty, excited faces. "The tracks is what I found, all right?"

"Shit," said Burke. He spit and rubbed the back of his neck.

"But, what the hell, that's what I was scouting for, ain't it?" Gadler asked. He took note of Mexican Carlos and the small wet puddle lying beneath his boots. "Has this one spilled his bladder?"

"I'm raising water," Mexican Carlos said, stepping away the dark spot beneath him.

"Never mind him," Burke growled at Gadler. "Tell us about the wagon tracks. How far away are they? Why didn't you stay on its trail?"

"I figured I best get the news back to the rest of yas," said Gadler.

"We would have come to you," said Burke.

"Yeah, and for all I know you might have thought I was cutting out on you, going to take all that gold for myself," said Gadler.

"That's not what we'd of thought," said Burke, knowing full well it was exactly what he would've thought. "How far are the tracks from here?"

"Eleven miles or so," said Gadler, "as the crow flies."

"We ain't crows, and we ain't flying!" Paylo suddenly raged, his Colt streaking up from his belly holster. "If I ever again hear you say 'As the gawddamned crows fly'!"

"Put the gun away, Paylo. Let's get the hell out of here, and track that wagon," said Burke. "For all we know that lawman is still dogging us!"

"If the lawman got to the bridge, he's lying down in the gorge right now, him and Ted Hugh counting all the rocks in their face," said Paylo, uncocking his Colt and lowering it. "If there's one thing I know for sure, it's how to fell a bridge."

"Still and all, no gunfire," Burke demanded, already gathering his horse's reins, the rest of the men doing the same. "Not until we get that wagon in sight. Then we'll do enough shooting to raise the dead." He stepped up into his saddle, jerked his horse around toward Morgan Gadler and stared down at him expectantly. "Well?" he said impatiently, feeling hot, sweaty and irritable with the bulletproof vest on beneath his shirt.

The tired gunman had hoped to sit down out of the searing heat and rest himself and his horse. But he saw that Burke would have none of it. "I'm coming," he said, raising his sweat-stained hat back onto his head and reaching for his saddle horn. Once in his saddle, he led the men along the dry wash the first fifty yards, then turned the lead over to Burke as they filed up onto the trail of hoofprints Gadler had left around a steep mound of sand.

Shaw followed the tracks of the horses until he saw all but one set turn and go down into the wash, while a single set rode on across the rolling sand hills toward the middle of the sand basin. One rider had gone on scouting the desert ahead for the others, he deduced.

He rode over to the lower edge of the wash and studied it closely before riding down into it. Only when he noted the tracks all leading off along the wash and out of sight around a nearby turn did he ease both horses down the cut bank. With rifle in hand he followed the tracks for the next hour, stopping only for a few minutes at a time to rest both horses along the way. He had to remind himself to keep an easy pace, sensing the distance between himself and the gunmen drawing closer with each rise and fall of his horses' hooves.

A mile ahead of him, Red Burke stood in his stirrups and stared through a pair of binoculars at the freight wagon and the two horsemen sitting at the edge of a long stretch of sand flats. "By God, sir," he said to Paylo, sitting on his horse beside him, "we've got them where we want them! I couldn't have hoped to catch them in a better spot." The two had left the others waiting five yards behind them.

"Let me see," said Paylo. He quickly finished wiping his gritty face and stuffed a wadded up bandanna inside his shirt. "I always knew I'd come upon a big chunk of riches someday. It's all that kept me going at times." He took the binoculars and looked out through them.

"Do you see them?" Burke asked, quickly getting

impatient with him. "Come on, *come on*, we ain't got all damned day." He snapped his fingers toward Paylo, wanting the binoculars back.

Paylo lowered the binoculars and handed them back to Burke. With a serious expression, he said, "I'm ready to ride in and kill all three . . . leave nothing alive but the horses pulling it."

"Now you're talking," said Burke. He raised his hand and waved the other five riders up around them. "All right, everybody, listen up," he said. "The wagon is out there. I recognized Juan Lupo driving it. There's two men on horseback escorting him."

"What's our plan?" Mexican Carlos asked, getting excited at the prospect of more gold than he had ever seen in his life about to become his. His horse spun in a full circle.

"Our plan is to get closer before they see us. Then we ride them down, kill them, get our hands on the wagon and take it somewhere safe where we can pillage it without interruption." He gave a dark grin. "Any questions?" he asked, knowing what an advantage he had riding into gunfire wearing the bulletproof vest.

Shaw had first watched the dark specs move across the sands flats in the harsh glare of sunlight. When he stretched the telescope open and gazed through it, he saw the dark specs grow into riders. He recognized Red Burke in the lead, riding his horse at a quick but restrained clip. *Saving it up for a charge*, Shaw surmised.

But he himself wouldn't have that option. He

needed to get close enough to start dropping them as they made their attack. He swung a bandoleer of rifle ammunition over his shoulder. Keeping his horse's reins in hand, he slid from his saddle over onto the barebacked speckled barb. Finding the hard-boned barb rested and ready to run, he batted his boot heels and felt the animal bolt forward. When both horses reached a fast pace, he turned loose the other horse's reins and let it run freely beside him.

In the middle of the sand flats, Juan Lupo had stopped the wagon and stepped down to check on the team horses. On his way back to the driver's seat, he looked out across the flats and saw the dark specks riding toward them at the head of a large cloud of dust.

"We have visitors," he said quickly, but coolly. Without waiting for a reply, he stepped back into the driver's seat, unwrapped and picked up the traces. Releasing the long oaken brake handle, he retrieved the Winchester from against the seat beside him and checked it. "I'll head straight for the foothills," he said, nodding toward the hazy purple hill line in the distance west of them. "You'll find me there among the rocks."

"You bet," said Dawson. He swung his horse in close, raised his Colt from his holster and fired two rapid shots into the air above the team horses' heads.

Hearing the shots and seeing the team horses break into a run, Burke spurred his mount into a hard gallop and shouted back over his shoulder, "Spread it! It's commenced!" He raised his rifle and fired on the run. Around him the others began doing the same, each of them fueled by the thought of a wagonful of minted gold coin, theirs for the taking.

Chapter 16

When Red Burke and his men began firing at the wagon, Shaw put the speckled barb into a hard run. His rifle in hand and ready, he held his fire until he circled to the right and put himself into a position that did not risk a stray bullet going toward Dawson, Caldwell and Juan Lupo. Once he knew his line of fire was safe, he raised his rifle just as Morgan Gadler spotted him and let out a loud yell to draw the others' attention to Shaw.

As Gadler turned his gun toward him and fired, Shaw let loose his first shot and watched the gunman fly from his saddle. Gadler hit the sand and rolled along, raising a cloud of dust until he stopped and lay facedown, dead.

As Gadler went down, Burke shouted at Paylo riding beside him, "There's that damned lawman who's supposed to be dead!"

Paylo only gave a sidelong glance, the two of them pounding along, their horses at a dead heat. The rest of the men rode spread out across the sand.

After Shaw's rifle shot, they divided their fire between him and the two lawmen who had taken prone positions in the sand, to protect Juan Lupo and the fleeing wagon.

Shots from the two lawmen ripped through the air, causing Mexican Carlos and the three other Mexicans to veer and spread out even more. With a loud yell, Carlos returned fire repeatedly, holding a big horse pistol with both hands. His reins lay tied together in his lap. His horse raced along at a full run.

"Got him," Dawson said to Caldwell, seeing the big horse pistol getting closer.

Before Carlos had gotten close enough for the pistol fire to be effective, Dawson's shot hit him high in the left shoulder. The impact twisted Carlos backward off his saddle, but his boot stuck tightly in his leather-cased stirrup. The running horse dragged Mexican Carlos away, screaming in a bellowing cloud of dust.

From his prone position, Caldwell aimed through the dust and fired just as Paylo sent a rifle shot past the two lawmen toward the fleeing freight wagon. Caldwell's shot ripped Paylo from his saddle and sent him rolling, dead on the ground. Paylo's bullet whistled past Juan Lupo's head, but Lupo neither slowed nor looked back. He kept the team horses running full bore.

Seeing Paylo go down, and not wanting to go down himself, Burke veered his horse into the thickest part of the rising dust cloud and raced away, feeling the bite of a bullet strike his protecting vest with a solid thump at shoulder blade level.

"Damned Mexicans!" he cursed to himself, having felt the wild shot come from the direction of Sergio, Ernesto and Antonio. Feeling a warm liquid on his shin, he looked down to see if was blood. But he saw no blood, only water from where a bullet had sliced through the canteen hanging from his saddle horn. "Hell, don't worry, you're bulletproof!" he said aloud to himself, spurring his horse on through the thick dust.

Avoiding the dust, the three Mexicans swung wide of the lawmen and tried to head around them toward the wagon. But the lawmen turned with them and kept firing. Approaching the two, Shaw swung around with Sergio, Antonio and Ernesto and slid his barb to a halt. He jumped down from the horse's bare back, dropped to a knee, took careful aim and fired, mindful of Juan Lupo being out in front of his target.

Caldwell and Dawson saw Shaw's shot slam Antonio in the back and send him flying sidelong from his saddle. Also rising from the ground into a knee-firing position, the two concentrated their fire on the Alevario brothers who had drawn closer together in pursuit of Juan Lupo. Shaw did the same. "*Ayiiii!*" Ernesto screamed as a bullet punched through his back and splattered blood on his saddle horn, his lap, and his horse's neck. Falling forward, he wobbled in his saddle and managed to shout to Sergio, "Oh, my brother, I am dead!"

Sergio caught a glimpse of Ernesto falling from his saddle beside him. "So am I, *mi hermano*," he said. He dropped his rifle and raced on, alone, knowing that behind him the three lawmen had turned their shots on him. He felt the hard impact of bullets hit him, followed by their cracking sound, resounding across the broad sand basin.

When the last of the three Mexican gunmen had fallen, Caldwell and Dawson scanned the desert floor for Red Burke, who seemed to have disappeared. "Shaw's got him," Caldwell said hopefully.

But they watched as Shaw searched in vain to find Burke in the roiling dust that rose high and wide across the basin. Finally, Shaw lowered his rifle and shook his head. Standing, he looked toward them and called out, "Catch up to Juan Lupo. I'll be right along."

On the other side of the thick, drifting cloud of dust, Burke spurred his horse, not slowing down until he came upon Mexican Carlos' horse. The animal walked at a leisurely pace; Mexican Carlos still hung from its stirrup by a single boot.

"Help . . . me," Carlos rasped, his halting voice barely audible.

Knowing he'd need water, Burke swung his horse over, took the other horse by its bridle and stopped it. Without stepping down, he lifted Carlos' canteen by its strap, shook it and hung it over his own saddle horn. "I can't be no help to you," he said, gazing down at the raw, bloody, sand-stripped face that struggled to look up at him.

"H-elp me?" Carlos repeated.

"Help you?" said Burke. "Pard, I can't even stop to help myself right now." He stepped down from his saddle, loosened Carlos' gun belt and pulled it from the man's waist. The holster was empty, but it was the bullets Burke was after. He swung the belt over his shoulder and glanced back at the dust cloud to make sure the lawmen hadn't spotted him yet.

With a bloody, skinless hand, Carlos tried to clutch Burke's leg. "Don't . . . take . . . my water," he pleaded.

"Get off me," Burke said, kicking his hand away. "Go squeeze yourself some damned water, you worthless sonsabitch."

"No . . . please . . . my foot," Carlos coughed and wheezed, his lips dry and sand-coated, his open mouth half filled with caked dust.

"Free your own foot," said Burke. "I don't owe you nothing." He turned to his horse and stepped up into the saddle while the dust still stood thick in the air. "The best thing you can do now is die as fast as you can, Mexican Carlos," he said with a dark chuckle. Then he turned the horse, punched his boots to its sides and rode away. By the time the dust had settled enough for Shaw to see across the basin, Burke had vanished into the wavering swirl of heat and sunlight.

Back atop the speckled barb, Shaw kept watch across the desert floor as he rode back and found his other horse looping along toward him at an easy pace. Stopping the horse he rode, he slipped back onto the saddle and led the speckled barb in the direction Dawson, Caldwell and the wagon had taken.

A half hour later he had followed the wagon tracks and hoofprints onto a rugged, sloping hillside. He stopped before a large rock that stood partially sunken in the ground with a narrow path leading around it. Looking up, Shaw saw Dawson step into sight and call down to him, "It's about time we heard something from you. Where have you been? Where's Jane Crowly?"

"One thing at a time," Shaw replied. He touched his hat brim and rode around the rock, leading the spare horse behind him. "Let's get together quick. I've still got scouting to do."

Behind the large rock, Shaw dipped water into his upturned hat from a wooden cask in the wagon bed and watered both of his horses in turn, while Juan Lupo watered the team horses from canvas water bags. While Shaw attended his horses, he filled Dawson in on Jane's gunshot wound and convalescence in Mal Vuelve. While the two men spoke, Caldwell laid out strips of jerked elk meat and opened an airtight of beans.

When he had finished watering the horses, Shaw shook out his hat and put it back on. Walking over to Caldwell, Shaw said to Dawson, "You remember we talked about who else might have had a stake in the depository robbery?"

"Yep, I remember," said Dawson.

"Well, here's a name for you to think about," Shaw said. "Garris Cantro."

"The Border Dogs?" said Caldwell, his face turning troubled.

"Cantro's Border Dogs . . ." Dawson shook his head slightly. "When were you going to tell us?" he asked.

"Just now," Shaw replied. "I could've waited 'til your birthday, but I know you hate surprises."

"Where'd you hear this from?" Caldwell asked Shaw, a strip of elk meat still hanging on his knife-point, untouched.

Shaw nodded toward the desert floor in the direction of the gun battle they'd had. "The one with the red beard is Red Sage Burke. I shot him and another man down, in Agua Mala."

"You shot him down?" Dawson asked with a quizzical expression.

"He was wearing a Korean bulletproof vest," Shaw said. "I expect he still is."

"A bulletproof vest?" Dawson asked in disbelief.

"I've heard of bulletproof vests," said Caldwell. "The Koreans wore them against the French."

"So I heard," Shaw said, remembering Jane telling him the same thing. "Anyway," he went on, "I winged a third man in order to get information from him, and that's the information I got. Cantro and his Border Dogs were in on the gold robbery, and they'll be coming to get it back."

"Hold up," Dawson said. He looked over at Juan Lupo and said to him, "John, you need to be hearing this."

Lupo had just finished watering the team horses. When he walked over and joined the three of them, Shaw recounted everything that had happened while he and Jane Crowly scouted the trail surrounding their expedition. He told Lupo about the shoot-out in Agua Mala. Then he went on to tell the three of them about tracking Red Burke to Suerte Buena, and about Burke taking up with the Alevario brothers in order to get the gold for himself.

"But now these Alevarios are dead, yes?" Juan asked when Shaw paused.

"The Alevarios, yes," said Shaw. "But Red Burke, I don't know. The last I saw him he was still alive, riding away in the dust."

"And . . . you are going after him?" asked Lupo. He watched Shaw take a sip from the canteen Dawson handed him.

"That's right," said Shaw, taking a tin plate of unheated beans from Caldwell, "just as soon as I've got enough grub to hold my belt up."

"You figure now that he sees he missed his shot at the gold for himself, he'll try to get back to Cantro with the news?" Dawson anticipated.

Shaw only nodded, eating hungrily. Beside him Caldwell held up an unopened airtight of beans and said, "I'll stick these in your saddlebags for the trail."

"*Gracias,*" said Shaw. "I'll find a chance to stop and eat after I know I've got Burke where I want him."

Juan Lupo gave a troubled look out across the desert floor and up along the hills above them. "Cantro and the Border Dogs . . ." He shook his head slowly.

"It's not getting any easier, is it?" said Caldwell, seeing the grim faces around him.

"There's more," said Shaw. "The man I kept alive

to get information from got away from Jane. She shot him, but didn't kill him. If he went back and told Cantro everything, we could have the Border Dogs already breathing down our necks." He chewed a final spoonful of beans, took another sip from the canteen and wiped a hand across his mouth.

"How are the team horses?" Dawson asked Juan Lupo.

"They are holding up good," said Lupo. Again he gazed off and up along the rocky hills.

"Good," said Dawson. To Shaw he said, "We'll get this wagon across the desert as fast as we can, and get out of everybody's face."

"You do that," said Shaw, already turning to his horses. "I'll keep myself between the wagon and everybody wanting a bite of it." He swung up into the speckled barb's saddle and took the reins to the other horse in hand. "The next time you see me, I hope to have Jane with me, healed up and kicking high."

"Watch your back trail, my friend," said Caldwell, touching his hat brim toward Shaw.

"And ours as well, scout," said Dawson.

Touching his hat brim in reply, Shaw said, "You can count on it." Then he spun the speckled barb and horse beside him, and rode away, around the rock and back down to the desert floor. Moments later the three watched him stir up a rise of dust below as he rode out onto an endless carpet of sand and was soon swallowed by the wavering heat.

"With so many wanting our wagon," said Juan

Lupo, "perhaps the best thing to do is to let them see it."

The two American lawmen looked at him, then at each other, with a questioning glance. "How soon before we get in range of some *federales* you know you can trust, Easy John?" Dawson asked.

"Very soon . . . I hope," Juan replied. "Meanwhile, I trust no one but the three of you."

Chapter 17

The billowing dust on the desert floor had settled when Shaw rode back to where he had last spotted Red Burke. From there he followed the hoofprints of Burke's horse. Near the edge of the sand basin he saw Mexican Carlos' horse still dragging Carlos around aimlessly in the sand. As he drew close, he slowed to a halt and stepped down from his saddle. Hearing a faint choking sound and seeing Carlos' body tremble violently, he jerked his canteen from his saddle horn and walked over, keeping watch for Burke lurking anywhere nearby.

"Wat . . . wa-water . . . ," Carlos moaned in a quivering, dying voice.

Shaw first freed Carlos' boot from the stirrup, then stooped down, twisted off the canteen cap, wet his fingertips and touched them to his burned lips covered over with a black crust of dried blood. "Try to lay still, Mister, I've got plenty," Shaw said quietly to the dying man, seeing the sore condition the sun and the dragging across the burning sand had left him in.

Holding the canteen a fraction away from the blistered, scalded lips, Shaw poured a thin trickle of water into Carlos' open mouth. Carlos strangled a little but managed to swallow and try to hold his face upward for more. Shaw slipped his free hand beneath the raw, hairless head and poured another thin trickle. As he poured the water, Shaw could see no shade, no place out of the baking evening sun.

"*Gracias . . . ,*" Carlos managed to whisper. With a burned and trembling hand he gestured toward the Colt in Shaw's holster. With a new round of shivering and convulsion, he gave Shaw a pleading look.

Shaw knew what the man was asking him to do, yet he gave no answer. Instead he held Carlos still and poured another trickle of water. Then he laid Carlos' head down gently and stood up. As Shaw picked up the tired horse's reins and pulled the animal aside, Carlos struggled to murmur "*Gracias*" again, this time in a weak and fading whisper.

As Shaw capped his canteen, he watched Carlos close his eyes and try to hold back another convulsion. Without another word, Shaw raised his Colt, cocked it and fired. The bullet struck Carlos in the center of his forehead. Carlos' head relaxed into the sand as a red puddle began to widen beneath it.

Shaw stepped back and took stock of the horse. "All right," he said, judging the horse to be hot and thirsty but otherwise sound, "you can tag along with us." He stripped the horse's saddle and bridle and dropped them both in the dirt. "But you'll have to keep up."

Taking the reins to the speckled barb, he walked

the horses along for the next ten minutes, letting the three animals get used to one another before stepping back up into his saddle. He heeled the barb to a walk, leading his spare horse. The third horse followed a few feet behind as they moved along, tracking the hoofprints in the sand.

By dark they had traveled up off the sand basin and into a stretch of sparse wild grass. The third horse began falling farther and farther behind, grazing and sniffing the air to the west where the hills supported small herds of Mexican mustangs. Soon the horse had wandered off on its own and disappeared from sight. Shaw looked back for it only once. Then he rode on, moving slow but steadily, tracking Burke throughout the night in the light of a wide full moon. . . .

Fifteen miles ahead of Shaw, Red Burke continued to push his horse harder and harder. But more than halfway through the night, when he saw the tired animal losing ground in spite of spurring and whipping it with his wrist quirt, he finally stepped down from his saddle. "Lazy sonsabitch," he growled at the weary animal, jerking it forward.

He continued along the trail until he reached the rope bridge; then he tied the animal to a tree and slept like a dead man. In the morning he awoke to a rumbling sound of horses' hooves on the bridge's plank walkway. "What the hell . . . ?" he whispered in amazement, crawling stealthily through the brush. At the edge of the trail he peeped out and saw the column of Mexican *federales* riding single file across the creaking, trembling bridge.

"Damn you, Paylo," he whispered gruffly, seeing the bridge still intact. "If you wasn't dead, I'll gut you sure as hell."

He watched in silence until the last of the soldiers had crossed. As two rear guards rode out of sight around a turn, he said, "That's right, get out of here!"

Standing, he dusted his knees and said to his horse standing tied to the tree, "Well, at least we don't have to ride all the way around." He walked over, untied the horse and jerked it roughly away from the tree and stepped up into the saddle. "Come on, I'll swap your worthless hide for a fresh mount as soon as we get back to Agua Mala."

Looking carefully both ways for any more *federales*, he nudged the horse out onto the bridge and started across at a walk. He could still feel vibrations from the crossing soldiers. Yet halfway across, Burke stopped the horse suddenly as he heard a loud snap and saw the planks at the far end of the bridge flip up wildly into the air.

The main ropes broke, whipping upward like an angry serpent. The whole bridge twisted to one side as another rope broke, and Burke's horse reared high with a loud whinny and turned on its hooves. Burke struggled to hang on as the animal spun and began running back in the opposite direction. But with the bridge bucking and twisting violently, Burke lost his seating, flipped up out of his saddle and slid down over the horse's rump.

Grabbing on to the fleeing animal's tail and holding on tightly, he screamed at the horse, "Go boy!"

Burke's spinning feet hit the walk planks at a hard run. He heard more planks flipping up behind him while the rest of the main ropes snapped and twanged and whistled in the air. As the horse raced off the doomed bridge, Burke felt the whole structure collapse and begin falling from beneath his feet. Still clinging to the horse's tail, he could see the animal taking him closer to safety with each step. But just as the horse's front hooves pounded onto solid ground, its rear hoof dealt Burke a solid kick and sent him flying backward.

He realized in a flash that the bridge was no longer beneath him. Eyes bulging, Burke caught a fleeting glimpse of the running horse's tail as the horse abandoned him. He let out a loud, echoing scream as he grappled with whipping, tangled ropes and flying oak walk planks.

Clawing, screaming, grasping, falling, Burke felt the collapsed structure drop straight into the open mouth of the deep chasm. Above him, as he fell, he saw more than half of the broken rope bridge writhing and undulating as it dropped and swung back toward the shear wall of jagged rock. His fall slowed, then stopped suddenly with a hard jerk as a tangle of rope encircled him and held him in it. He almost breathed a sigh of relief, yet, before he could, the bridge slammed against the rock wall and the impact of it snapped him upward in the tangle of rope like something tied to the end of a bull whip.

When his upward flight ended and fell, much of the tangled rope holding him unraveled downward, spinning him like a top. When it stopped, Burke stared down at a spinning world of jagged rock and rushing water still lying more than a hundred feet below him. On a rocky bank he saw the body of Ted Hugh, the man he'd hurled off the bridge, lying broken in a dried circle of blood. "Oh no!" Burke said aloud, "I can't die here . . . not like this." Broken planks and loosened rocks and dirt rained down around him.

At the end of a long loop of rope circled under his arms he swung back and forth slowly above the rushing stream, ten feet out from the receding rock wall. When the swinging slowed and finally stopped, he stared straight up, from the end of his rope at the end of the fallen bridge, bobbing like an ill-handled puppet.

"By God," he said in a disbelieving voice, "I'm— I'm still alive!"

But no sooner had Burke's words left his mouth than his upturned eyes widened in terror as he caught a glimpse of a rock the size of a goose egg hurtling downward. The rock dropped suddenly and mercilessly, smacked him squarely in his forehead and knocked him cold. As he slumped unconscious, his feet dangling, one of his boots slipped free of his foot and tumbled to the water below.

A full two hours passed before Red Burke opened his eyes and the memory of his situation came flooding back to him. He'd awakened with a start, feeling a heavy weight and sharp points atop his bowed head. When his eyes opened he stared into the upside down bald face of a black buzzard perched atop

him, its talons gripping his forehead as it leaned
forward and craned its neck at a steep angle. The
carrion hunter's fierce yellow eyes peered into his
with a questioning stare.

Burke screamed, kicking and shaking his head
spasmodically, and sent the big bird flying away in
a flurry of batting wings. He looked down at the
swaying world beneath him, a single bare toe standing out through a hole in his dirty sock. His head
pounded from the large bloody whelp the rock had
left between his eyes. But he ignored the pain and began searching his wits and the terrain surrounding
him, looking for a way out of his dilemma.

If he raised his arms high, he could wiggle free of
the loop of rope and drop to the water below, but it
was too far, and too rocky. After a moment of silent
thought, he decided his only hope was to swing himself against the rock wall, get a grip on it and climb
upward through the tangled remnants of the collapsed bridge.

His head pounding, his left boot missing, Burke
struggled until he began to swing in and out toward
the rock wall. After several full minutes of hard
work, he managed to get close enough to the wall to
kick himself out for a deeper swing to it. When he
swung back to the wall, this time he grabbed on to
the walk boards and rope railings lying flat down
the steep rocks.

Once he'd secured a footing for himself among
the broken oaken planks, he wiggled out of his long
loop of rope, but held on to it and climbed upward a
few feet and stepped his bare foot over into the loop

and pushed himself upward for another foothold. After a moment of consideration, he tied a knot higher up in the loop of rope, stuck his foot into it and pushed himself farther up.

Using the dangling rope and the collapsed bridge for his support, with each hand over hand and foot over foot, he inched himself higher up the side of the rock wall like a slow-moving spider, weaving and creating his rope web as he went.

After two hours of climbing and struggling and knotting the rope, he found a narrow ledge in the rock wall and crawled onto it. He lay panting and aching, and closed his eyes against the pain on his forehead. Dying would be easier, he thought, gasping, drenched with sweat.

He'd already loosened his long riding duster and let it fall. He reached around up under his shirt to untie the wet, heavy bulletproof vest, but his fingertips could not reach the strings. *To hell with it . . .* , he told himself, giving up. He might need the vest anyway, if he managed to get out of this hole alive. The vest might be as important to him as the Colt on his hip, he thought, and he sure as hell wasn't chucking that away.

His hands and bare foot bloody from the jagged rock and oak splinters, he arose from the ledge, reached out and grabbed on to the rope and bridge debris and started climbing again. After another full hour of gut-wrenching pulling and tugging, with loose dirt and rocks pelting down around him, he took heart as he felt a breeze and looked up to see the edge of the crumbled bridge only another fifty feet above him.

Burke stopped long enough to cling to the wall and look down. He chuckled aloud to any unseen entity that might be listening. "It takes a hell of a lot more than this to lick ole Red!"

With a renewed energy he climbed faster, harder, and within twenty minutes he swung his arms over the upper edge onto solid ground and hung there, catching his breath and feeling relief surge through him.

"Damn it to hell. I've done it . . . I've done it," he said under his breath, shaking his head slowly. With all of his strength he heaved himself up over the edge and rolled up onto his feet. Standing in a crouch, his palms on his knees, he took deep breaths, laughing to himself. "Red Sage Burke," he said proudly, "what sonsabitch can stop you now?"

"What took you so long?"

Burke straightened with a snap, his hand poised near his holstered Colt. Shaw sat on a rock a few feet away, calmly holding an airtight of beans in his left hand.

"You *do not* want to touch that gun, Burke," Shaw said quietly through a mouthful of beans, "not after working so hard to stay alive."

Burke stared at him, knowing no bullet could harm him. He saw Shaw's two horses as well as his own standing calmly beside the rock.

Shaw swallowed his beans and set the airtight down on the rock next to him, a spoon handle sticking up. "I got tired of waiting, thought I better eat something."

"I best tell you," said Burke, feeling cocky and self-confident, "whatever you think you're getting from me, you ain't getting. Not after what I just went through."

Shaw wiped a hand across his mouth. "I don't want anything from you, Burke. Those men you were riding with are all dead. I just came here to finish things up, make sure you're dead."

"*Uh-uh.* There again," said Burke, raising a ragged, bloody finger for emphasis. "It ain't going to go the way you think it is. I can take any-damn-thing you can shoot at me." His hand poised tense at the butt of his Colt. "Your bullets ain't sending me to hell. I'll send you."

Shaw gave him a bemused look. "You talk like a man with a handful of aces. If I didn't know better, I'd almost speculate you're wearing a bulletproof vest."

"What I'm wearing is none of your damned business." As Burke spoke, his hand made its play for his Colt.

Shaw's revolver came up and fired. The first bullet slammed Burke in the chest. The outlaw fell back a step, but he only gave a grimace, then a dark grin. Shaw's shot only knocked his aim off a little, he thought. But his bullet streaked wildly past Shaw's head. Before he got another shot off, Shaw fired again, the bullet striking almost in the same spot.

Burke grunted and staggered farther back with the impact. But he almost laughed aloud at Shaw for not realizing that a shot in his chest wouldn't kill him. He cocked his gun and aimed it unsteadily at Shaw. "So long, fool!" he said, ready to pull the trigger.

"Adios," Shaw replied. His third shot again hit the outlaw in almost the same spot. Burke couldn't believe this man hadn't learned by now. But again the impact of the slug pushed him back a step, and before Burke could pull the trigger, his bare foot stepped back off the edge and the outlaw fell from Shaw's sight wearing a stunned expression. This time there were no ropes or walk planks to stop him.

Shaw walked to the edge and looked down just as Burke hit the stream. The rushing water caught his body and swept it away over jutting rock, leaving a streak of blood widening in its wake. Shaking his head, Shaw returned to his rock, sat down, picked up the airtight and finished the remaining beans. When he'd finished eating, he stood up, gathered the reins to the speckled barb, his spare horse, and Burke's horse and swung up into his saddle. Riding the long way around the trail, he set out for Mal Vuelve.

PART 3

PART 3

Chapter 18

Mal Vuelve, Mexico

Jane Crowly had regained her strength, although her chest still felt as if she'd been struck by a ball-peen hammer. That was all right; pain was something she knew how to overlook. Pain didn't bother her, be that pain physical or emotional, she told herself, blowing smoke toward the dirty ceiling. *So, what the hell . . . ?* Pain was just a natural part of her life. It always had been. *Ignore it . . . ,* she told herself.

Anyway, she'd been down too long. She missed Lawrence Shaw. She missed having his hands on her, feeling his hard body next to hers . . . and all the rest of it, she thought, blowing more smoke upward, watching it swirl in the darkness. She'd always been drawn to gunmen; she didn't know why. Even though she and Shaw had made love only that one time, and she had to admit neither of them had acted very lovey-dovey afterward, she missed whatever it was that Shaw brought out of her.

She thought of their affair—if that's what she could call it. In spite of it being only that one time, in an abandoned adobe in the desert, amid a storm, gunmen everywhere wanting to kill them, she liked to think it was something special—something wild and beautiful. She smiled to herself recalling that night, and blew another thin stream of smoke upward into the looming gray swirl. The patch of dried red blood on the bandage circling her chest had grown smaller with each changing. *Get up . . .* , she told herself.

In her room in LaPrey's Cantina and Brothel, she had spent much of the night listening to creaking beds and the voices and drunken laughter of *federales* in the rooms on both sides of her. The Mexicans had not seen her, nor were they looking for her. But she had rested enough to be able to ride, and ride she would. There was too much going on for her to keep Shaw, Dawson and the others waiting on her.

Jeez . . . She shook her head.

All right, they weren't waiting on her, she admitted to herself, letting the thin black cigar hang from her lips as she pushed up and sat on the side of the bed. Hell, they probably didn't wonder if she was dead or alive. But she was a trail scout, the same as Shaw. She knew Shaw relied on her, and she took her work seriously, the same as he did. She stood up in the darkness and reached over for her clothes hanging over a chair back.

Dressing herself, she picked up the Colt from the nightstand beside the bed and shoved it down securely into her waist. Then she picked up her hat and boots from beside the bed, eased over to a wooden-shuttered window, opened it and climbed out. "You randy devils . . . ," she murmured, hearing a bouncing bed and the sounds of impassioned voices from the room next to hers.

Looking all around, she leaned against the adobe wall and pulled on her big miner's boots, then slipped along to the last window and rapped on the shutter quietly until LaPrey stuck his head out and said, "Who is there?"

"It's me, Janie," she said quietly. "I'm leaving."

"You are leaving?" said LaPrey. "But you cannot leave. You still need to rest. Lawrence Shaw will skin me alive."

"No, he won't," said Jane. "Listen to me. If he comes back here looking for me, tell him I'm headed down to the sand hills, but I'm going back the way we came, through Suerte Buena. He can find me along the trail."

Seeing she had her mind made up, LaPrey shrugged and said, "I do not like this, but I will tell him." He gave her a toss of his hand. "Adios, dear Janie."

Jane touched her hat brim toward him and slipped away toward the livery stables in the grainy hour before dawn.

In moments she had slipped her horse from the stables without being seen or heard. She walked the animal out of town onto the trail, stepped up into the saddle and rode away, taking the trail back toward Suerte Buena instead of riding the same road the larger column of Southern Mexican soldiers had taken toward the swinging bridge the day before. There were starting to be too many *federales* riding the high trails to suit her. Besides, she thought, if the gold wagon was making any kind of time at all, by now they would be crossing the desert farther west on the rolling sand hills below Suerte Buena.

She rode steadily until midmorning when, as she rounded a turn in the trail, she stopped suddenly and found herself staring into the faces of Bale Harmon and Roy Heaton.

Sitting slumped with a pained expression on his face, Heaton said, "It's Jane Crowly, the low-down bitch who did this to me."

Jane jerked her horse's reins, trying to spin the animal and ride away. But from either side of the trail behind her, Corey Trent, Elvis Pond and Elijah Chase sprang out of hiding, grabbed her horse by it bridle and held it in place. "Sonsabitches!" Jane shouted, kicking at the men and reaching for the Colt.

Elvis Pond leaped up, grabbed her around her waist and threw her to the hard ground before she could draw the gun. As she tried to scramble to her feet, Pond's boot toe dealt a swift kick to her lower belly and doubled her over into a ball.

"Pull her up," Harmon said to Pond and the others, still seated atop his horse. Beside him, Heaton said in a strained voice, "Let me get my hands on her throat." He started to step down from his saddle, but Harmon stopped him, saying in a commanding voice, "As you were, Heaton. Stroud left me in charge. I'll say who puts their hand on her and who doesn't."

Pond and Chase jerked Jane roughly up from the ground and stood her up straight in spite of the pain in her chest and lower stomach. "You trail turds . . . are making a big mistake, messing . . . with me," Jane said haltingly. "I ain't telling you . . . nothing, I don't care what—"

Upon getting a nod from Harmon, Pond stepped forward, spun around and punched Jane in the face. She crumbled backward. But Chase held her up and shook her back and forth like a rag doll. "She's got a tough ugly mouth, but she can't take a hit worth a damn."

"Damn it, Elvis, what's wrong with you?" said Harmon with a slight chuckle. "I didn't mean for you to knock her head off. I meant for you to slap her, or something. That's not the way to hit a woman."

Heaton cut in, saying, "Who ever accused Jane Crowly of really being a woman?"

Elvis Pond stared blankly at Harmon. "Want me to hit her easier?"

"No," Trent cut in before Harmon could answer, "she's had enough." He gave Harmon a glare as he snatched the Colt from Jane's waist and pitched it to Elijah Chase. "There's no cause for hurting this woman just because you don't like her or her ways."

"Her *ways* ought to be changed," said Heaton, still bitter over the gunshot wound he blamed her for, even though privately he knew he'd caused it by jerking the rifle barrel while she held it cocked and ready to fire.

Bale Harmon looked Jane up and down and chuckled again. "You might have a point there, Roy," he said to Heaton. "Some women need saving from themselves."

Pond's right cross had knocked Jane out, but she had already begun coming to. She shook her head slowly, trying to collect her senses. She mumbled profanities at her captors in a dazed and incoherent voice. Raising his voice for Jane to hear, Harmon said, "Keep your filthy mouth shut or I'll have Elvis hit you again."

Pond stepped forward and drew back his fist in anticipation. "No, Elvis! Not now," said Harmon. "If you want to do something, reach down her britches and tell us what you find."

Pond stuck his hand roughly down Jane's waist. "This ain't right," said Trent. Stepping away from Jane and Chase he gave Pond a shove. Pond backed off, giving him a cold, hard stare.

"Easy, Trent," Harmon chuckled. "Elvis is only following orders. I told him to do a little bush scouting, so he did."

"Stroud isn't going to like this," said Trent, "neither is Cantro."

"I say they don't have to know it ever happened," said Harmon. "What say you?" His hand rested on a rifle across his lap.

"I didn't feel nothing down there," Pond said to Harmon. Wanting no more to do with this, Chase turned Jane loose and stepped away from her. But

Pond grabbed her and held her back against his chest.

"Nothing at all? You're sure?" Harmon asked Pond, his eyes and face taking on a strange, flushed look. "She really is a natural woman?"

Pond just stared at him, holding Jane's arms pinned behind her.

"Never mind," said Harmon. "I expect I'll have to check for myself." He swung down from his saddle and stepped over in front of Jane Crowly.

Trent and Chase looked at each other. "I don't like where this is heading," Chase said quietly.

"Nor do I," said Trent, under his breath.

Coming to, Jane recoiled at the feel of Harmon's hand down her trousers. Jerking back away from him, her eyes snapped open. "You rotten sonsabitch!" she shouted. "Keep your slimy paws off me!"

"Oh?" Harmon's hand came up out of her trousers. He quickly backhanded her across her already-injured face. Blood flew from her lips. "What's makes you so damned particular, after all I've heard about you?"

Jane's head rocked sideways; but when she righted it she spit blood and saliva into his face. "Go on, hit me again, you sonsabitch. Have your fun! My *man* is going to kill you!"

"Your *man*?" Harmon gave a dark laugh, wiping his shirtsleeve across his face. "What kind of *man* would have the likes of you?"

"Lawrence Shaw, that's *what* man," Jane said defiantly. She spit again.

"Lawrence Shaw—yeah right, you and the Fastest Gun Alive," Harmon said. His hand rolled into a large, tight fist this time. He punched her hard. She fell back and slumped against Elvis Pond. "Hold her steady, Elvis!" Harmon bellowed. He punched her again; again she spit blood at him.

"Leave her alone, Harmon!" said Trent. His Colt came up cocked and aimed. So did Chase's. "We're taking her back to Stroud and Cantro," Trent added. "She's no good to us dead!"

"I expect you're right," Harmon. But he hit her again twice before stepping back and wiping his bloody fist on his shirt. "The lousy bitch is too knocked out to feel it now anyway." He looked at Pond, still holding the unconscious woman and said, "Take charge, Elvis. Get her back into her saddle and keep her beside you. If she gives you any trouble on the way back, punch her again."

"Can I do anything else?" Pond asked.

"I don't give a damn what else you do to her," said Harmon. "Just keep her alive so Stroud and Cantro can talk to her."

Riding into Mal Vuelve, Shaw saw a spotted pig running across the dusty street squealing loudly. Two young soldiers pursued the fleeing animal while a stout sergeant with a drooping mustache barked orders at the men. The sergeant stood out front of LaPrey's Cantina and Brothel, his hands on his hips, watching the chase. But his eyes turned to Shaw and measured him carefully as Shaw rode at a walk toward the cantina, leading his spare horses behind him. "What do we have here?" the sergeant said to the corporal standing beside him.

"More *americanos*, my sergeant," the corporal replied, watching Shaw warily.

"*Si*," the sergeant said quietly, "but this one wears a badge. Go bring him to me . . . in a way that will show him who is in charge here."

Even though Shaw was already riding toward the cantina, the corporal knew what the sergeant was asking of him. "*Si, mi sargento*," he said with a sly grin. He stepped forward and gave a hand signal to four riflemen who stood guard at the front of the cantina. "Follow me," he commanded the young soldiers.

Overhearing the sergeant, LaPrey stepped through the open doorway. "Uh, Sergeant, this man is not one to approach in such a manner."

"Oh, and why is that so?" the sergeant asked without turning to LaPrey.

In the street, before Shaw could reach the cantina, the corporal and the four armed soldiers ran out and surrounded him, forcing him to stop his horse and the two spare animals behind him. "Halt, *americano*!" the corporal called out, walking forward with an official bearing. "Where do you think you are going?"

Shaw sat at ease in his saddle, his hand on his thigh close to his Colt. "To LaPrey's," Shaw said in an even voice, not the least rattled by the rifles pointed at his chest. He nodded toward the cantina where LaPrey and the sergeant stood. Both were watching with rapt attention.

Noting the badge on Shaw's chest, the corporal took on a stiff, authoritarian tone of voice. "Ah, you are an *americano* lawman, I see."

"Yep," Shaw said, offering no more on the matter until he saw the corporal's attitude.

"You are here in my country to hunt down the border outlaws, I take it?" the corporal asked. Shaw looked past the corporal and saw the sergeant and LaPrey talking. As LaPrey spoke close to the sergeant's ear, the big sergeant took on a startled look.

"That's right," Shaw said. "I do so with the blessings and the written authorization from *Generalissimo* Manual Ortega."

"Do you have this written authority in your possession?" he asked haughtily.

"No," said Shaw, seeing what was at work here. He relaxed and let his hand fall from his thigh, closer to his Colt.

"Ah . . . then that is too bad," said the corporal. "Perhaps you have *la General's* permission, perhaps you do not. Without such written authorization," he added, "it becomes my duty to ask your business in Buena Suerte and decide whether or not to make you welcome—"

Hurrying forward from the cantina, LaPrey at his side, the stout sergeant cut the corporal off, saying, "That will be all, Corporal! Take your men back to their posts. I will speak to this man myself."

Shaw sat and watched the corporal order the riflemen back to where they had been standing. As soon as they had left, the big sergeant looked up at him and said, "You must forgive the corporal, Senor Shaw. I'm afraid that searching for the stolen depository gold has made us all a little edgy and cross."

"I understand," said Shaw.

"*Por favor*, step down and join us inside, out of the sun. I will have my soldiers take your horses, and water them."

"*Gracias*," said Shaw. He stepped down from his saddle and handed the sets of reins over to a young soldier that the sergeant had summoned. "But I won't be in town long. I came here searching for a friend of mine." He looked at LaPrey.

"Your friend left town this morning early," LaPrey said. "I'm afraid I couldn't say anything to make her change her mind."

"Ah, the friend you search for is a woman . . . ," the sergeant said with sympathy. He shook his head with a sigh. "These women, what are we to do with them?"

"Beats me," Shaw said, going along with whatever picture the Mexican had drawn for himself. The three walked toward the cantina.

"I am Sergeant Vitarez," the big sergeant said. "Tell me, Senor—aside from searching for the woman, are you also searching for the stolen gold, like everyone else?"

"No," Shaw said, remembering Juan Lupo's warning to trust no *federales* regarding the gold until they had gotten the valuable cargo moved closer to Mexico City. "I'm chasing outlaws all along the border. This woman happens to travel with me."

"I see, she travels with you," said the sergeant, dismissing the subject of the woman. "But surely you have heard of the stolen gold?"

"I've heard it," said Shaw. "I'm just not searching for it. That's the job for you and your army."

"It is good to hear someone say that, Senor," said the sergeant. His gaze tightened on Shaw. "Provided that it is the truth, of course."

Chapter 19

At the bar, Shaw sipped from a water gourd as the sergeant and LaPrey drank rye whiskey from wooden cups. Shaw kept his words guarded and didn't even mention Jane Crowly again until the sergeant heard the squeals of the fleeing pig return, and he hurried out front to bark orders at the soldiers chasing it. As soon as the big sergeant was out of sight, Shaw said flatly to LaPrey, "Where is she?"

"She left before sunup this morning," LaPrey said, sounding worried. "But I swear I made her comfortable and welcome, just the way I knew you would want me—"

"Which way?" Shaw asked, cutting him off. "Nobody's mad at you."

LaPrey breathed easier. "I am so glad to hear that. I have been afraid that you would blame—"

"Stay with me on this, Clute," Shaw said, again cutting him off. "Which way did she go?"

"She said to tell you that she is riding back to the desert floor through Suerte Buena on the same trail the two of you rode," said LaPrey, trying hard to say it just the way Jane had told him to. "I believe these soldiers arriving here made her nervous." He gestured toward the riflemen standing out front as another column of men began to pass. "They left the sergeant, his corporal and four guards here to meet another column while their own column rides on to the search the trails for the men who burned the cantina and church in Suerte Buena."

"There's already one column here and another one is coming?" Shaw asked for his own reference, knowing Dawson, Caldwell and Juan Lupo would want to hear about it.

"Yes, it is so," said LaPrey. "I knew it was important for you know this," he said in a lowered voice. "I did good, *oui*?"

"Yes, you did good, Clute," Shaw said, understanding what Jane intended to do. She had turned back in order to avoid the *federales* who'd suddenly shown up along the high trails. He fished a ten-dollar gold coin from his pocket and slipped it into the Frenchman's hand.

"Thank you for understanding," said LaPrey, grasping the coin. He watched Shaw turn up the water gourd and finish it. "And now you are leaving Mal Vuelve?" he asked, in surprise.

"Yep," said Shaw, "now I'm leaving. Just as soon as my horses are watered."

"But, *monsieur*," he said with a sly grin, "if it is a woman you thirst for, I can give you what you desire. Even the twins are available, for a price, of course." He grinned and jiggled the gold coin on his hand.

"Obliged," Shaw said wryly, "but Janie's the only woman I'm interested in right now."

"Oh . . . ?" LaPrey looked at him in stunned disbelief.

"Is there something wrong with that, Clute?" Shaw asked. He gave the Frenchman a flat stare. He wasn't about to explain his and Jane's relationship. He didn't quite understand it himself.

"Oh no, *monsieur*! Nothing at all!" said LaPrey. "It is just that a man with your reputation . . ." He gestured a hand up and down at Shaw. "You must have your pick of the women, *oui*? Is it not so?"

Shaw continued to stare at him, not answering.

When the sergeant returned, he walked in with the corporal and the four young guards following him. Seeing the look on the sergeant's face, LaPrey said, "Uh-oh," and eased away from Shaw's side and disappeared.

"Senor Shaw," said the sergeant, "before I allow you to leave Mal Vuelve, I am afraid I must ask you where you got these." He stopped in front of Shaw and held out his palm, holding several of the stolen gold coins the soldiers had found while rummaging through the saddlebags on Burke's horse.

Shaw's eyes immediately went to the doors and open windows, seeking his way out should it come to that. He did not want to kill any soldiers if he could keep from it. These men, like himself, were here to uphold the law. "All right," Shaw said. "Those had to come from Red Burke's horse. He's one of the men who burned the church and cantina in Suerte Buena. I took his horse after I killed him."

"You killed this Red Burke we are chasing, yet you do not tell me so as soon as you ride in?"

"That's right, I killed him," said Shaw. "I should have told you, but I didn't." He paused, then said, "His body is at the bottom of a gorge where the rope bridge collapsed this morning."

"The bridge is down?" the sergeant asked, looking stunned.

"Yep," said Shaw, "I figure Burke had something to do with that too."

The sergeant considered everything, eyeing the Colt standing on Shaw's hip, knowing that he had earned the name of being the Fastest Gun Alive. "I believe you, Senor," the sergeant said finally. But then he snapped his fingers at the corporal and the four guards. The guard's rifles came up and pointed at him from less than six feet away. "But I must ask you to stay here in Mal Vuelve until my *capitán* returns, in order for him to hear this for himself."

"I understand," Shaw said.

The sergeant, the corporal and the four young guards all looked relieved. But only for a second; then Shaw's Colt was up, cocked and aimed, only inches from the sergeant's belly. "Except I don't have time for this, Sergeant," he said. To the corporal and the guards he said, "Guns, on the floor, pronto."

"What do you want us to do, *mi Sargento*?" the corporal asked with a worried expression.

"Have them drop their rifles, you fool!" the sergeant shouted. "Do you not see the gun pointed at me?"

"Lay down your rifles!" the corporal barked quickly at the guards.

The rifles were stacked quickly on the floor, and the corporal opened the flap on his holster, raised his pistol and pitched it to the ground. "All right," said Shaw, "now let's all get out of here, onto the street, nice and easy like." He called out over his shoulder, "Clute, I know you're back there hiding. Go get my horses and bring them around front."

Clute stood up slowly from behind the bar and said to the sergeant, "I want you to know that I had nothing to do with—"

"He knows that," said Shaw, stopping him. "Now get my horses before I put a bullet in you." He threw in the threat for LaPrey's sake.

Clute said as he hurried toward the rear door, "You heard him threaten me, Sergeant! I do this against my will."

"Get going, Clute," said Shaw, "or I'll do more than threaten you."

Shaw kept the soldiers covered until Clute returned with the three horses. When Clute came back in through the front door, the three horses standing at the hitch ring out front, Shaw said to one of the soldiers, "You, stack those rifles in Clute's arms."

While the young soldier did as he was told, Shaw lifted the sergeant's pistol from its flap-topped holster. He stooped and picked up the corporal's pistol, then wagged his Colt toward the door and said, "Now everybody out front, to the water trough."

"The water trough?" the stout sergeant said indignantly. "You go too far, Senor."

Shaw ignored him.

Out front, Shaw gestured his Colt toward the trough. "Drop them," he ordered Clute.

The Frenchman looked at the sergeant first and said meekly, "You see that I must do as I am told, *oui*?"

"Drop them," the sergeant said with resignation.

When Clute had dropped the rifles into the trough, Shaw unloaded both pistols with one hand, then pitched them into the water. "I know you'll be on my trail. But this will slow you down and keep me from having to kill you." He backed a few feet to his horses, took their reins and stepped atop the speckled barb.

A moment later, LaPrey and the soldiers stood watching him ride away at a gallop in a rise of dust. No sooner was Shaw out of sight than the sergeant turned to the corporal and shouted angrily, "Well, what are you waiting for? Have your men get their rifles and get them dried and into working order!"

"Are we going after him, *mi sergento*?" the corporal asked.

"Of course we are going after him," the sergeant barked. He paused for a second in consideration, then added, "Just as soon as *el capitán* returns and orders us to do so."

Shaw rode hard along the trail toward Suerte Buena. Knowing the soldiers would be riding right behind him, he hoped to meet up with Jane along the trail or find her resting her horse in town. They had to get back down to the desert floor and let the others know that in addition to the Border Dogs coming, there were now two columns of *federales* patrolling the hills and desert trails. Running into either group with the wagonload of stolen gold would be a serious problem.

After what he'd done in Mal Vuelve, he was going to be dodging *federales* for a long time, he reminded himself, veering off the main trail the last two miles and riding up along a broad ridge overlooking the dusty streets of Suerte Buena.

From the cover of tangled vines and foliage, Shaw lay flat on the ground and scanned the town slowly with his telescope. He saw a line of horses at the hitch rings out front of the burned cantina. The cantina had already been hastily cleaned of debris and partially reroofed to accommodate travelers along the high trails. At one end of the row of hitch rings, a man stood watch over the horses. He leaned against the front of the cantina with a rifle in the crook of his arm.

These were no ordinary travelers, Shaw told himself, judging the quality of the riding stock and seeing the rifle and shotgun butts standing in saddle boots. *The Border Dogs . . . ?* he asked himself. As if in answer to his question he saw Roy Heaton, Elvis Pond and Bale Harmon walk out of the cantina. Heaton led Jane Crowly by a rope tied around her neck. He walked slightly stooped, his free hand held against his stomach wound. Shaw saw a look of dark hatred on his face for the woman who'd given him that wound.

Uh-oh . . . What have you gotten yourself into, Janie . . . ? Shaw asked silently, seeing her hands tied in front of her, and her bruised and battered face. He winced and tightened his focus. He watched them walk along to the livery barn and go inside, Heaton giving a sharp jerk on Jane's rope, clearly enjoying his job.

Shaw had no idea what Jane might've done, but whatever it was she hadn't deserved a beating like this, he thought. He lowered the lens from his eye and collapsed the telescope between his gloved hands. He had to go down there and get her. It was that simple, he told himself. Backing out of the vines and foliage to the horses, he stepped up into his saddle and turned the horses onto the switch-back trail. . . .

Inside the livery barn, Elvis Pond took the rope from Roy Heaton and tied Jane to a post in the middle of the floor. He patted her bloody, swollen cheek and walked away. Jane stood with her head bowed and listened to Garris Cantro question one of two young Mexican soldiers sitting on the straw-covered floor tied to a stall post. Pond, Heaton and Harmon stood quietly waiting for Cantro to turn to them.

But Cantro was in no hurry. He raised the soldier's chin with the toe of his boot and asked, "Do you know who I am?"

"*Si,*" the terrorized young soldier said, "you are Senor Cantro."

"And these men?" Cantro asked. He gestured toward Pond, Heaton and Harmon.

The young soldier hesitated, then said with trepidation, *"Los Perros Fronterizos?"*

"That's right, we're the Border Dogs," said Garris Cantro. He stared down at the young man intently. "We live *here*, in these desert hills and plains. The Mexican government knows we live *here*. We've paid good money to all the right people to be *here*. Comprende?"

"Si, comprende," the man said.

"See, men, he understands all that," Cantro said, half turning to his three gunmen with a smirk on his bearded face. Turning back to the soldier, he dealt him a sharp kick to the jaw and barked angrily, "Then what in the hell was the idea, attacking me and my men on our way here?"

"We only follow our orders, Senor Cantro," another soldier cut in.

"Orders from who . . . and why?" Cantro demanded, turning to the other soldier.

"From our *capitán*," the soldier said. "We were told what you and your men did here, burning the church, the cantina."

"I can't believe this," said Cantro. He turned to Heaton. "Did Red Burke do all this to set me up, Roy?"

"I can't say for sure," Heaton answered hesitantly, "but it looks to me like he did. He was running awfully wild the last I saw of him."

"What was the idea, Roy?" Cantro asked, turning and walking over close to him. "You three figured to get the *federales* down on me, keep me and the soldiers both busy while you found the wagon and took the gold for yourselves?"

"No—no, sir," Heaton said shakily, "leastwise that was never my intention. I can't say what Burke and Sid Nutt might have had in mind. But I was playing it straight as a string, doing what you told us to do . . . try to find that damned wagon."

Cantro stepped back, but still gave him a questioning stare. "These soldiers say we've been blamed for every-damn-thing but the weather. If I find out you and Burke and Nutt did this to slow me down getting to the desert and finding that wagon I'm going to kill you real slow-like."

"I—I wouldn't blame you if you did, sir," said Heaton. "But so help me God, I'm innocent."

"We'll find out," said Cantro. He turned to Jane. "Now, Jane Crowly. Let's see what you can tell me about finding that wagon."

"Go . . . to . . . hell," Jane replied in a pained and muffled voice. Her nose was swollen and red, her eyes black and puffed. Her lips were swollen, split and covered with dried blood.

"Did you do all this to her, Elvis?" Cantro asked.

Harmon and Heaton both looked frightened, as if worried that Elvis Pond would point the finger at them.

But to their surprise, Pond replied to Cantro in his sullen tone, "That's right, just me."

Heaton and Harmon both looked relieved. Then they were both stunned to hear Cantro say, "Good work. I like a man who can get things done." Turning back to Jane, Cantro said, "We're going to leave you here to think this over a few minutes while we go eat. When we get back I'm going to ask you again and again where I'll find that wagon. Each time you don't tell me, I'm going to let Elvis decide what part to carve off you next."

Cantro stood close enough for Jane to spit blood at him; but he dodged it and looked down at the dark bloody spittle on his boot toe. "Well," he chuckled, "I always heard you're a filthy ornery bitch-cur. Today we'll see just how tough you are."

Turning on his heel, Cantro gestured Heaton, Harmon and Pond toward the door. Leaving a rifleman behind to watch the prisoners, the four filed out and walked back to the cantina, where workers were busy putting on a new roof while inside men continued on with their drinking. No sooner were they on the dirt street than Harmon said to Cantro, "The fact is all three of us beat the hell out of that she-man, not just Elvis."

"I thought as much," said Cantro. "You two are lucky I don't kill you both for it."

Heaton and Harmon gave each other a puzzled look.

"But, sir," said Harmon, "you praised Elvis for it."

"That's different," said Cantro. "Elvis Pond is a whole other breed of dog. Right, Elvis?"

Pond's response was only a short grin.

In the barn, one of the soldiers on the ground ventured a look up at Jane, saying, "*Señora, por favor*, tell them what they want. Do not let them kill you for the gold!"

The guard only listened without saying anything.

The soldier continued. "There is a second column of soldiers riding in from the west. They will find the gold anyway, before these men find it."

"Mind . . . your own . . . business," Jane murmured through her swollen lips.

Watching, the guard only laughed under his breath and drew on a long fresh cigar. Ten minutes later, the cigar half finished, he heard a knock on the rear door and stepped over and said without opening it, "Who's there?"

"It's me. I brought you some roasted goat," said the voice on the other side. "Have you et yet?"

"Hell no, I ain't," said the guard, swinging the door open at the prospect of food. "I'd sure fill my mouth with some roast—"

As the door swung open, Shaw's rifle butt slammed him hard right across the bridge of his nose. The blow sent him flying backward to the ground.

Jane lifted her head and looked at Shaw with her eyes almost swollen shut. "Lawrence . . . is that you?"

"Be quiet, Janie," Shaw said. He untied her hands and slung the rope off her neck.

"Give me . . . a gun . . . Lawrence," she said. "I'm going to go kill some sonsa—"

"Not now, Janie, you're coming with me," Shaw said. He slipped a knife from his boot and cut the rawhide strips holding the soldiers. The young men stared at him, awed at the way he'd handled the guard. To the first soldier he said, "Listen to me. When you get away from here, head back toward

Mal Vuelve. You'll run into Sergeant Vitarez and his guards. Tell him I cut you loose. Maybe it will make up for me poking a gun in his belly."

"You poked a gun in the sergeant's belly?" the soldier asked in disbelief. "Oh, Senor, Sergeant Vitarez will never forgive you, no matter what you do. He is one tough *hombre*, that one."

"So am I," Shaw said. "Tell him these men are his enemy, not me."

"*Si*, we will tell him, Senor," the Mexican said, the two of them rising from the floor, rubbing their freed wrists.

Chapter 20

Outside of the livery barn, Shaw told the soldiers, "You two take that horse." He nodded toward Burke's horse standing saddled and ready to go. "You'll have to ride double, but not for long. The sergeant and his men will be coming along soon enough."

"*Gracias* again, Senor," said one of the soldiers. "I don't know how we can thank you enough."

"Just get going," said Shaw, "explain things to Vitarez for me."

"*Si*, it will be done," said the other soldier, both of them grabbing the horse's reins and pulling it along into the brush and cedar behind the barn.

In spite of still having two horses, Shaw decided it was best to keep Jane Crowly on his lap until she became steady. Shoving her up onto the saddle, he swung up behind her and eased the two barbs into the brush, headed in the opposite direction of the two soldiers. As he carried her along in his arms, he felt her slump in and out of consciousness against his chest. "Give me . . . a gun," he heard her whisper mindlessly under her breath.

"Don't worry, Janie, you won't need one. They're going to pay." He drew her closer, careful of hurting her battered face, and rode on toward the trail down to Agua Mala.

A half hour after Shaw and Jane had left, Elvis Pond walked into the barn carrying a tray of food for the guard, Roddie Layne. When he found Layne lying knocked out on the dirt floor, he cocked his head slightly, then sat down and began eating. Halfway through the meal, he heard Layne moan and begin to awaken.

"Looks like somebody coldcocked the hell out of you," Pond said. He made no effort to help the addled, bloody-faced man to his feet. Instead he nodded at the food and said, "I didn't know if you was going to live or die. No reason for food to go to waste."

"Hel-help me, up . . . ," Layne moaned, reaching a hand up in Pond's direction.

Still chewing, Pond stood up and walked over and lifted Layne to his feet. He inspected the swollen, bloodied nose and whistled under his breath. "You're going to be damned sore for a while."

"Hell, I expect . . . I know that," Layne said, coming around slowly. He staggered toward the door. Pond walked over and steadied him. They walked out the door and toward the cantina, the shadows of evening beginning to fall long across the dirt street.

Upon seeing Roddie's face and hearing his story, Cantro and the rest of the men inside the cantina spilled out onto the street and climbed up into their saddles. "Everybody rides tonight," Cantro called over his shoulder.

"What about me?" Roddie Layne asked, holding a wet cloth to his broken nose.

"You can shoot and you can ride, so mount up," said Cantro. Again he shouted, louder this time, "Everybody rides tonight!"

"I found hoofprints going off deep into the brush, sir," said Corey Trent, him and Elijah Chase coming back from behind the livery barn with torches in their hands.

"We'll start from there," said Cantro. Seeing the men mounted and ready to ride, he turned his horse to face them and said, "We can't let these two get away. They're going to lead us to the gold. They know where that wagon is as sure as the world is flat. They might start out in the brush, but they've got to hit a trail to ever make it down to the desert floor. We'll stay close and let them guide us. Now everybody get spread out in the brush and find their tracks."

In moments one of the mounted men called out, "Sir, over here. I've got two sets of tracks headed west, and one headed east."

Riding over quickly, Cantro said, "This way. They're headed toward Agua Mala. We're going to push on through the night until we find them. I'm betting they're headed down to the sand hills. They're going to lead us straight to that wagon." He batted his boot heels to his horse's sides and rode away. The men followed along, loosely forming up a military column as they rode through the brush and followed the hoofprints up onto the main trail.

A half hour ahead of Cantro and his men, Shaw stopped in a moonlit clearing in a switchback turn and eased Jane down to the ground. Then he slid down himself, lifted his canteen from his saddle horn and helped her over to a rock and seated her. "I look like hell, don't I?" Janie said in a pained, half-conscious voice.

"You'll be all right," Shaw said. He uncapped the canteen, poured some water onto the bandanna he jerked from around his neck and dabbed carefully at her battered face. She winced and sliced her breath in pain.

"This ain't right, Lawrence, them doing all this to me," she said, her voice trembling with the pain and with rage. "I'll carry this beating for a long time to come," she said. "Not that I was any beauty girl to begin with, eh? I'm homely as a gray cat anyway."

"Don't talk like that," Shaw said, wiping blood from her cheek and from a cut under her swollen eye.

"Hell, it's the truth," she said, trying to open her eyes up at him.

"I don't like that kind of talk," Shaw said. "I don't know what to say to you when you talk like that."

"You don't have to *say* anything. I'm just spouting off some truth on the matter." She sighed and turned her face up for him. "As looks go, I didn't stand to lose much anyhow."

"That's enough, Janie, stop it," Shaw said. In the moonlight he saw a long trailing tear run from her eye down her bruised and swollen cheek.

"I'm sorry, Lawrence," she said, gasping as he touched the wet cloth to her injured nose. "I—I suppose I'm just afraid . . . you won't love me anymore."

Shaw made no response. What could he say? He didn't love her. He'd never told her he did. What a time to bring it up, he told himself, dabbing the wet bandanna gently, getting some of the dried blood from her battered face.

When he didn't answer, she reached up and took his wrist. "I'm sorry . . . I shouldn't have said that. I've put you on the spot, haven't I?"

"Janie," Shaw said, "this is not the time or the place."

"I know," she said. "I could kick myself sometimes. I just can't learn to ever keep my mouth shut." She turned loose of his wrist and shook her head slowly. "If things ever go good for me, I find a way to screw them up." Her voice sounded muffled and stiff with pain.

"Take it easy," Shaw said. "You don't need to be talking right now." He looked back along the trail in the moonlight. "We need to get going. Can you ride?"

"That's a hell of a question," she said indignantly, her voice turning stronger. "Hell yes, I can ride. Would you ask Dawson or the Undertaker something like that if they were beat up?"

"Yes, I would," Shaw said. He pressed the wet bandanna into her hand and said, "Here. Carry this." Then he swept her up almost against her will and carried her to the horses.

Jane looked down at him through swollen eyes when he'd lifted her up into her saddle. "I went a little soft there for a minute, but I'm all right now. I don't want you thinking you owe me anything."

"We'll talk about it later," Shaw said.

Jane started to say more, but she fell silent as the two of them heard the sound of horses moving along the switchback trail beneath them, heading in the opposite direction. "*Federales*?" she whispered.

"I hope so," Shaw whispered. "Wait here." He handed her the reins to the speckled barb and slipped over to the edge of the trail in a crouch. Stooping beside a rock, he looked down in the pale moonlight. As he rode slowly along the trail below he made out the light tan color of the Mexican soldiers' uniforms and the outline of their garrison caps.

The second column . . . Good enough, he thought.

Back at his horse, Jane asked as he stepped upward into his saddle, "Good news, or bad?"

"It's more soldiers," Shaw said. "For now it's good news. They're going to be riding straight into Cantro and his Dogs. It'll get him off our backs for a while." He backed his horse a step to keep Jane in front of him, where he could watch over her. "If they get into a fight, it'll give us a chance to reach the wagon without them on our tail."

"Then what are we waiting for?" Jane said bravely, seeming to put aside her injury and pain.

Garris Cantro drew his horse up sharply in the moonlight when the column of Mexican soldiers sat facing him six abreast on a wide stretch of trail. "Whoa, Arnold!" said Cantro, his horse circling to a halt beneath him. Behind him, Arnold Stroud quickly brought the men to a halt and sent them scrambling to take up the same abreast position as the soldiers facing them.

"*Hola* the trail, Senor Cantro," a young Mexican captain said, sitting calmly but prepared for anything.

"*Hola* to you, Captain Fuerte," said Cantro. He composed himself quickly. "What brings you here to the badlands?"

"The stolen gold, what else?" said the captain with a stern expression.

"Ah yes, that stolen gold," said Cantro. "I heard all about that. I'm surprised your army hasn't had better luck finding it by now."

"I'm also here to find the men who are killing and plundering all along these hill towns," Captain Fuerte said.

"Yes, I've heard all about them too," said Cantro. "I wish you luck hunting them."

"They are Border Dogs," the captain said bluntly, and with confidence.

"Easy, Captain," said Cantro. "No men of mine have had anything to do with—"

"Three of your men were shot down in the Raw

Leg Cantina," the captain said, cutting him off. "One died, one stood up and ran away, and one was taken prisoner by two *americanos* ... A fast gunman and the woman, Jane Crowly."

"They weren't my men, Captain," Cantro insisted. "If they were, I'd have their hides for doing something like that." He let his hand rest on the Winchester rifle across his lap. "You know how much I value the trust I've established with the Mexican government."

"I know you have paid high-ranking officials with money you steal from the other side of the border," Fuerte said coldly. "That is what I know." As he spoke he raised a hand and summoned two soldiers to the front of his ranks. The soldiers escorted two civilians riding between them, one of them Cactus John Barker, the owner of the Raw Leg Cantina and Brothel in Trabajo Duro. The other civilian wore a battered stove-pipe hat and kept a nervous eye on Cantro's men.

"Uh-oh," Heaton whispered to himself, seeing the cantina owner's face. He backed his horse a step and tried to put himself out of sight behind Arnold Stroud.

"Senor Cantro, do you know these two men? They are witnesses," the captain said, gesturing toward Cactus John and the other civilian.

"Witnesses?" Cantro scoffed. "I know Cactus John Barker. But he was Bexar John Barker 'til he gut poisoned half of Bexar County with snake head whiskey. Then he ran all the way to Trabajo Duro while they were all too sick to hang him."

"Nothing but damned lies," said Cactus John. "I built a sterling reputation making Kentucky sour mash with my own two hands." He glared at Cantro. "And I'm damn proud of it."

"Sure you are," said Cantro with sarcasm in his voice. "I know this one too," he said, staring at the other man. "His name is Paul Harrod—they call him the Bird." He glared at Harrod and said to Cantro, "Ask him how many missing chickens it took for him to get his name. You couldn't scrape together enough eggs to make breakfast 'til they threw him out of Colorado." He shook his head and spit in contempt. "Witnesses? Ha!"

Harrod stiffened with indignation. "I admit I once dealt fast and loose with other people's poultry. But that was years ago. I saw what Red Burke did in Suerte Buena, and I heard him say he did it under orders of Garris Cantro—"

"I won't have chicken thieves and whiskey benders pointing fingers at me or my men," said Cantro.

"Nevertheless, they are my witnesses," the captain said stubbornly. To a soldier carrying blackened torches he said, "Provide light for the witnesses."

Torches flared, and when they had been passed along to the two escorting soldiers, the men rode forward slowly, the two civilians between them. Cantro whispered to Stroud, who had inched up beside him, "Prepare to attack."

When the two soldiers rode close enough for the circle of light to spread over most of Cantro's men, Heaton ducked his head slightly and tugged down on his hat brim. But the two witnesses looked at each other and nodded. Without a word, they turned and rode back to the captain, the two soldiers carrying the torches on either side of them.

"He's in among them," said Cactus John.

"Are you certain?" asked the captain in a lowered voice.

"I'm damned certain," said the cantina owner. "He tried to duck his face, but I got a good enough look at him first."

"I don't recognize any of these men from what happened in Suerte Buena," said Harrod. "But that doesn't change what I heard the one called Burke say about them riding for the Border Dogs."

"I see," the captain said with contemplation. "Both of you, go to the rear."

The two turned their horses and rode back along the outside edge of the troops. "I don't like the idea of tangling with these Confederate guerillas," said Cactus John on their way. "They're still fighting their damned war."

"I know," Harrod said quietly. He glanced back over his shoulder at the flickering torchlight on the trail. "I once nearly lost an eye over a careless remark to a soldier, and he was just a Union Regular. I hate to think what these Border Dogs are apt to do."

Captain Fuerte waited until the civilians were safely in the rear; then he said to Cantro, "The man who was in Trabajo Duro with Red Burke is in your ranks, Senor Cantro. So he must be one of yours."

"Being one of mine doesn't mean he's in the

wrong, Captain," said Cantro. "We best put this thing behind us and get on with what we were doing."

"What I am doing is upholding the law here in these badlands," said the captain.

"Yeah? And I happen to be chasing Jane Crowly and that gunman I told you about. You're interfering in my business."

"It cannot be helped, Senor Cantro," said the captain with determination. "I must insist that you and your men hand over your guns and come with me. I have many more questions about why this Red Burke has gone around using your name while breaking the laws of my country."

"We don't hand over guns, Captain," said Cantro. "In fact, just the thought of it makes me want to shoot somebody." Behind Cantro, his men levered rifles and cocked hammers and shifted position. Seeing them prepare to attack, the Mexican soldiers did the same.

At the rear of the column Harrod turned to Cactus John and said, "Do you feel like we've done all we can here?"

"There ain't a doubt in my mind," Cactus John said, already backing his horse for a quick turnaround.

Farther along the moonlit high trail, Lawrence Shaw and Jane Crowly listened intently to the sudden eruption of gunfire in the distance behind them. "Sounds like Cantro and his Border Dogs just said howdy to that column of *federales* we saw," Shaw said.

With swollen lips Jane still managed a smile of satisfaction. "I just hope they don't kill the ones who did this to me. I've got bigger plans for them no-good sonsabitches."

"So do I, Janie," Shaw said almost to himself, the two of them riding the downward trail toward the wide stretch of sand hills below.

Chapter 21

————

Captain Fuerte's soldiers were young, but seasoned and battle savvy. The fighting had started at a distance of only fifty feet, but within seconds both sides reeled back, pressed by the high volume of gunfire. As the space between them broadened, both soldiers and Border Dogs found cover over the rocky edge of the trail and down the steep hillside. Bodies of both sides lay broken and bleeding in the trail beneath a looming cloud of burned powder.

"Keep the horses covered!" shouted Stroud, hearing the whinny of a wounded animal among the rocks behind him. Three men had taken the reins to all of the horses and hurried away with them, to the shelter of taller rocks embedded in the sloping earth like a fortress wall. Beside Stroud, Cantro fought savagely. The two of them had taken cover behind a half-sunken boulder, and Roy Heaton hunkered down beside them.

"Get word back to the horse guards," shouted Cantro to Stroud above the steadily pounding gunfire. "We're not going to allow ourselves to be pinned here by Fuerte's larger numbers. Tell them to get those horses back up onto the trail and meet us a hundred yards forward."

"Yes, sir," Stroud shouted in reply.

"You're going to attack? In the dark? Our own guns will kill us!" Heaton shouted, gripping Stroud's forearm.

"No, *we're* going to attack, Heaton," Stroud said boldly. "This includes you." He jerked free of Heaton's grip on his arm. "Don't worry, our men know how to shoot straight ahead." Having emptied his rifle, he laid it aside and drew his Colt. Arnold Stroud felt more at home in this kind of battle situation than he'd felt anywhere in a long time. He shouted at Cantro, "Shall I have the men form a Roman wedge, sir?"

"Yes, Arnold, this is just our move from here," shouted Cantro. "You and I will spearhead that wedge."

"Jesus!" said Heaton, looking sick at the thought of charging into a wall of bullets.

To Heaton, Stroud shouted, "Get back there and give the horse guards the message."

"Now?" said Heaton, his eyes wide in terror, hearing what sounded like angry wasps zipping past inches above their heads.

"Yes, now!" shouted Stroud. The tip of his Colt came around and jammed into Heaton's chest. "Now or *never*!"

"Easy, easy! I'm gone," said Heaton. He turned quickly and crawled away slowly on his belly.

Stroud fired a bullet into the rocky ground only an inch from his head. "Get moving, Heaton!" he bellowed at him amid the relentless explosions of the Mexicans' rifle fire.

Thirty yards away on the rock-strewn hillside, Captain Fuerte also lay behind the cover of a land-stuck boulder. But he lay sprawled on his back, his tunic open, a soldier stooped over him pressing a bandage to the bloody wound in his side. Hovering over him a young sergeant said, "We can keep them here as long as we choose to, *Capitán*."

Fuerte considered it. He looked down at the wound on his side and asked the soldier dressing it, "How bad am I shot, Corporal?"

"It did not go deep, *Capitán*. Thank the Blessed Mother. But you will have to be—"

"Help me to my feet," the captain said. "I must be able to get up and ride."

The corporal and the sergeant exchanged a dubious glance.

"But, *Capitán*," the young sergeant said. "These men can go nowhere until you give me the word. We can hold them here or kill them all. You do not need to ride! This night is yours."

"*Si, Sergento*, I heard everything you said," Fuerte replied, "but it is not my wish to hold them here."

"Then but say the word, and we will kill all of them, *mi Capitán*," said the sergeant.

Captain Fuerte stared down, ignoring his pain, watching the corporal finish dressing the wound as he spoke to Sergeant Gasperez. "If we kill them here, *Sargento*, perhaps it will end the trouble for people of the badlands; perhaps it will not. I do not know if Cantro was responsible for the trouble here." He looked up at the sergeant. "But if they are searching for the gold, as I believe they are, following them to it and taking it back from them will be good for all of *Mejico*." He gave a smile in spite of his pain. "Will it not?"

"Of course, you are right, *mi Capitán*," said the sergeant. Bullets whistled overhead and zinged wildly off the boulder. "We will let them leave and pursue them, then?"

"Do not let them through too easily, or they will know our intentions," said the captain. "But let them fight their way through."

"*Si, mi Capitán*," said the sergeant. "It will be as you command."

Captain Fuerte turned to the corporal, who had just finished bandaging his side. "To my feet, *Corpóreo*. My men must not see me lying on my back."

While the fighting continued with no letup, Stroud, with only a hand signal, brought his Border Dog troops forward one, two and three at time until they managed to find cover in a way that left them spread out into a wedge with Cantro and Stroud at the foremost point. "Man!" said a newer, younger gunman named Marcus Prine to one of the older Border Dogs, "this ain't my kind of fighting at all! This is the same as fighting a war!"

"All killing is like fighting a war," the older gunman, Basil Kirkland, grimly replied.

"You know what I mean," said Prine. His hands trembled on the stock of his rifle.

"Yeah, I do," said Kirkland. "But this kind of fighting is a good thing for us now and then." Raising his Winchester rifle and aiming at a muzzle flash in the dark he added, "It serves to separate the wheat from the chaff, so to speak."

No sooner had Kirkland pulled the trigger than bullets whistled past them in return. "Damn it!" said the newer gunman, ducking closer to the ground. "How am I going to know which one I am?"

Kirkland laughed and shouted above the gunfire, "If you get blown away, you're the chaff." He stared in the direction of Arnold Stroud, awaiting Stroud's signal for them to attack. "But stick close to me; I'll turn you into wheat," he added.

"You got it," said Prine, his hands trembling but ready, wrapped tightly around his rifle stock.

At Stroud's signal, the Border Dogs rose and charged with a fierce rebel yell. From the trail, slipping along quietly, leading the horses, the horse guards looked down at what appeared to be a glittering, loosely formed arrowhead cutting a swath along the sloping hillside through the Mexican gunfire.

At the head of the wedge, Cantro and Stroud advanced at a trot, firing as they went. In spite of the heavy return fire, the two leaders deliberately measured their pace in order not to get too far ahead of their men. A bullet grazed Cantro's thigh; another nipped at Stroud's upper arm. But the two moved methodically, firing as soldiers fell before them and tumbled down over the rocks on the steep sloping hillside.

Behind, some of their own men fell, but the two led the fiery wedge through the soldiers until Cantro stooped behind a rock where a wounded Mexican soldier lay with both hands holding his bloody abdomen. As Cantro and Stroud peered down at him, their guns smoking in their hands, the young soldier's eyes pleaded for mercy.

"Keep quiet, it'll soon be over," Cantro said to the soldier, beneath the heavy firing both in front and behind them. Stroud pulled a pistol from beneath the flap of the wounded soldier's holster and pitched it away.

"*Entiende?*" Stroud asked, staring into his frightened eyes.

"*Si* . . . I understand," the young soldier said in a pained voice.

Having fought their way through the soldiers, Stroud waited for a lull in the firing to pass while many of their men reloaded. When the firing grew intense once again, he stood and shouted out his order this time, instead of relying on a hand signal. "Move out!" he bellowed back along the hillside through the heavy gunfire and the screams of the wounded and the dying.

From above, the horse guards watched the fiery wedge on the dark hillside as it seemed to flatten and form a flickering, undulating line. Upon Stroud's order, the men turned as one and began ascending the rocky hillside, fighting behind themselves. The Mexicans offered no letup as the gunmen worked their way upward and began spilling onto the trail. Scattered in the darkness everywhere on the hillside, the pained voices of wounded continued to resound in the night.

The horse guards hurriedly stuck reins into the men's hands indiscriminately, knowing they could sort out the horse later. Halfway down the rocky hillside, Cantro and Stroud hurried the men past them and covered them until the last of them topped the edge. "Well done, Arnold," said Cantro, when he'd given the last man a shove.

"And you as well, sir," said Stroud. They ran up and joined the others, not realizing the firing had all but stopped, much of what was left not coming close, but zipping upward ten yards to the side.

"Sir, have they lost their aim?" Stroud asked as they hurried to the upper edge of the rail and grabbed their reins from a waiting guard.

"No," said Cantro. "Fuerte is no fool. He thinks we'll take him to the gold."

"Which we will, if we don't manage to shake them off our trail, sir," said Stroud.

"Indeed we will, Arnold," said Cantro, "if we make a run for it."

"I see, sir," said Stroud. "But we are making a run for it."

"You bet we're not, Arnold," said Cantro. "They're going to have to fight us from their saddles every mile of the way."

Shaw stopped his horse at the edge of the wide desert basin. Jane's horse stopped alongside him on its own. Jane sat slumped in the saddle, as she had for the past half hour, her bruised and battered face shadowed beneath her floppy hat brim. In the east the sun had begun to glow along the edge of the world. It had been a long time since the heavy gun-fire in the distance behind them had ceased. But Shaw had still noted random fire now and then coming from along the trail.

He had a picture of Cantro and his Border Dogs fighting the *federales* on the run. That was the Border Dogs' style—guerilla fighters, he reminded himself, and they had sharpened and honed their deadly craft since the great Civil War. There would be riders coming before long. He was certain of it.

"Janie, wake up, we're down from the hills," he said sidelong to her.

Jane jerked up her head, startled. "Huh? What? I'm not asleep. Where are we?"

"At the bottom of the hills trail," said Shaw, gazing out at the rolling sand hills lying ghostly pale and purple in the predawn light. "Whoever the Border Dogs ran into, they're still fighting up there," he said with a nudge of his head back over his shoulder.

"How far back you figure?" Jane asked, trying to wake, but having a hard time with the pain of her injuries still seeking the soothing comfort of sleep.

"Not far enough," said Shaw. "Two hours, maybe less. But they're on us. They have us marked for the gold. They won't let up."

"Then neither will we," Jane offered with determination. "It's a full day's ride across." She straightened in her saddle, booted her horse up a notch and rode forward onto the beginnings of a coarse white carpet of sand. "We best pick up the wagon tracks before Cantro gets down to us."

On the far side of the basin lay another long stretch of blackened hills like the ones behind them. Shaw nudged his speckled barb along behind her, riding the horse at a quarterwise canter, taking a last searching look back into the dark hills behind them.

Chapter 22

Riding diagonally, knowing the wagon tracks had to be out there, Shaw and Jane Crowly pushed forward onto the barren desert floor. Reaching into the rolling hills, they traveled across the coarse sand carpet until it grew finer, thicker and whiter beneath their horses' hooves. By sunrise they had ridden through sand-banked dry washes, patches of creosote, stretches of mesquite and remnants of wind-tossed bracken and wild brush and scattered chimney cactus.

At midmorning they looked back at their trail while they rested the horses in a shallow dry wash shadowed by an ancient rock shelf lying striped of the sandy earth that had once engulfed it. On the sand at Jane's feet the unique trail of a snake led up into a crevice in the rock shelf. "Sidewinder...," Jane commented to Shaw in a dry, tired voice, cautioning him as to the snake's presence.

"I see it...," Shaw replied, echoing her parched, windless tone. He stood staring back through his telescope, scanning their tracks all the way back to the base of the hill line. Above them the sun had taken on its scalding, ovenlike countenance for the day, its glare already too harsh and pressing for the human eye to negotiate for any longer than a few seconds at a time.

"Any sign . . . ?" Jane asked after a moment. She had poured a few precious drops of canteen water onto the bandanna and sat pressing it gently to her split and swollen lips.

"Yep, I see them," Shaw replied.

"Which bunch . . . ?" Jane asked, rising to her feet with effort.

"Cantro and his Dogs," said Shaw, not at all surprised. "But I expect he hasn't seen the last of the *federales*. Not if they figure he's onto the stolen gold."

Jane tried to lower her hat brim and stare out with her swollen, naked eyes. But she gave it up and cursed under her breath. "Damned sun . . ."

Through the glass Shaw saw Cantro and Stroud, both men wearing bandages over their flesh wounds, riding at the front of a strewn-out column of men. Many of the men following them wore similar bandages. One man rode wobbling in his saddle, his hat missing, his blood-stained shirt open wide and a thick, heavily bloodied bandage on his chest.

"They're right on our tracks, Janie, just like we knew they would be," Shaw said quietly. "They'll be hard to lose from here on." He raised his telescope an inch and gazed up the meandering rocky trail leading down to the desert floor. "No sign of any soldiers yet, but they'll be coming soon enough."

Jane picked up the reins to her horse and dusted the seat of her trousers.

"Yep, they will," said Shaw. He collapsed the telescope between his palms and stuck it down into his saddlebags. "There should be runoff water still left in the rock tanks," he said. "We might have to start thinning them down some from there."

"We'll have to let them get awfully close for us to do that," Jane warned. "Are you sure you want to give away our lead?"

"They're on to us anyway," said Shaw. "When we find the wagon so do they. At least there'll be less of them to fight once the gold is on the line."

"Gold . . ." Jane shook her head. "Except for its glitter and shine, fighting and killing is all I've ever seen in it." She grabbed her saddle horn, swung up and tugged her floppy hat down onto her head.

"You'll get no argument from me on that," Shaw said, swinging up into his saddle beside her.

They rode on at a diagonal direction until in the early afternoon they'd reached the same coarse, thinning carpet of sand that lined the other edge of the sand hill basin. Feeling the horses growing weary and winded beneath them, they stepped down from their saddles and led the animals over a mile across a strip of barren silver-gray slate that lined the base of the hills.

Studying the hard rock Shaw noted the scrape of fresh hoof and the wheel marks and with much effort said to Jane beside him, "Here they are, headed for water . . ."

"Same as us . . . ," Jane replied with the same breathless effort.

They scanned the brutal wavering land as they followed the faint signs left by their party, until finally they saw a lone bird lift up from a sunken spot on the flat earth at the foot a steel-gray overhanging hillside.

The tanks . . . Shaw pointed a tired hand but spoke only to himself, too tired and hot and dry-mouthed to speak aloud.

When they reached the sunken rock basin they found a shallow pool of water still left from the heavy storm. A stream of braided water that had run down the hillside had already been reduced to a thin trickle. In days the runoff pool itself would be boiled away by the fierceness of the desert sun, yet leaving a shaded store of cool water beneath the earth's surface.

"Thank God . . . ," Jane said in spite of her pain. She let her horse's reins fall from her hands and staggered the last few feet and dropped onto her knees. With no regard for her battered face she stretched flat on her stomach in the tepid water.

Beside her, Shaw let the speckled barb drink while he sank two canteens into the water and let them fill. He took off his hat, dipped it full and turned it upside down over his head. "Rest yourself in the shade," he said to Jane, standing, gazing up the jagged hillside. "I'm going to see what I can spot from higher up."

Too tired to respond, Jane only nodded her head and lowered her face back into the soothing water while at her side her horse drew its fill.

Shaw capped the filled canteens, hung them from his saddle horn and took the telescope back out of his saddlebags. He shoved the telescope inside his shirt up under his poncho. Drawing his rifle from his saddle boot, he let the speckled barb continue drinking as he walked around the water and climbed forty yards, almost hand over foot, up the loose black gravelly hillside.

From a rocky perch against a standing rock spur, Shaw shoved aside a brittle stand of misplaced mesquite brush and raised the telescope to his eye. At the bottom of the distant hills they'd crossed in the night, he saw a ragged column of soldiers pushing onto the desert floor, an hour behind Cantro's men, he speculated. Closer in, he saw Cantro and his Border Dogs pushing hard toward the tanks, unwavering from the trail he and Jane had left across the sand basin.

Swinging the telescope away from Cantro and his men, Shaw searched southwest for any sign of the wagon tracks leaving the hard slate surface and heading on across the sand basin. "Where are you, Dawson . . . ?" he murmured aloud, more able to talk now that he'd gotten some life-sustaining water back into his parched body.

Giving up on finding any wagon tracks in the sand just yet, he turned back to Cantro, knowing that sooner or later the wagon had to ride off the hard ground and make the crossing through the

powdery sand. He had no doubt he would find the
tracks farther ahead.

He raised his rifle to his shoulder and took a prac-
tice aim on Garris Cantro riding at the head of the
column. Then he lowered the rifle and looked all
around. This was the ideal place to start picking
men off, he decided. But cover was scarce. He stood
and climbed higher and looked down into a deep
draw to his left, whose steep wall ran all the way
back down to the slate floor. *All right . . .* He could
fire from here, then flee down the other side. *Good
enough . . .*

Below, Jane finished soaking herself and sat dripping, staring up the overhanging hillside through
purple swollen eyes as Shaw turned and climbed
down and walked around the water to her. "Any
sign of wagon tracks?" she asked, sounding better
herself, the water renewing her energy.

"Not a trace," Shaw said. "But they've got to cross
somewhere along here." He pointed along the hill
line. "There's a cut-in a hundred yards ahead. We're
going to take the horses there and have you wait for
me."

"Whoa, hold on," Jane said. "I'll go take the
horses around there with you. But I want to be at
your side if there's shooting to be done. I'd like to
get my sights on the sonsabitches who did this to
me. Especially that damned Roy Heaton."

Shaw saw the determination in her eyes. "Fair
enough," he said evenly, knowing this was not the
time to argue. "As soon as Cantro and his men get

close enough, I'm going to take down any scouts before we go. It'll buy us some time and keep them at bay while we look for the wagon."

"Are you going to try for Cantro himself?" Jane asked. "It seems like that would set them back on their haunches for a good while."

"Cantro's smart," said Shaw. "He won't bring all his men forward, not to a watering hole in open country, not without scouting it out first. He'll hold his men back out of rifle range until he knows it's clear here."

"He can't hold back for too long," Jane said, "not with a column of angry *soldados* on his tail."

"That's what I'm betting on, Janie," said Shaw. "The more they kill one another, the less killing we have to do. I'm going to press them against each other as much as I can." He looked her over, her blackened, swollen eyes, her busted nose. "Are you ready to ride?"

"*Ready?* Hell, I'm waiting on you," she said.

When they'd ridden their rested and watered horses along the base of the hill line and turned into the draw, they hitched their reins around a rock spur. Rifle in hand, Shaw climbed upward along a steep path. He offered a hand back to Jane, but she shoved it way and climbed right along behind him.

Reaching the point where he'd been earlier, Shaw sat down and raised the telescope to his eye. Gazing out he watched Cantro and Stroud lead the men closer and finally slow to a halt before riding into rifle range. Looking out with her swollen, naked eyes, Jane squinted at two riders who left the rest of the column and rode forward.

"You called it right, Lawrence. Here comes his scouts," she said.

"Yep," said Shaw, "and look at who the one on the left is." He handed her the telescope for a closer look.

Careful of her swollen eyes, she looked out through the lens, then said under her breath in a growl, "It's him, that rotten bastard!" She watched Heaton spread away from the other rider as the two rode closer.

"What about the other one?" Shaw asked. "Did he have a hand in the beating?"

"No," Jane said, "leastwise I don't recognize him. He wasn't with the ones who did this." She lowered the lens and said, "You've got to give me Heaton."

Shaw looked at her. "Are you sure?"

"I've never been more sure about anything in my whole damned life," she said. She lay the telescope on her lap and held her hand out for the rifle.

"Every shot has to count, Janie," Shaw cautioned before handing the rifle to her. "Can you do it?"

"*Huh*. I expect I can," she replied haughtily. "I've dropped grizzly and running buffalo from farther off than this."

"That's grizzly and buffalo, Janie," said Shaw, still holding the rifle. "This is a man."

"After what Heaton and his pals did to me? Give me that rifle," she said, snatching the big Winchester from him. "I'll kill him sure as hell."

Shaw watched her cock the rifle smoothly and raise it adeptly to her shoulder. She appeared as familiar with what she was doing as any man he'd seen shoot. "Roy Heaton first . . . ," she said quietly, relaxing, settling for the shot, a knee cocked and the rifle steadied on it.

Shaw waited and watched. After a moment of hesitation she let go of her breath and had to take another one and resettle. She cut a glance toward Shaw and said, "I've got him now."

Shaw watched again as Heaton and the other scout drew closer. "Take your shot, Janie," he said quietly, in order not to throw her aim off. He continued watching, waiting in silence.

She hesitated even longer. Shaw saw her having trouble and was ready to reach over for the rifle. Finally she slumped, lowered the barrel and said in a voice close to sobbing, "Hell, I can't shoot him. . . . I—I just can't."

"Give it to me," Shaw said, quietly but firmly, taking the rifle from her hands.

"Adios, Heaton," he said under his breath, raising the rifle, taking close aim and squeezing the trigger. Jane sat with her head lowered as if in shame as the shot exploded beside her. What felt like two full seconds later, Heaton flipped backward silently from his saddle and rolled in the dirt while his horse veered slightly and began to slow.

"Damn you, Lawrence," Jane whispered. Her eyes were full of tears as she lifted her head and gazed out at the body lying sprawled in a rise of dust.

As Heaton went down, the other rider cut sharp and raced away across the basin floor. Farther back out of range, Cantro and the others watched as the second shot exploded and a long second later the rider flew sideways from his saddle and slid to a halt, dead in the dirt.

Cantro scanned the hillside above the sunken water hole and said to Stroud, "Just as we expected. They want us to pay dearly for this water, eh?" He looked back at the men who had taken turns beating on Jane. "I expect there's some vengeance in the works too."

"We can't stay here long, sir," Stroud said just between the two of them.

"Right you are, Arnold," said Cantro. He swung away from the ranks, rode a few yards and looked back along the trail behind them. "This blasted dust," he said under his breath, unable to see how close the soldiers had gotten to them over the past hour. Riding back to Stroud he said, "Whoever Jane Crowly's friend is, he thinks he can hold us here until the soldiers begin nipping at us from the rear."

"What will it be, sir?" Stroud asked.

"Or else he wants us to charge," Cantro continued, "so he can pick some of us off before he makes his getaway. He knows we don't want to kill him until he leads us to the gold." He grinned and shook his head. "I wish I had a dozen men like this one. . . ."

Sitting on the hillside, Shaw watched Cantro and his men ride off to the left without coming any closer into rifle range. "He's not going to charge us,

Janie," he said, sounding almost disappointed. "He's going to get some distance, ride into the hills and come at us from some cover. Good plan," he said, "better than letting me pick his men off, and better than fighting the soldiers out on the open desert." He stood up and offered a hand down to Jane. "Let's go, Janie. Cantro's tipped the odds back into his favor for now."

"Just go on without me, Lawrence," Jane said, too ashamed to look up at him. "I'm no damned good for nothing or nobody. Leave me here. . . . I'll feed myself to the coyotes."

"We don't have time for this, Janie," said Shaw.

"I mean it, Lawrence," she said, staring away from him. "I can't even kill the sonsabitches who beat me like a dog. What kind of weak, sorry fool am I?"

"You're no fool, Janie," Shaw said. "And I'd call you anything but weak."

"Then can you *please* tell me what the hell is wrong with me?" she pleaded. She turned up her battered face to his.

"Janie, it's no easy thing, killing a human being. I'd think there was something wrong with you if it came easy to you," said Shaw. "Can we get going?"

"You would?" she said, without making a move toward leaving. He saw tears stream down her bruised, puffy cheeks.

"Come on, Janie, get up," Shaw coaxed. "There's worse things than not being able to take a man's life. If I could go back and change anything, I wish I could be that way myself."

"Bull!" Jane said, but she took his outstretched hand and rose to her feet. "You're just trying to make me feel better."

"Think what you will, Janie," Shaw said, the two of them climbing over a crest of rock and heading back down to their horses. "We'll talk more about it later. Right now we've got to get out of here."

"The only person I ever shot and killed on purpose was a woman, you know," she said, almost sobbing again. "The poor Widow Edelman . . . and I shot her in the back!"

"I know, Jane," said Shaw. "You did it to save my life, and I'm grateful to you for it."

"Well, it's the damned truth," she said, as if Shaw had somehow discredited her for mentioning it.

There was no talking to her, Shaw told himself. Being with Jane had been a mistake—a mistake that could be fixed only one way, he thought.

Chapter 23

Once in their saddles, Shaw and Jane left the deep draw at a run. Skirting along the base of the hills across the hard rock surface, they kept watch for any sign of the wagon crossing the sand basin. When they finally saw the wagon tracks and the hoofprints of the team horses and Dawson's and Caldwell's saddle horses, Shaw pointed them out and the two swung over and rode alongside them.

"It's about time," he called out to Jane, the two of them not even slowing down. Instead Shaw looked back along the base of the hills for a moment as gunfire began to erupt from around the water hole. "I hope the wagon has already made it across and headed up into the hills," he shouted. "They'll be sitting ducks out on these sand hills." He looked forward, his eyes following the wagon tracks. "Maybe we'll get lucky and they'll all kill each other back there."

Jane also looked back toward the gunfire, batting her boots to her horse's sides. "You're traveling with the wrong damned person if you expect any good luck to come looking for us."

Shaw didn't reply. They rode along the trail of the wagon and horses until a rise of sand stood sheltering them from the hills alongside the water hole. Knowing they were out of sight and out of range for the time being, Shaw slowed the speckled barb's pace and cut away from the wagon trail to the top of another higher sand rise, where he could look down across the rolling land ahead of them.

Kneeling with the telescope steadied on his raised, crooked forearm, Shaw scanned back and forth slowly through the waver of heat and harsh glare of fiery silver-white sunlight. Finally he stopped scanning suddenly and eased the lens back on a retake and said, "Got them."

"Good!" Jane said. "How far are they from the other side?"

Shaw grimaced. "Seven or eight miles," he said. "Too far to outrun Cantro or the soldiers, unless they start running real soon." He stood and dusted sand from his trousers. "We'll start sending them warning shots."

"How hard can they run anyway with a load that damned heavy?" Jane asked. "If they're not careful they'll run them wagon horses to death."

"I know," said Shaw. He shoved the telescope into his saddlebags and swung up into his saddle. "But we'll give them the warning. Juan Lupo will have to decide how hard to push the horses." Behind them the fighting back and forth had grown closer and more intense, sounding as if the fight had left the water hole and was moving in their direction.

Before Shaw could ride forward, Jane grabbed the speckled barb by it's bridle and said out of the blue through puffed, swollen lips, "In case the worst befalls me and I don't make it through this, I want to tell you now that I'm sorry I put you on the spot. You know, all that talk about love and what-not?"

"Forget it, Jane," Shaw said. He couldn't believe she'd bring it up at a time like this.

"I was out of my head, hurting, scared," she said. "I know you don't love me." She shrugged. "I wouldn't expect you to. Hell, who'd love a peculiar ole prairie cur like me?"

"Janie, this can wait. We've got to go," he said firmly.

"I know I've got a damned dirty mouth and my manners are crude and unladylike," she continued without pause. "I know I don't toe nobody's mark but my own—" She stopped short and looked at him more closely. "That's it, ain't it . . . it's my curs-ing all the damned time. That's what has distanced you from me."

Shaw just stared at her, not knowing what to say.

"Because if that's it, I can change, Lawrence!" she pleaded. "I know I can change . . . and I will change. I swear I will. . . . You just watch and see."

"I don't want you to change, Janie," Shaw said. "It won't make any difference."

"You say that because you don't think I can," said

Jane, still holding on to hope. "But if it means you and me will be together—"

"Enough . . . ," Shaw cut in. He took her wrist and made her turn loose of his horse's bridle. "Janie, look at me. I think the world of you. But do I love you? No, I don't. I mean, not in the way we're talking about." He took a quick glance back in the direction of the gunfire, then went on. "The only woman I ever loved is dead. I wish I could forget her and love somebody else, anybody else. But I've tried, and I don't, I can't, and that's the whole of it. So there."

She stared at him through swollen slits of eyes. "I see," she said quietly, without attempting to mask her hurt and disappointment.

Shaw paused for a moment, then gave a curt nod in affirmation of his words and said, "Now . . . can we get going?" He swung his rifle up from his lap, pointed it skyward and fired two shots as they rode forward down the tall sloping sand hill and back onto the trail of hoofprints and wagon tracks.

Ahead of Shaw and Jane Crowly, Dawson, Caldwell and Juan Lupo heard the two rifle shots and looked back toward the sound. They had been hearing the distant sounds of gunfire and had no doubt that a running battle raged all the way back to the water hole. But the two deliberate rifle shots sounded much closer and seemed to carry a different meaning.

"Shaw and Jane?" Caldwell asked Dawson and Lupo, the three of them stopping for moment and gazing intently into the swirling heat that prevented them from seeing clearly so far away without benefit of Caldwell's field lens, which lay in the wagon seat beside Juan Lupo.

No sooner had Caldwell asked than two more shots resounded one after the other. "Yep," said Dawson, "I'd say it's them. Judging from the gunfire going on behind them, I'd say Shaw is telling us to hightail across the open ground and find ourselves some cover, pronto."

Lupo raised Caldwell's telescope, pulled it open and searched back until he saw Shaw and Jane top a rise of sand. "*Si*, it is them," he said, "and they are headed for us as if the devil is on their tails."

"And we best head on across here in the same manner," Dawson said as two more rifle shots resounded. "All right, Shaw, we hear you," Dawson muttered to himself. "Don't waste all your bullets warning us. . . ."

In the distance behind the wagon, Shaw slipped his smoking rifle back into its boot, pulled open the telescope and gazed out through it. "Looks like they got the message, Janie," he said, watching the wagon begin to move much quicker across the sand, the horses and the rolling wheels stirring up a rising cloud of dust.

"Good," Janie said, "with all this damned gunfire back here I was afraid they'd think it's just the Fourth of July."

From the swirling white heat ahead of them two shots exploded from Dawson's rifle, acknowledging

Shaw's warning. Shaw gave a tight grin. "Now cut straight for the hills. We'll meet you there. . . ."

When the wagon reached the base of the hills and started up a steep, rocky trail, Dawson looked back and saw two black dots that were Shaw and Jane Crowly riding toward them on the wavering blanket of silver-white sand. In the distance beyond the two black dots he heard the sounds of gunfire as the Mexican soldiers and the Border Dogs fought fiercely along the desert floor.

"This trail is much too steep and rocky for these horses," Juan Lupo called out over his shoulder, bouncing and swaying in the hard wooden seat.

"We don't have time to search for a better trail," said Dawson, his and Caldwell's horses climbing the trail on either side of the wagon and riding past him to scout the rough, treacherous hillside.

At a rough fork overgrown with mesquite brush and short, coarse cedar, Juan turned the wagon and bounced along another fifty yards until Dawson waved back and stopped him. As Juan brought the team horses to a halt and set the brake handle, Caldwell rode over to Dawson and said, "We might just as well have left Cantro a sign pointing the way here." He gestured at the two clear wagon tracks running back from the wagon.

"This is as far as we'll ever make it, unless the soldiers and Cantro's men kill each other off on their way here," said Dawson. "The five of us won't stand much of a chance here," he added, judging their defensive position.

Stepping down from the wagon, Juan Lupo walked up to the two of them, his rifle hanging from his hand. "Perhaps we would fair better if we made a run for it and took our chances on the desert floor," he said quietly.

"We might yet," said Dawson, looking down through the sparse cover of scrub cedar and pine and seeing Shaw and Jane's horse running along in the hoofprints and wagon tracks they'd left behind.

Lupo started to say more on the matter, but a commotion caused the three of them to turn their guns toward the steep hillside in time to see a battered stove-pipe hat roll out onto the rock trail. Dawson called out into the brush and tangled cedars, "You in there! Come out with your hands high!"

"Don't shoot! We're coming out!" a frightened voice called out from within the brush.

The three lawmen watched as Cactus John and Paul Harrod stumbled out onto the trail, their hands in the air. "Who the devil are you?" Lupo asked, amazed to see two men on this remote trail.

"I'm Cactus John Barker," said the cantina owner, looking back and forth, hoping to be recognized. "If any of yas have ever been to the Raw Leg in Trabajo Duro, you'd know that it's my place."

"I'm the Bird," said Harrod, standing beside him bareheaded, his stove-pipe hat lying on the rough ground at his feet. "I'm with him." He gestured toward Cactus John.

"What the blazes are you doing out here?" Lupo asked, eying them both closely.

"That's the same question I've been asking myself

this past week," said Cactus John. "I agreed to ride out with the *federales* to see if I can help them find the polecats who shot up the Raw Leg and burned down the church and brothel in Suerte Buena."

"You mean Red Burke and his pals," said Dawson.

"Yeah, that's right," said Cactus John, looking surprised. "How'd you know?"

"A friend told us," said Dawson. He looked at Harrod and said, "Pick up your hat."

"Thank you," said Harrod, stooping and snatching the hat from the ground. He wiped and straightened its battered brim. "We ran away late last night when the fighting started all the way up there." He pointed upward toward the top of the hills. "How we ended up on this trail is anybody's guess."

"This trail runs up to where?" Dawson asked.

"I heard Cantro say they'd come from Suerte Buena," Cactus John replied, "so it must run that far at least . . . probably farther, all the way to the other side of Ciudad de Almas Perdidas. But don't go taking my word on it. Hell, I've been half lost ever since I left *Tejas*." He grinned and lowered his hands a little. "Is it safe to say that if you fellows were going to kill us, you already would have?"

"We're not going to kill you," said Caldwell as he stepped down from his saddle. He searched the two men in turn and lifted a four-shot derringer from Cactus John's vest pocket.

"A fellow in my line of work learns to always keep a little shooter nearby," Cactus John said with a grin.

"Would a wagon this size make it up the trail?" Lupo asked, looking for a way out of their present quandary.

"Not with me in it," said Cactus John. "I'd jump out first. It's rough and steep and half missing in spots. I'm surprised we didn't break our danged necks riding it all night."

"But a man can amaze himself when there are guns firing at him," Harrod cut in, placing his hat atop his head and tugging it down.

"Who is the leader of the *federales*?" Lupo asked, his mind at work.

"A young captain by the name of Fuerte," said Cactus John. "A good enough fellow, but a little too ready to start shooting, for my money."

Lupo looked at Dawson and Caldwell and said with relief, "I know this captain. I met him in Mexico City. He is known as a man to be trusted."

"Even under these circumstances?" Dawson asked, careful not to mention the gold in front of strangers.

"That I will not say for now," said Lupo. He asked Cactus John, "How many men does Cantro have riding with him?"

"I didn't do a head count," said Cactus John, "but I'll put it at twenty or more. Of course I won't guess how many he lost last night."

Harrod cut in, saying, "I hate to impose, but do you have any water to spare, maybe a bite or two of something to eat? We've been going all night and most of yesterday with nothing in our bellies."

"*Si*, we can spare you some food and water," said

Lupo, raising his canteen and pitching it to him. "But I will warn you, after you eat you should get out of here. There will be more fighting before this day is over."

"You won't have to warn me twice," said Cactus John, holding his dusty hand out for the canteen when Harrod finished with it. "We've got horses cooling up there." He gestured toward the steep hillside. "As soon as we can shove something down our gullets, we're all for hitting the high trail back to Trabajo Duro. I came here thinking it was my civic duty."

"Civic duty—huh!" said Harrod. "If I ever do something like this again, I want somebody to kick me squarely in the rump. There's nothing *civil* about Old Mexico, and I know it."

Chapter 24

As Shaw and Jane topped a rise of sand on the last mile-long stretch toward the hills, two rifle shots resounded from less than a hundred yards away. When Shaw saw one bullet hit the ground near the speckled barb's hooves he knew the rifleman was too close for comfort. The other shot fell short and went unnoticed. As Jane turned and looked at him with concern in her eyes, he slumped suddenly in his saddle. "I'm not hit. Keep going. I'll be right along."

Jane caught on to his idea. "You'd better be," she said, kicking her horse and heading on, hoping to get herself out of the rifleman's range. As soon as she rode away, Shaw lay slumped on the barb's neck and rode the animal down over the crest of a sand hill. When he knew he was out of sight, he slowed the animal and leaped from the saddle. He hit the ground and lay there. But the barb circled and rode back and stuck its muzzle against his face. "Get out of here," Shaw hissed, slapping it away from him.

The barb jerked its muzzle away, ran off a few yards and stopped and looked back at him.

Moments later, two newer Border Dog gunmen, Harvey Bowes and Eddie Crew, stopped at the top of the rise and looked down with caution at Shaw's body lying sprawled on its side, facing toward them in the hot sand.

"Damn, Eddie, you nailed one!" said Bowes.

"Yeah, I did, and *you* didn't," said Bowes with smug little snap to his voice.

"You better make sure he's dead before we get too close," said Bowes, ignoring Crew's remark. "I understand this man is deadly."

Eddie Crew had started to raise his rifle and fire another round for good measure. But now he decided against it. "Oh, he's dead," said Crew, "no need in wasting bullets. If it ever took me over one shot to kill a sonsabitch I'd go to a different line of work."

As they rode in closer and looked down at Shaw, and at the speckled barb standing a feet away, Bowes said, "Hell, I got to shoot something to have a hand in this game." He raised a Remington from his holster, cocked it and started to aim at the barb. But before he got the shot off, Shaw's Colt swung up and fired.

On his horse beside Bowes, Crew saw the shot lift Bowes from his saddle and fling him to the ground in a spray of sand. Realizing he'd not yet levered a new round into his rifle, he let the useless weapon fall from his hands and didn't even grab for his pistol. Instead he grabbed his reins, turned his horse and headed back over the rise, the horse kicking up a cloud of fine sandy dust behind them.

Shaw's next shot punched him mid-high in his right shoulder and sent him twisting from his saddle and landing with a loud thump on the hot sand. By the time Shaw had walked up the rise, his smoking Colt in hand, Crew was bowed on his knees, his cheek in the sand, his right arm hanging limp. With his left hand he tried to push himself to his feet. Shaw stepped over and kicked his arm from under him. Crew rolled onto his back with a pain-filled moan.

"Oh God, it hurts," he said, almost sobbing.

"I bet it does." Shaw planted a boot on the young gunman's bloody chest and held him in place, his Colt staring down in his face. "Can you think of any reason why you're not lying dead beside your pard?"

"Yeah . . ." The gunman understood. He winced and said through his pain, "But I don't know nothing."

"Everybody knows something," Shaw said.

"If I tell you anything . . . will you let me go?" Crew asked.

Shaw looked at the wide spread of blood on his chest, and at more of it pumping up out of the bullet hole. "Are you sure that's what you want?" he asked grimly.

The young man looked away and deliberately didn't answer.

"How many guns does Cantro have riding with him after last night?" Shaw already knew, but he wanted to make sure the man wouldn't lie to him.

"I don't know," Crew said. "We separated from the others . . . last night and rode down . . . a different trail."

"That's why you're so close, then?" Shaw said, making sense of it.

"Yeah," the man said. "We figured . . . it would look good, us getting the jump . . . on everybody else."

Shaw only nodded. "Who are the men that beat Jane Crowly?"

"It . . . it wasn't me," Crew said. "I don't hold with that . . . kind of thing."

"Who was it?" Shaw asked.

"It was Roy Heaton . . . Elvis Pond and Bale Harmon," the wounded gunman said. "Pond does all of Cantro's . . . beating and torturing for him. Harmon is . . . just a mean prick."

Shaw noted the names, realizing Heaton was already dead. "Cantro had them do it?"

"Everything . . . is Cantro's doing. Trent and Arnold Stroud don't like it, but Cantro . . . is the leader," the man said, starting to fade from loss of blood.

Shaw only stared at him. "Where will I find Cantro and these men? Where will I find the main camp?" He could see the gunman was fading fast.

"You won't," the man said. "Best you'll do is find them at Ciudad de Almas Perdidas. Cantro, he likes to *fiesta* there." Shaw saw him drifting away. "I . . . guess I won't be joining him there. . . ."

Shaw let his Colt drop into his holster. "The City of Lost Souls," he said aloud, as if to remember it should he need it for future reference. He walked toward the speckled barb. The horse looked him up and down curiously, as Shaw approached. "Easy, boy . . . ," Shaw said, reaching out for the horse's dangling reins. "You didn't throw me; I jumped."

Jane Crowly had ridden back down to the edge of the hill trail and waited for Shaw to arrive. As he rode up, she asked anxiously, "Are you all right, Lawrence? You had me worried to death here."

"I'm good," Shaw said. "I didn't want them getting too close, nipping at us all the way here."

"I figured as much," said Jane. "That's why I rode on and let you have them. Otherwise I would have stayed right there and—"

"I understand," Shaw said, stopping her. "Those two came down a different trail. The others are still an hour or more behind us, fighting on the run." He nodded up the trail where he saw the wagon tracks leading. "What's going on with everybody?"

"We best get on up there," Jane said. "Easy John is starting to talk out of his head."

"Yeah? How's that?" Shaw asked, nudging the speckled barb upward onto the rocky trail.

"He's talking about turning the gold wagon loose on the desert floor instead of getting all of us killed over it." She gave a crooked, swollen-faced grin. "There's parts to his plan I have to say I look upon most favorably."

"After all we've gone through escaping Fire River with that gold, he wants to give it up?" Shaw said. "I don't buy it." He nudged the barb on upward, Jane right beside him.

"That's because you don't care as much for living as some of us might," Jane said. "But what do I know? I'm just the dumb ole girl on this little *swor-ray*."

Shaw started to tell her he didn't like hearing her talk that way about herself. But he stopped himself from doing so, thinking, *What's the use . . . ?* "So, you're all for getting out of this alive," Shaw said instead.

"Yeah, crazy me, huh?" said Jane.

Shaw only smiled. On the way up the trail to the turnoff he considered Lupo's reasoning on the matter until he reached a conclusion.

As they turned toward the wagon, Shaw watched Lupo, Dawson and Caldwell turn toward him and Jane. Reaching for Shaw's horse, Dawson said, "Glad you made it, Shaw. We're just talking about what we ought to do."

Caldwell and Lupo gave Shaw a nod as he and Jane swung down from their saddles. "So I heard," Shaw said, taking an uncapped canteen that Caldwell held out for him and swigging from it. He stared at Juan Lupo and said, "Jane tells me you want to give up the wagon."

"*Si*, I think it is best to do so," Juan said defensively. "We have done all we can do. It is time we stopped this chase and admit we're defeated."

"I see," said Shaw, with a slight nod. "Is that why they call you Easy John, because you give up so easy after such a long, bloody fight?"

Juan flared, but he kept himself under control. "I am only trying to save the lives of you and your friends. *Si*, I give up easy this time, when everyone's life is on the line."

"I wish to hell you'd been with Santa Anne at the Alamo!" Jane cut in through split and swollen lips. "It would have saved us all a lot of hard feelings."

Juan Lupo ignored her and said to Shaw, "What would you have me do? I am letting all of us off the hook!"

Dawson and Caldwell only watched and listened, having no idea what Shaw was trying to prove.

"What about your country?" said Shaw. "You said all that mattered was that your poor country get its gold back to maintain its sovereignty and help its struggling people." As he spoke he walked past Lupo and stopped at the edge of the wagon.

"Do not question me on this," Lupo said, his voice growing stronger than Dawson had ever heard it. He turned, facing Shaw from ten feet away. Dawson eased forward and stopped a step behind him. "Step away from the wagon, Shaw," Lupo warned, his hand pausing near the butt of his gun. "I do not value the gold as much as I value the lives of all four of—" He stopped short. A long boot knife appeared in Shaw's gloved hand, reached out and slashed a rope holding down the corner of the tarpaulin covering the gold.

"You don't value the gold, because there's no gold to value," Shaw said. He picked up a bag, slashed it with his knife and let a stream of sand and small stone fall to the ground.

Juan grabbed for his gun butt, only to find his holster empty. He heard the hammer of his revolver cock behind him, felt the barrel jam against his back. "Stand fast, Easy John," said Dawson. "We're learning a lot here."

Shaw reached down into the wagon bed, picked up a gold ingot and held it up for inspection. "Just enough gold to make it all look real." He tossed the ingot to Caldwell, who looked at it closely. "What about it, Undertaker?"

"Yep, it's real," said Caldwell.

Shaw reached back into the wagon, moved a couple of top-layer ingots and picked up a stone and tossed it to the ground. "But this isn't," he said. "Neither are the rest underneath the top layer. Easy John just salted the wagon with enough gold to make a getaway if it came to this."

"*Si*, you are right," Juan said sternly in his own defense, "and now we must all agree that it has 'come to this.'"

Dawson backed away from Lupo, but kept the gun aimed at him. "You've had us escorting a salted wagon full of rocks all the way from Fire River?"

"No," said Lupo, "I only switched the gold for rocks the day you two followed the Apache away from us. I had most of the day to do it. Forgive me, but I saw a time when something like this would happen. It was my duty to lead everyone as far away from the gold as I could, in order to protect it." He looked ashamed but continued. "I had to distract, mislead and deceive everyone in order to save my country's gold."

"Save it for your-damn-self, you mean," Jane said gruffly. "I ought to beat your brains down to your boot wells!" She took a threatening step toward Lupo, but Caldwell stopped her.

"Settle down, Jane," said Caldwell. "He wasn't trying to keep it for himself. If he was, he would have cut out long before now. He wouldn't have stuck himself here with us in a slow-moving wagon. Like he said, he was drawing everybody farther away from where the gold is hidden. He could have taken our horses and lit out on us any time, in the night, while he was on guard and we were asleep."

"He could have killed us in our sleep," Dawson added. He rubbed his chin and considered it. "Caldwell's right," he said. "I don't like what's been done to us, but we're off the spot." He looked at Lupo and said, "All right, Easy John, no more tricks. Let's get the wagon back down the trail and get ready to cut it loose."

"Like hell," said Jane. "Let him ride it down and cut it loose himself. I've gotten a belly full of Easy John Lupo and his tricks."

"If none of you want to go with me, I understand," Lupo said. "I am grateful to you for all you have done." He gestured toward the trail Cactus John and Harrod had ridden down on. "We are told this trail leads all the way to the Ciudad de Almas Perdidas. You are all free to take it and ride away."

Shaw looked up the steep rocky trail in dark contemplation. Then he turned to Dawson, Caldwell and Jane and saw the looks on their faces. To Lupo he said, "What, leave now and miss all the fun?"

Chapter 25

Perched high on the hillside, Shaw lowered his telescope for a second and gave a sharp whistle down to the others when he spotted the first of Cantro's men charging hard across the sand hills. The riders followed the wagon tracks toward the jagged hill line. Looking farther back through the glaring afternoon sunlight he saw the Mexican soldiers pressing hard from less than two miles behind.

At the base of the hills, Dawson turned from looking upward at Shaw and said to Lupo, "Get ready, Easy John, they're coming."

Without reply, Lupo climbed into the wagon seat and released the long wooden hand brake.

"Get a good look before you give it up," Caldwell advised with a concerned look on his face.

Lupo gave him a short grin.

"And be careful," Caldwell added.

"I am always careful, Undertaker," Lupo said. "You be careful yourself. Someday perhaps we will work together again."

"I hope not," said Caldwell, his rifle in hand. He stood holding the lead team horse by its bridle until they heard Shaw let go the first round with his Winchester.

"All right, they're close enough," Dawson shouted to Caldwell and Lupo. "Get out of here."

Caldwell turned loose of the big horses' bridle, stepped back and slapped his rifle barrel on its rump as Lupo slapped the leather traces to all of the horses' backs and sent them bolting out onto the desert floor.

Above on the hillside, Shaw's first shot had dropped one of the Border Dogs' front riders dead in the sand. He took close aim for his second shot as Lupo pushed the heavy speeding wagon tauntingly in front of the riders and led them off along the sand hills past Shaw and the others' line of fire.

Farther back on the desert ground, Cantro stood in his stirrups and stared through a pair of battered binoculars at the front riders, two of them having been shot from their saddles. "There's the wagon!" he shouted to the men around him, disregarding the two dead men on the ground ahead of them. "They're making a run for it!"

"All right, men! Ride it down!" shouted Arnold Stroud to the men behind him. His horse reared high and came down into a hard run, kicking up a cloud of sand behind its hooves.

"They're going for it . . . ," Shaw murmured aloud to himself, levering a fresh round into his rifle chamber. He took a close aim and fired; another front rider fell, this one taking his horse down with him and rolling forward in a tangle of limbs and hooves. When the horse stood and shook itself off and ran away, the rider lay dead where he'd fallen.

Cantro led the charge, headed straight after the wagon, most of the men spreading out and following him. With the gold wagon in sight, the Border Dogs threw caution to the wind and raced wildly through a line of deadly fire coming from Dawson, Caldwell and Shaw on the hillside. Behind them the Mexican soldiers pressed down on them, the Border Dogs offering no return fire to protect their rear.

A thousand yards ahead in the wagon, Lupo looked back and saw Cantro and his men charging hard. Now was the time to abandon the wagon, he told himself, lashing the traces around a wooden rail on the edge of the seat designed for just such a purpose.

As the six horses thundered as one up over a sand hill and started down the other side, Lupo rose into a crouch. Taking a deep breath, he hurled himself sidelong out of the wagon and rolled a full ten yards diagonally down the soft, hot hillside in a spray of powdery white sand.

At the end of his roll, he scrambled onto his feet and into a run and disappeared over the top of a sand hill just as the Border Dogs came pounding up over the hill in pursuit of the wagon. Blowing and fanning dust from his face, Juan gave a dark chuckle, realizing no one was coming to look for him. Apparently they hadn't even noticed his footprints in the sand. "Ah, gold," he said to himself, closing his eyes for a moment. "It blinds everyone in its brilliance."

Standing, he walked up to the crest of the hill and watched the last of Cantro's men race toward the wagon. He stood at the crest of the sand hill facing the direction of the approaching soldiers. He did not want them to ride over the hill and come upon him all at once and start shooting. Instead he waited until he saw they were within shooting range of him, and he raised his arms high in the air.

Captain Fuerte, riding hard, spotted the lone figure standing hatless, arms upreached, a hot wind blowing his black tails sidelong. "Don't shoot," he bellowed as the men alongside him took aim on Lupo. "We do not kill unarmed men. He surrenders; take him prisoner." He veered his horse toward Lupo and said to the three men nearest him, "Follow me. I will see for myself what he has to say." He rode closer, studying Lupo's face until recognition came to him. "Juan Lupo?" he said, riding closer.

"*Si*, it is I, *Capitán* Fuerte," said Lupo, feeling better by the minute.

"Are you hurt? What are you doing out here?" Fuerte asked.

"I have found the stolen gold, *Capitán*, and under the authority granted me by *Generalissimo* Manual Ortega, you and I are delivering it safely back to Mexico City," said Lupo. "Now, go get the wagon and bring the gold back to me. We have a long ride ahead of us." He raised a finger for emphasis. "Do this well, *Capitán*, and we will both stand side by side while you receive the highest medal of valor and honor our country has to offer."

"*Si*, Juan Lupo, it will be done," said the serious young captain.

Lupo stood for a moment as the captain and the three soldiers rode away. This was simple enough, he told himself, walking toward an abandoned horse where it stood near the body of its fallen rider. If the captain returned with the wagon, he could be trusted enough to go back and retrieve the gold. If the captain didn't return . . . well, the gold was still safely buried where he'd left it. Lupo smiled to himself. *Life does not always have to be so hard. . . .*

When the firing had moved across their front and continued on across the desert floor, Shaw climbed down to where Jane stood waiting. "I hope Lupo made it," he said. "That's about all I've got for him."

Jane handed him a canteen; he sipped a mouthful and spit a stream. "That's all you've got for him?" Jane asked with a curious look. "What the hell does that mean?"

"It means just as it says," Shaw said, wiping a hand across his lips. He stepped over to his horse and shoved his hot rifle into his saddle boot. "I saw him talking to the Mexican captain the last time I looked. I figure it's all out of our hands now."

"What about Cantro?" Jane asked. "What about what his men did to me? Am I supposed to forget all that?"

"You tell me, Janie, are you?" Shaw said.

"That's no damned answer," Jane said.

"It's all the answer you get," said Shaw. "When it comes right down to it, I don't think you're going to want those men's blood on your hands from now on."

"Like hell I don't," she blustered.

Shaw stared at her. "Do you, Janie? *Really?*" he pressed. "Because if you do, I'll take you to them and watch you kill them." He said it in a way that let her know it would be her doing the killing, and the living with it afterward.

Jane fell silent for a moment. Without answering him, she asked with another curious look, "Are you leaving, right here, right now, like this?"

"Yep," said Shaw. "Right here, right now, like this." He swung up into his saddle.

"But what about us?" Jane said. "We were going to talk *later*, remember?"

"This is later, Janie. We are talking," Shaw said. Before he could say any more, Dawson and Caldwell came riding up from the edge of the trail and he turned the barb to face them.

"We just saw the soldiers take back the wagon from Cantro's men. They're headed back to Lupo with it. This is turning out to be a good day for Juan Lupo all the way around." They stopped and looked down at Shaw. "We're going to fade back and get out of sight up the next hill trail."

"Good luck," said Shaw, fishing through his pocket for the dented-up deputy badge Dawson had given him. "I'm headed up right here." He flipped the badge up to Dawson.

"What do you want me to do with this?" Dawson asked, catching the badge instinctively.

"Use your imagination," Shaw said, adjusting his saddle. He turned to Jane. "You're welcome to ride with me as far as Suerte Buena."

"I don't want to go to Good Luck," said Jane. "Where are you headed from there?"

"I can't say," said Shaw. His eyes told her a lot, but none of it made her feel welcome.

Jane turned to Dawson and Caldwell. "Do you mind if I ride along with you two a ways?"

Dawson looked at Shaw, saw the consenting look on his face and said to Jane, "Sure, Jane, ride as far as you want with us."

Jane turned to Shaw, took the speckled barb by its bridle and led it a few feet away for privacy. "Look, Lawrence, I gave things some thought too. I don't think I'm ready to settle down just yet. I've still got lots of places to go and sights to see. You know me, I ain't ready for anything like everybody else wants, not yet anyway."

"I know," said Shaw, letting her see it her way, make it her parting, not his.

"No hard feelings? Amigos for always?" she said with a crooked smile on her battered face.

"You know it, Janie," said Shaw. He backed the speckled barb a step and began to turn it onto the steep rocky trail.

"When you want this badge back, it'll be waiting for you," Dawson said. "How's that for imagination?"

"That wasn't what I was going to tell you, but I'm

obliged," Shaw said. He touched his hat brim toward Dawson and Caldwell and nudged the horse forward.

"He'll be back for it; you watch," Dawson said quietly between himself and Caldwell. "For some reason, he's just not wanting to wear it right now. . . ."

Shaw rode the rest of the evening, taking his time on the rough, nearly washed out trail. He spent the night under the stars without a fire and told himself he didn't miss Jane Crowly. In the morning he rode on. At a point where his trail gave view of another high trail to the east he watched Garris Cantro and his remaining men pass from sight to sight and disappear on toward Suerte Buena.

Border Dogs, headed home . . .

He stayed two days in Suerte Buena, Cantro and his men already gone, ducking soldiers along their way, he figured. When he left, he took supplies with him and spent another night under the stars, this time with a fire, and hot food and coffee. All right, he admitted, he had missed Jane the first few nights, but the loneliness had gotten better now.

"You're a hard gal to miss, Janie . . . ," he said, speaking into his coffee. She was crazy, he told himself, yet so many people he knew would fit that charge, that it was hard to judge her too harshly for it. Anyway, he was glad she was gone.

For over a week he wandered the high trails, knowing that by now, Lupo and his wagonload of gold should be well on their way to Mexico City. He knew that by now Dawson, Caldwell and Jane were off the far end of the desert and headed back across the badlands toward the border. He knew that by now Garris Cantro and his men were back where the dying gunman had told him he would find them.

In the afternoon heat, he found himself stopping the speckled barb at the edge of the City of Lost Souls. He gazed along the dusty street and saw a long wooden table set up beneath a faded green canopy out front of an ancient cantina. The tile roof of the cantina had been trimmed with colorful streamers of cloth, with flowers interwoven into it.

Fiesta . . . , Shaw thought. At the head of the otherwise empty table he saw Cantro sitting, staring at him, surrounded by gunmen backing him on either side.

Shaw stepped the speckled barb forward, and rode on until he saw he'd ridden close enough to be under Cantro's skin, but not close enough to unsettle him. He stopped and stared at Cantro, making him speak first. "All right," said Cantro, "I found out that you're Lawrence Shaw."

"I am," Shaw said, and he fell silent again.

"The Fastest Gun Alive," Cantro said with a bit of a dark chuckle.

"I am," said Shaw.

"I always wondered how any one man can be the fastest," Cantro said.

"It's just how it is." Shaw's poncho hung dusty and limp.

Behind Cantro the men started to spread out a little, but Cantro stopped them with a raised hand. At the doorway of the cantina stood two men Shaw had not seen before. The two stepped out front cautiously and stood watching curiously. "Just how it is . . ." Cantro nodded, repeating him in contemplation. "Well, *Fastest Gun Alive*, you made a fool's mistake coming here, after costing us all that gold. I don't see you getting out of here alive."

Shaw ignored his words. "I want Elvis Pond and Bale Harmon." He searched the faces of the gunmen.

"The hell you say." Cantro stood up and leaned on his palms on the table edge. "Just what do you want them for?"

"For beating Jane Crowly," said Shaw. "She's my woman. It was wrong what they did. They have to pay for it."

"Hold on, Shaw," said Cantro. "I'm the leader. I allowed it. Are you going to kill me too?"

Ignoring his question Shaw searched the faces and said calmly, "Elvis Pond. Bale Harmon. I'm here to kill you. Step out."

"Let us blast this fool," a gunman near Cantro whispered to him.

"Shut up," said Cantro, "this is going to be interesting." To Shaw he said, "Do you realize that one word from me and you're dead?"

Shaw met Cantro's gaze. "Are all your men cowards, or just the two I'm going to kill?"

"I'm no coward," said Elvis Pond, stepping away from the others with his gun hand poised near his holstered Colt. "Neither is Harmon," he said. A few feet away, Bale Harmon also stepped away from the others, his gun hand poised and ready.

"That's right, Shaw," said Harmon. "If you think you can take two at once, make your move. I beat Jane Crowly, so what? She's not your woman anyway. She's nothing but a damned she-male, is what I always heard."

"Hold it right there, all three of yas," said Cantro. "I'm short of men right now. I can't risk it. I'll tell you what, Shaw, you ride out of here, we'll act like you just stumbled in by mistake—"

"Hold it, Cantro," one of the two men standing out front of the cantina called out. "What's this man talking about? Did someone here beat up a woman?"

"There's nothing to it, Major Zell," said Cantro. "It's all a misunderstanding."

The two men stepped forward and looked Shaw up and down. "Lawrence Shaw, eh?" said the one who had spoken out. "I've heard of you." He wore a thick black beard and had a scar down his face. "I've always heard you're a man who travels on his word."

Shaw just stared at him.

"I'm Major Martin Zell," the man said. "This is Mr. Liam Bowes, my second in command. I lead the Border Dogs. What's this about?"

Cantro cut in, looking strange and worried now that Zell and Bowes had stepped in on the matter. "Major, this is nothing. I needed some information. I thought this Jane Crowly woman had it. I gave Elvis and Harmon permission to smack her around some, that's all."

Zell looked at Shaw for a reply.

"I saw her face. That's why I rode here," Shaw said.

Zell grimaced. "We don't beat women, Cantro!" He glared at Pond and Harmon. "If you two did it, here's where it brought you." He looked at Shaw and said, "Two against one?"

"It suits me," Shaw said, turning his eyes from Zell to Pond and Harmon.

Zell called out to the other men, "Let no one interfere. If these men are all three square with it, so am I."

"I'm square," said Elvis, staring at Shaw. "I want his trigger finger when I'm done."

"I'm square," said Harmon. "Let's get on with—"

Two shots exploded from Shaw's Colt almost as one. Both men flew backward and hit the ground dead, in spite of the bulletproof vests they wore hidden beneath their shirts.

"Both of them, clean through their foreheads!" a gunman called out, running over and looking down at the bodies.

"You didn't give them a chance, Shaw," Zell said, stunned.

"I didn't come here to," Shaw said. While his Colt was still smoking he swung it up and shot Garris Cantro in the same spot as he'd shot the other two. Cantro flew backward in his big, heavy wooden chair and sprawled dead in the dirt.

Zell stood speechless as every gun in the street came out cocked and pointed at Shaw.

"Good Lord, man!" said Zell. "You leave me little to defend you with! He told you he was in charge.

He told you he allowed it. You didn't so much as flinch! Why did you kill him?"

Shaw stepped over closer, his Colt still smoking, three shots left in it, pointed loosely at Major Zell's stomach. "Because he was in charge . . . because he allowed it," he said. Then, in a lowered tone, he said between the two of them, "Killing Cantro is on the house. You don't even have to thank me."

Zell gave him a strange, puzzled look. In the length of a second, Shaw had read why Zell and his second in command were here to begin with. "Everybody, hold your fire," Zell commanded. "Hold this man blameless for anything that has happened here today. This was all Cantro's doing. Things are going to be different from now on."

Shaw emptied the spent rounds from his Colt and reloaded. When he turned to step back into his saddle, Liam Bowes said, "Shaw, I lost a cousin out there the other day. I want you to know I'm not going to foster any hard feelings over it. Do you understand me?"

Shaw only nodded. He stepped up into his saddle, turned the speckled barb and rode away. At the far edge of town he looked back on the City of Lost Souls and let out a hard, tight breath. "Damn it, Janie . . . ," he said to the dusty street and the dead men lying on it. He looked up across at the sky. Unaccustomed as he was to hearing such words come from his mouth, he said under his breath, "Damn it all to hell. . . ."

Ralph Cotton brings the Old West to life—
don't miss a single page of action!
Read on for a special sneak preview
of the next Lawrence Shaw adventure,

GUN COUNTRY

Coming from Signet in March 2010

Badlands, New Mexico

On the cold, wind-stirred desert night, his senses had abandoned him for a time; it was as if he'd vanished into the swirling emptiness around him. He may have fallen asleep in his saddle, for all he knew. During the missing time the pain inside his head had disappeared into a warm, furry blackness. But with the first dark, silvery streak of dawn his senses had returned, and with them the insistent pain.

He rode on, his aching head bowed and turned against a moaning wind.

He knew who he was, he reminded himself. He knew his name, his age, flashes of details and particulars of his life. *Oh yes, he knew. . . .* But he'd had to grapple with it for a time in order to get the information back clearly into his mind. For a time when his memory had come and gone he'd almost hoped he might lose it altogether. But that was not to be the case, he told himself.

At daylight, Lawrence Shaw, also known as Fast Larry, also known as the Fastest Gun Alive, rode upward into Colinas Secas from the southwest, off the dusty badlands floor. He wore a battered stovepipe hat and a long, ragged swallowtail coat. A broad, faded red bandanna mantled the bridge of his nose and had shielded most of his face against the sharp wind-driven sand. Behind him the cold desert wind still moaned in the grainy light like a field of lost souls.

At the edge of town Shaw stopped his speckled barb and jerked the bandanna down below his chin, stirring a rise of dust on his chest. Beneath him the barb chuffed and shook itself off. "Easy, boy," he murmured to the dust-coated animal. "We'll get you fed and stalled first thing."

He patted a gloved hand to the barb's withers. Dust billowed. At a hitch rail out front of a dimly lit saloon, Shaw eyed three horses huddled together with their heads lowered against the cold wind. He saw shadows looming in the saloon's dusty front window. With pain throbbing in his head, he veered the barb away from the saloon and rode on at a walk. He had no idea who the men were inside the saloon, but he had no doubt they were the sort of men who could lead him where he needed to be.

Inside the window, three gunmen stood sharing a bottle of rye whiskey. Seeing the stranger turn his horse away, one of the gunmen, an Arkansan named Thurman Thornton, said proudly, "Well, well, it appears this drifter doesn't desire our company." He wiped his wrist across his lips and passed the bottle sidelong to the other two.

"I suspect he might be faint of heart," a gunman named Bell Mason replied, "if just the sight of our horses scares him."

"Suppose we ought to wake Dex up and tell him? See what he wants us to do?" Thornton asked.

"Naw, Dex is passed out with the whore," replied a third gunman named Roland Stobble. He took the bottle, threw back a drink and passed it on.

Beside him Bell Mason took the bottle and said, "Hell, he'll just tell us to run this scarecrow out of town. It looks like we already done that." He gave a short, dark grin. "We didn't even need permission," he added with sarcasm and threw back a drink.

"Yeah," said Stobble, eyeing Thornton with a sour expression. "Do you ask Dex's permission to go to the jake, or do you figure that out on your own?"

Thornton ignored the remark, still looking out the dusty window. "I can send any scarecrow hightailing. I don't need no help, or permission."

The three watched the ragged dust-covered stranger appraise a seedy hotel from his saddle as he rode on past the saloon and turned the speckled barb toward the livery barn at a tired walk.

"Ah, look, he's going to attend to his horse," said Stobble in a mocking tone. "Ain't that commendable? You got to always admire a man who puts his horse's needs ahead of his own." He gave a dark chuckle, took back the bottle from Mason and threw down a drink.

"I'll tend his horse," Thornton threatened, staring out toward the livery barn as Shaw and the speckled barb walked out of sight. He adjusted his coat and started to walk toward the front door.

"Whoa, hang on," said Stobble, blocking his way with a raised arm. "What's your hurry? It's raw and cold out there. Listen to that wind."

"So?" said Thornton, stopping abruptly.

"So let's let him come to us, if he gets his nerve up." Stobble shrugged.

"What if he doesn't?" said Thornton. "What if he goes someplace else?"

"Where the hell else is he going to go?" Mason cut in, sounding agitated by Thornton's slow-wittedness.

"What's wrong with you, Thurman?" Stobble asked Thornton with a goading smile. "Are you still floating around on them cactus buttons?"

"Never mind what I am or ain't floating on," said Thornton. He settled back into place and let his coat fall open again. "When he does get here, I'll send him hightailing out of town, you watch."

"Oh, we'll watch sure enough," said Stobble. "You can bet on that."

"Send him hightailing?" said Mason. "Hell, that ain't nothing. My poor old grandma could send him hightailing. I thought we might get a chance to see some fireworks."

"I can do that too," said Thornton confidently. "It makes me no difference."

"You mean you don't mind killing a man before breakfast?" Stobble goaded.

"Before breakfast, after supper, during dinner, I don't care," Thornton said. "Dex said not to let any strangers into town. Far as I'm concerned, I'll drop this saddle tramp when he walks through the door."

"All right, that's more like it," said Stobble. "To hell with sending a man *hightailing*." He gave Mason a knowing grin. "Show us some action."

Inside the livery barn, Shaw slapped his hands up and down his coat sleeves; the speckled barb shook itself off again and chuffed and blew as dust swirled about them.

From inside a stall a man grumbled and coughed and stood up from a blanket spread on a pile of fresh hay. He held a flickering lantern up against the morning gloom. "Damn it," he said, "drag yourself and that dirty cayuse out back and dust him down! I've swallowed too much of this blasted desert as it is."

Shaw turned and faced him, his swallowtail coat hanging open down his chest, his big bone-handled Colt standing tall and clean in its holster. He stared at the livery man without saying a word.

Uh-oh . . . With an appraising look, noting both the gun and the stranger's cool, confident presence, the livery man said in an apologetic voice, "Pay me no mind, Mister." He chastised himself out loud. "Damn it, Radler. I expect swallowing a little dirt is better than having a bunch of it shoveled into my face."

"Is that your name, *Radler*?" Shaw asked the old man quietly. As he spoke he opened his coat enough to reach into a vest pocket and pull out a gold coin.

"Yes, sir, it is," said the old man. "Caywood Radler, if you want to know the whole of it. You can call me Radler; most folks do." He caught himself and added nervously, "That is, unless you prefer calling me something else. I'm not what you call a stickler on formality. I go along with most anything."

Shaw flipped him the gold coin. "This is for me and the horse. I want a stall big enough for both of us while I'm here."

Radler caught the coin with his free hand and gave him a puzzled look. "Mister, we've got a hotel in Colinas Secas, a saloon and brothel, too. A man ain't held to sleeping in a stable." He looked Shaw over in the thin glow of the lantern.

"I saw the hotel on my way here," Shaw said in a flat tone. "I'll take the livery."

"I do pride myself on running a good, clean livery barn," the old man said as he stepped away and hung the lantern on a post. He hefted a wooden water bucket, carried it to the barb and set it down before the horse's probing muzzle. He slipped the horse's bit from its mouth, lifted its bridle and let it draw thirstily from the bucket. "But I don't want you to feel like I said anything against the hotel."

Shaw only stared at him.

"A fellow has to be careful what he says these days in Colinas Secas . . . or Dry Hills, if you prefer not to call the town by its Mex name," he continued. "Either which name you want to call it is all right by me. I just don't want you to get the wrong idea—"

"What's got you strung so tight, hostler?" Shaw asked, cutting him off.

"I don't want no trouble, is all, sir," the livery man said. "I saw what happens to anybody who gets in you boys' way—"

"'Us boys . . .'?" Shaw asked, again cutting the frightened man short. "What *boys* is that?"

"Why, Dexter Lowe's boys, of course," said the old man. He blinked in surprise. "Who else's boys would I mean?"

"Let's stop asking each other the same question," said Shaw. He began to get the picture. "I'm not one of Dexter Lowe's men." He studied the old man's nervous, watery eyes. "Are Lowe and his men holing up here in Colinas Secas?" Dexter Lowe and his gang were one of the countless gangs that Shaw, U.S. Marshal Crayton Dawson and Deputy Jedson Caldwell had been sent to break up along the border badlands.

Radler looked stunned, but he refused to offer a reply. "Look, Mister, I'm an old man. I've got no business meddling where I don't belong. Lowe told us all what would happen if we said anything about him and his boys being here . . . so I *ain't* saying nothing. For all I know you might be here to see if I can keep my mouth shut, like I was told."

"I understand," said Shaw, the sound of his own voice making his head throb deeper in pain. He thought about his old battered U.S. Deputy Marshal badge. "Now what about that stall?" As he spoke he loosened the barb's saddle cinch, lifted the saddle from the horse's back and slung it over a rack while the barb continued drinking. He knew he could reach into his pocket, pull out his badge and ease his mind, but he wasn't going to do that, he told himself.

Showing Radler he was a lawman would settle the old livery man's fear, but keeping the fact a secret seemed to always work to his advantage, he reminded himself, turning and pulling his ragged dust-coated bedroll down from behind his saddle.

"This one here is freshly cleaned," Radler said, gesturing toward the closest stall standing with its door open, its floor partly covered with clean straw.

"I'll take it," Shaw said. He could feel Radler's curious eyes on him as he beat the rolled blanket against a support post, then unrolled it and stepped inside the stall.

"Yes, sir," said the old man. "A fellow wants to sleep in the barn, who am I to wonder about another man's peculiarities?" He stood watching until the barb raised its dripping muzzle from the empty water bucket. Giving the horse a nudge on its rump, he followed it inside the stall where Shaw stood fashioning his sleeping blanket into a hammock.

"Now I've seen it all," he said, watching as Shaw tied the gathered blanket ends along the stall rail. "Mister, you must be a man who has slept his share of nights with heathen animals."

Shaw turned around, sat down in the drooping hammock and leaned against the wall planks. "You don't know the half of it," he said tiredly. He took off the battered stove-pipe hat carefully and pegged it on a post atop the rail. The livery man winced at the sight of a blood-stained bandage covering the top of Shaw's head.

"Lord God!" the old man said. "Was you scalped?"

"Scalping would have been a treat," Shaw said. He touched his fingertips gently to the bandage. Upon seeing the bandage, the livery man noted that is was wrapped around Shaw's head nearly down to his ears. But beneath the hat brim the otherwise white gauze wrapping had turned brown under a coating of trail dust.

"Somebody shot you?" the old man ventured. "You was shot in the head and lived? My God, man! You must hurt something fierce!"

"Only when I talk about it," Shaw said, giving the man a look.

"I understand; say no more." Radler dropped his inquiry, growing less fearful now that Shaw was off his feet and making himself to home in the barn. "I'll get this cayuse rubbed down right away," he said. He couldn't keep himself from staring at the blood-stained bandage.

"Not yet," said Shaw, stopping Radler from reaching down and picking up a handful of clean straw from the floor. "He likes to stand for a few minutes first, collect his thoughts."

"Really . . . ?" Radler eyed him, wondering whether he was joking. "Then he's one hell of a horse."

"Yes, he is." Shaw fished another coin from his pocket and flipped it to the old livery man. "Before you rub him down and grain him, suppose you go to that saloon and bring me back a bottle of rye." He winced at the pain in his head.

"Oh, you need whiskey for all the torment you must be in," said the old man.

Instead of replying, Shaw said, "Stand it on the post for me while I catch some shut-eye."

"Want me to wake you up as soon as I return with it?" Radler asked.

"That wouldn't be a good idea," Shaw said firmly. Turning and slinging a dusty leg up onto the hammock, he sank down, folding his hands and carefully tucking them behind his bandaged head.